Death in the Face

A Hector Lassiter novel

CRAIG MCDONALD

BETIMES BOOKS

First published in the English language worldwide by Betimes Books 2015

www.betimesbooks.com

ISBN-13: 9780993433108

Cover design by JT Lindroos

ALSO BY CRAIG McDONALD

PRAISE FOR
THE HECTOR LASSITER SERIES

"With each of his Hector Lassiter novels, Craig McDonald has stretched his canvas wider and unfurled tales of increasingly greater resonance."   —Megan Abbott

"Reading a Hector Lassiter novel is like having a great uncle pull you aside, pour you a tumbler of rye, and tell you a story about how the 20th century 'really' went down."
—Duane Swierczynski

"What critics might call eclectic, and Eastern folks quirky, we Southerners call cussedness — and it's the cornerstone of the American genius. As in: "There's a right way, a wrong way, and my way." You want to see how that looks on the page, pick up any of Craig McDonald's novels. He's built him a nice little shack out there way off all the reg'lar roads, and he's brewing some fine, heady stuff. Leave your money under the rock and come back in an hour."   —James Sallis

"Craig McDonald is wily, talented and — rarest of the rare — a true original. He writes melancholy poetry that actually has melancholy poets wandering around, but don't turn your backs on them, either."   —Laura Lippman

"James Ellroy + Kerouac + Coen brothers + Tarantino = Craig McDonald"   —Amazon.fr

*This novel is for
Daniel Wells*

"You only live twice;
Once when you're born,
And once when you look
Death in the face."
—Ian Fleming
(after Matsuo Basho)

PROLOGUE

1967

The man sat in the packed movie theater in Las Cruces, surrounded by people, yet very much alone. A novelist and screenwriter of some note, he winced and shook his head at the mockery Roald Dahl had made of his British friend's last, fully realized novel. It was utterly appalling, a goddamn *travesty*.

The screen villain, a short and portly little man with a scar down the right side of his face, somehow managed to seem fey despite his piratical wound. He was a mincing antagonist a world away from the one described in the superior James Bond novel. The little man hissed, "They told me you were assassinated in Hong Kong."

Scottish actor Sean Connery, looking bored, even a bit pained to have to say the words, burred back, "Yes, this is my second life."

The man who sat watching the movie with pale blue eyes had for many years been accused by critics of writing what he lived and living what he wrote.

Indeed, on this dreary October day, the novelist's life was about to imitate his dead friend's writings, it could be said. Just like the titular hero had at the beginning of this over-budgeted and over-blown film adaptation, the fiction writer meant to bring off his own false but quite permanent end.

As the film credits rolled, the tall man with the pale blue eyes rose and strode squinting into the New Mexico sun, lighting up a Pall Mall as he made his way toward the turquoise 'fifty-seven Bel Air.

This was the last day that he would ever spend living with his given name—his looming "death" was a long-in-coming gift to himself.

CONTENTS

PART I

"EVERY DAY IS A JOURNEY..."

NEW YORK,
IDLEWILD AIRPORT:
1962

1

PEOPLE DYING WHO NEVER DIED BEFORE

Hector Lassiter sat in the airport lounge, nursing his second Old Fashioned, and thinking about death.

His corner of the darkened portion of Idlewild's departure area was quieting for the night, at last settling down save for the rustle of the occasional custodial worker changing a trash bin's liner, emptying an ashtray stand, and the burr of a vacuum cleaner pushed around here and there from distant somewhere.

He was booked on a flight to England scheduled to board in just under an hour. In his present, gloomy state of mind, fifty-nine minutes seemed near on infinity to the novelist.

Plans called for Hector to join an old friend in England. Together they would press on to Japan for a two-week, barnstorming tour of the former Axis stronghold.

The excursion was partly at his chum's instigation. Ian Fleming—at last gaining dubious fame and significant money for his long-running James Bond thrillers—was heading east on a research trip for a projected Asian-set 007 novel.

Hector, though far longer established as a novelist and occasional screenwriter, wasn't tagging along for background or a setting for any novel or screenplay of his own, but rather by arrangement on Ian's part for Hector to *cover* the British thriller writer's in situ research for *Playboy Magazine*.

The notion of writing about a fellow writer's fact-finding trip tore at Hector, far more than he cared to admit. So he tried again to kid himself it was an endurable excuse to see Ian. It was also a secret favor to the author's wife, Ann, a long-ago acquaintance of Hector's, pre-dating his friendship with Mr. Fleming.

Ann increasingly feared for her self-destructive mate's mounting liquor and nicotine binging, as well as an equally alarming spike in Ian's always-present penchant for sustained melancholia.

Hector consoled himself at least this time he wasn't going on his own nickel as he had in 1937, the last time he'd agreed to babysit a fellow author bent upon a volatile overseas sortie.

That last lamentable junket found Hector stalking Ernest Hemingway through Civil War-torn Spain. Hector was still living under the shadow of a Francisco Franco-decreed death warrant fostered by fallout from *that* sorry mess—a standing execution order that had-too long kept Hector from returning to one of the favored countries of his youth.

This time, things would surely turn out differently, he kidded himself.

But there was more: A fellow author memorably declared that after the age of forty, a man should only go to a new place if his freight was fully paid by another. In this instance, at least Hector's tab was seen to by that impertinent men's magazine with its nude centerfolds and seemingly deep pockets.

Dwelling on all that, Hector shook his head, staring into the sweet-smelling muddle of his cocktail. The fingers of his left hand drummed a paperback copy of Ian's *From Russia with*

Love, recently touted as one of President Kennedy's favorite novels, an eyebrow-raising admission that instantly rocketed Ian's books to the top of the U.S. bestseller lists.

Ian.

Melancholy.

Self-destructive despair.

A mounting preoccupation with death.

Hell, Hector brooded, still staring into his highball glass, why shouldn't any of that be? It *was* getting to be that sorry time of life, after all.

Ian Lancaster Fleming was fifty-four; Hector Mason Lassiter was now sixty-two.

Although there was no denying younger Ian had contrived to put far greater mileage on his face and dealt more palpable punishment to his whippet frame than beefier Hector ever dared contemplate, the elder author felt more the goner on this storm-swept night.

Ian drank far harder and smoked infinitely more, of course. But when it came to friends—or at least contemporaries, if not outright *peers*—the sharpening arc of attrition was exacting the more pitiless toll from Hector of late; that was undeniable. There was simply no getting around the grim facts: Assessed with a cold eye, the older author figured that sorry mortality rate probably owed mostly to the vagaries of his undeniable, advancing age.

And, hell, it was autumn, after all. Some of the season's inherent melancholy surely had to contribute to Hector's present maudlin mood, or so he tried to make himself believe.

Hemingway had memorably declared fall the time of year that unfailingly put fiction writers in piercing awareness of death, the season that so feverishly "made all the scribbling boys put pen to paper like grieving, sorry sons of bitches."

Hem: Now there was *another* big one who had recently gotten away, damn it. Jesus Christ, poor Ernest was more than one year dead, yet still a stubborn and profound drag on Hector's daily morale.

William Faulkner had also died in July, Hemingway's birth—*and death*—month, as it happened. Not for the first time, Hector undertook a fast and wrenching rough tally of The Lost: Herman Hesse, e.e. cummings and Karen Blixen—all gone and for keeps in this sorry year of Our Absent Lord. There would be no more words from any of them, not *ever*. Hell, even ditsy, imminently resistible Marilyn Monroe had passed, and, like Hem, seemingly by her own hand.

Another Hemingway line, one not original to Papa, abruptly crossed Hector's mind: "People dying this year who've never died before."

You stop that now, Hector scolded himself. *You're already flying across the ocean to babysit a dangerously maudlin writer. For Christ's sake, don't you go and turn into one yourself. Don't you dare do that.*

He smiled ruefully and shook his head. This trip wasn't *all* about Ian and death, not really.

One of *those* odd coincidences that somehow contrived to stubbornly typify his picaresque life had also recently sprung itself upon Hector. That development had impelled him to fly East far more than any request from the Flemings or found money from *Playboy*.

About a week before Ian and Ann and Hugh Hefner came knocking, a man in Japan who ran a venerable inn phoned Hector to say a long-languishing trunk had been discovered in a forgotten corner of his Western tourist-focused hotel. That trunk—perhaps more of a footlocker, judging from the man's description—was labeled as having been the possession of Hector's first wife and fellow novelist, Brinke Devlin.

Before they had met in Paris in February of 1924, the slightly older Brinke had been a globe-trotting writer of a sort long-ago prefiguring Ian or any of Fleming's lately burgeoning would-be knock-off scribes.

Throughout the early 1920s, Brinke had restlessly moved country-to-country—hell, continent-to-continent—voraciously soaking up local color and settings for her sexy, clever series of mystery novels featuring the dapper, *bon vivant* sleuth she'd dubbed Connor Templeton.

It was Hector's understanding the old trunk contained some of Brinke's clothes—Hector let himself entertain the prospect they'd still carry her musky, delicious scent—a diary *and* an unpublished manuscript for a Templeton novel. It seemed an absolute jackpot.

The simple prospect of fresh words recorded in Brinke's graceful hand—fiction or nonfiction, God, that hardly mattered, not at all—was more than enough to send Hector dashing off to Japan to claim the goods.

Yes, this trip wasn't *all* sloppy seconds, not *fully* a bitter repast of reflected glory and growing sadness.

If that Japanese inn-keeper was on the up-and-up, Hector had a real chance to hear Brinke's voice in his head again, to savor her intimating new things to him through her precious prose. Here was a chance to have his life's greatest love freshly restored in a real sense, talking to him and confiding insights through her writing. It was also a chance to further leverage Brinke's literary long game by perhaps putting a new work out there in her name.

Thinking now of lusty, luscious Brinke inevitably set other notions and urges moving inside Hector, all undeniably animal.

Specifically: his lone companion in the concourse's quiet, darkened little bar.

Lone companion?

Probably they weren't anywhere nearly that solitary, of course. Almost always these days, there seemed to be some J. Edgar Hoover minion, furtively watching from the shadows, stalking Hector.

True, he hadn't yet spotted any of his usual Bureau tails on this damp night, but history being the harshest of teachers, *they* were almost certainly lurking somewhere in Idlewild this evening, spying on him, relaying Hector's movements to that evil little frog-faced bastard, John Edgar Hoover.

Sighing, Hector drained his highball glass and fully turned his attention to the pretty, black-haired woman sitting kitty-corner from him at the L-shaped bar. She wore a tailored charcoal suit—the matching jacket was presently off. A silky tan blouse clung to proud breasts and flattered broad, straight shoulders. She'd be tall standing, Hector guessed, probably five-ten, or maybe even an inch better than that, even without those wickedly sharp-heeled, black pumps he'd seen she sported as she first approached the bar.

The stranger's glistening, raven hair echoed Brinke's. So did her smoldering eyes. *Maybe*, Hector kidded himself, *that's a sign*.

This woman looked to be perhaps thirty years old on the high-end as he assessed her in the low and undeniably flattering lounge light. Hell, she might be younger, or, maybe even a shade *older*, he reckoned upon closer inspection.

She was almost certainly European. He deduced that from the way she held her cigarette between thumb and forefinger, clutched at its end.

The brunette had flawless if slightly sunburned skin, not quite yet fading to a tan. Her nails were cut short and unvarnished, and her hair was brushed straight back, disappearing in a heavy fall behind those prideful shoulders that begged caressing and kissing. No sign of hairspray, not given the way her fingers easily streamed through that long, dark mane while pressing open a paperback with her cigarette hand.

Hector had gotten a glance at the cover of that book a drink-and-a-half back—her own spy novel, something new by Eric Ambler. He couldn't fault the fetching stranger her reading tastes.

At least it wasn't Ian's Bond, thank God—commuters now always seemed to be clutching those omnipresent Signet paperbacks just like the one Hector carried, devouring Agent 007's wild escapades while awaiting trains, planes and buses.

Hector checked his battered old Timex: fifty minutes until boarding likely commenced. More had been started in less with an attractive woman now and again in his time; or at least that had been so when Hector was in his natural prime.

Given the emptiness of their little wing of the usually bustling New York airport bar they now had nearly same as to themselves, they almost certainly were booked on the same flight.

Perhaps if they hit if off there'd be space on the plane to permit moving around of seats. If so, possibly a lounge conversation might stretch into more on the plane, and something still more from there might ensue—during or after a potentially shared London Heathrow landing and a lingering layover.

But he was surely getting far ahead of himself indulging such lusty fantasies about all that.

And, regardless of all that may or may not lay in wait, in the end, Hector simply wasn't up to being alone in his head anymore, not on this moody, loss-haunted night. Shirley

Bassey crooning on the lounge sound system: *Burn My Candle.* Even the music could be worse—it might as easily have been flavor-of-the-moment Bobby Vinton or the infernally over-played *Moon River.*

Intent upon rolling those familiar, capricious dice, Hector caught the bartender's attention, pointed at his glass for a refill, then nodded across the bar, indicating where he expected his fresh drink to be delivered.

Confidence?

Hubris?

Hector told himself, *No guts, no glory.* He slid his copy of Ian's thriller into his sports jacket's pocket along with his old Zippo and virgin pack of Pall Malls and rose to risk an introduction.

He said, "May I intrude on your reading?"

A smile, open and inviting; warm dark eyes appraised him. She fingered her nearly emptied wine goblet and put down her book. The dregs of something red swirled in the glass. She said, "My God, please *do*. I'll shamelessly confess that for some time I've been hoping you would do this very thing." A silky British accent. She sat up a little straighter and moved her purse to make room. "You're Hector Lassiter, aren't you?"

"Uh, yes…" Made, again. He cursed to himself.

"I've read you, as you'll surely have guessed by now," she said. "I thought I recognized you from the photos on your books. You really rather resemble the actor, you know, William Holden? But I expect you hear that a lot. Anyway, I quite relish your novels."

Quite relish? Jolly good. Hector smiled his thanks and tapped her copy of Ambler with an index finger. "I quite relish this fella's works, too."

"So do I, mostly, but maybe not this time," she said. "I fear this one of his just isn't reaching me. It's a bit too fragmented, I think."

Everyone was a critic.... He said, "What are you drinking, and won't you please have some more on me?"

Another smile. There were almost imperceptible laugh lines around her broad, sultry mouth and the faintest of crow's feet accented wide black eyes he could see better in the low lounge light. Yes, he thought, definitely thirty, at least. Maybe verging thirty-five or perhaps a bit more. But still quite beautiful.

And anyway—and *again*—who the hell was he to judge, sitting, as he did, on the wrong side of sixty?

"Yes, please, that would be quite wonderful," she said, "and it's Cabernet." The bartender hadn't started mixing Hector's next drink yet. He caught the man's attention and said, "Belay my refill, buddy, please? Two glasses of Cabernet Sauvignon, instead." He said more softly to her, "What vintner, by the way, or does that matter at all?"

"It really does, I fear," she said. "More than a bit of a wine snob you've got on your hands, Mr. Lassiter. Tonight, it's Miguel Torres."

"That will do very nicely indeed," he said.

A somewhat sheepish smile. "It's not cheap, I know. Sorry if..."

Hector liked the way her accent and smile made those last, apologetic words come off. Her being remotely sorry for the cost of the wine was entirely disingenuous of course, yet charmingly, even enticingly so. This stranger wore her expensive tastes well.

Dell Shannon was their background music presently: *Runaway.*

In keeping with the lyrics of the moody song, a steady rain kissed the window overlooking the concourse, striking the panes, then trailing in meandering streaks down the glass. Distant rumbles of thunder shook silverware.

As they waited for their wine, He said, "You still have me at a cruel disadvantage. What's your name?"

"Cruel? Hardly." She assessed him candidly, then said, "Haven Branch." She caught him looking at her left ring finger and gave him a knowing half-smile. She reached out and pointedly turned his left hand for a better view. Her fingers lingered on his palm longer than needed. "Not even a tan line on that naked ring finger to raise eyebrows," she said. "So glad we got *that* out of the way. Good news for both of us, or don't you agree?"

Oh, he agreed, plenty. Hector shifted his arm to make room for the delivery of their drinks. He checked his watch and decided to settle his bill in advance. He said impulsively, "The lady's is mine, too."

She thanked him again and tapped her glass against his. "To what, then?"

"You started this toast, so you have to do the honors."

"How about to absent friends?"

Morbid, but undeniably appropriate given his present dark state of mind. Hector countered with, "Sticking to the Royal Navy tradition, 'Ourselves.'"

They tapped glasses again and sipped their wine. Heady stuff, indeed.

Hector realized on top of his other drinks, he'd need to throttle back after this one or else risk a serious buzz. He also had some mild blood-sugar concerns to keep an increasingly wary eye on these sorry years. He settled their mutual tabs and turned back to face her. "You read a lot?"

"Yes, but mostly thrillers—you know, your kind of novels."

"Where bound?"

"England for a day or so, then pressing on to Japan."

Better and better. He smiled and said, "As am I."

"Maybe we could arrange to sit together, at least to our shared first stop?" Another smile. "That might be wonderful."

It might be. But give voice to hope? Dare to share your plans out loud? Do that, and you risked hearing God's capricious chuckle.

So very little ever went according to uttered plan in Hector's stormy experience.

Take their meeting tonight for example:

By their journey's still-distant end, both would be regarded as quite dead to the rest of the world.

2

STRANGERS ON A PLANE

Playboy had sprung for first-class seating for Hector— exactly *that much* was working in his favor. Haven was also flying first-class, but across the aisle in a row of four. The author's actual neighbor was a fidgety, nervous looking little Asian man—a fortyish Japanese who quickly pulled down the window shade at his side. *Well, there goes what little there was of the view,* Hector thought.

To steel himself for the long transatlantic flight, Hector rejected the stewardess' offer of another straightforward cocktail, asking instead for an Irish coffee. The little man next to him ordered club soda, then dug out a Vick's inhaler he proceeded to thrust up each nostril, noisily sniffing at it one side, then the other, then back again.

Hector sighed, sipping his coffee and whiskey. It was going to be a long journey with this man at his side. Hector watched as Haven Branch talked quietly and emphatically with their stewardess, who in turn vigorously nodded. He had a sense Haven was showing or displaying something to the flight attendant whose fetching rump otherwise blocked the author's view of whatever was in Haven's hand.

More head shaking ensued, then, with a faint smile, Haven rose and squeezed past the tallish, rather fey man seated alongside her. The man scowled at Haven, looking far more put out than it seemed circumstances warranted.

Their stewardess, lithesome, paled-skinned and redheaded—an endearing, faint bridge of freckles dappled her prettily upturned nose—leaned across Hector, a generous breast brushing his drink arm. She softly tapped his neighbor on the shoulder. She said, "Sir, I'm afraid I have to ask you to move. It's only just across the aisle. Sorry, but it really must be this way." Another smile. "And, anyway, you don't seem terribly keen on a window seat." She indicated his already closed window shade.

The Asian man started to balk, but his English failed him in the moment; the titan-haired flight attendant held her ground.

Looking perturbed, the little man squeezed past Hector, almost upsetting his spiked coffee. He plopped angrily into Haven's vacated seat. The blond man glared at his new neighbor, then back at Haven as, facing Hector, she gracefully brushed past the author's legs and assumed the Asian man's empty seat.

As she did that, the stewardess smiled and nodded at Hector, looking more inquiringly at him for some reason. Just what had Haven said to her about him, he wondered.

"I hope you don't mind my presumption in getting that chap moved," Haven said, "but I'm frankly arrogant enough to think we'll both be *much* happier for my having done so."

Much, almost assuredly, he thought. Hector smiled and presumed to order Haven another glass of red wine. "You're on safe enough ground, no fear there," he said. "But what in God's name did you say to secure this blessed swap?"

Haven accepted her glass of wine. Once again, the hostess studied Hector with amplified interest. Haven offered her glass for another tap, then said, "Given what you do for a living, can't you leave a woman *some* mysteries of her own?"

"Fair enough," Hector said, bumping his drink against hers.

She sipped her wine and nodded at the paperback balanced on his leg. "I take it that one's good? I mean, your foppish president says it's so, right?"

It was a reference to that list that had been released of Jack Kennedy's supposedly favorite novels of the year. The word through back-channels was an aide or someone had actually suggested Ian's title's inclusion to the mix in a cynical bid to make blue-blooded Jack appear more the everyman.

Hector shrugged. "Just like JFK, even a stopped clock is right twice a day, you know."

A soft smirk. "So I'm to gather you're a Republican or whatever, of some sort?"

Hector shrugged. "*Whatever* if anything. Not a Democrat, anyway. Probably not anything, really. I've never much been one for politics."

He relented. "But *I* like Ian's writing just fine. I'm flying to England to meet Mr. Fleming, as a matter of fact. Then we're pressing on to Japan together. A writers' Asian holiday, so to speak."

It tinged on name-dropping, particularly in light of Ian's lately burgeoning fame. Well, what the hell? It also had the virtue of being true.

"My God, I'd love to be a fly on *that* wall," she said. The wine at last seemed to be reaching her, its effect there just a bit in her silky but thickening voice. "Japan—I seem to remember reading you were part of your country's war effort. Were any of those patriotic efforts undertaken there?" She closely studied him over the rim of her glass.

Hector chose his next words carefully. He'd nearly been court-martialed by General George S. Patton and his minions in the aftermath of the last war for blurring certain critical lines.

"Mostly I was in the European theater," Hector said. "Never made to it the Pacific when all that was really active, and thank God for that. And I wasn't any kind of fighting man, *per se.*"

That last was a downright lie. And, loathe as he was to run a highlighter over his age to the younger Haven, he nevertheless said, "I was a bit long in the tooth for front line stuff, even then. At the end of the day, I was pretty much just a war correspondent. Ian and I *did* make a bit of a run into Japan shortly after the surrender, but it was just for a couple of days on a kind of silly lark. Nothing really came of any of that. Quixotic nonsense."

Fruitless though that last trip may have proven, all of that was still buried under layers of secrecy, even after all these years, bolstered on Ian's end at least, by the Official Secrets Act, and on Hector's by Patton's drumhead court and its no-statute-of-limitations' disclosure order that could land Hector's ass in some military jail, even now, if he ever publically spilled the beans.

Throughout the war, Hector had quietly been an agent for the Operation of Strategic Services. His OSS duties had actually led to Hector's first meeting with Ian, and, yes, that had happened in Japan during that other, still secret trip—but he simply couldn't confide any of that to Haven, even if he had felt impelled for some reason to do so.

He said, "You used the phrase, *your country.* You're British, at least English by birth, I take it?"

"London-born, but elsewhere bred," she said. "I don't ask this based on accent, but rather from memory—you're a Texan, isn't that so?"

"Born in Galveston," Hector confirmed. "Grew up on the Gulf Coast."

"Mr. Fleming says Texans are the best of Americans, you know. He's written that more than once at any rate. Bond's CIA friend, Felix, is a Texan, yes?"

Felix Leiter. Yes. "So you have read at least some of Ian's Bond books?"

"Of course, just not that one you're reading presently," Haven said. "Since the success of the film back home—you know, *Doctor No*—your friend is growing quite famous in Britain. His novels are unavoidable if you're any kind of reader at all."

"Ian *has* arrived," Hector said softly, fighting a wave of professional jealousy. The first Bond movie hadn't landed in America quite yet. He said, "I'm invited to visit the set of the next Bond film, the one they're making of this book next year. I'm asked to go to Istanbul with Ian for a few days." Hector held up the paperback copy of *From Russia with Love*. "Still deciding on that trip."

"Then I'm quite jealous," Haven said, smiling. "Sean Connery is...well, that handsome, strapping Scot is really quite something. He's much more attractive to me than the Bond in the books, who I find something of a dark neurotic. As those sorts of characters go, I'll confess that I really much prefer Heath Dirk."

Heath had been Hector's recurring character through a series of eleven novels in the 1930s and '40s. "I'll confide now that I was utterly distraught when you offed him," she said. "I was really angry at you for a time, mister. Dear God, *nobody* does that, not to that kind of continuing character, you know."

Hector well knew. Hell, that was the very reason for doing that thing as his interest in Heath waned. He'd be damned if he'd ever continue to write about a character who no longer engaged him. Always the envelope pusher—that was Hector on a good day at his writing table.

He traced the rim of his glass with a forefinger. "Name for me a book series where the eleventh volume in the arc was even half as good as the first installment, or even the fifth or sixth novel. And, old Dirk? He'd well run his course, at least for me. My God, I really didn't want to be writing him forever, not like Dame Agatha and that fussy damned Belgian of hers, or Estelle Quartermain, and her Albanian accountant-cum sleuth. None of that endless, ageless hero stuff for me, thank you very much. I loved Dirk too much to ever consider doing that to the poor bastard."

"I can't read either of those female writers anymore, either. No patience for their mysteries, even if they are my countrywomen, more or less. Thrillers are what I love. Your kind of books."

Hector said, "Forgive me, but this is threatening to turn into shop talk, at least from my perspective. I'm far more interested in you, Haven. So, you're going home?"

"That's right. Very briefly, then flying on to Japan."

"What brought you stateside?"

"A cousin's wedding. She went to school here. Promptly fell in love with a Yank. By now they're honeymooning in the Bahamas. I'm not convinced the union will endure, however. Anyway, I just flew up from Florida." That explained her mild sunburn, not yet faded to a tan.

Their discussion was abruptly interrupted by static, then pre-flight instructions.

The storm outside was also picking up. As they at last took to the air, the weather worsened. The Pan Am jet was buffeted by the wind and engulfed in frantic forks of lighting as it made its ascent.

Haven took his right hand in hers, gripping tightly. Hector reassuringly squeezed back. They kept holding hands for quite some time, even after their plane mounted far above the storm clouds and the roughness of the ride smoothed out.

Haven let go first; Hector brooded on that.

About three hours into the flight, his new friend was dozing. Hector unfastened his lap strap and rose on cracking knees to head to the restroom to splash some cold water on his face and otherwise freshen up. The forward facilities adjacent to the flight cabin were already occupied and sporting a longish line of fellow first-class passengers, fidgeting from impatient kidneys denied relief when the jet was still bucking through the storm front. Hector headed toward the back of the plane.

After splashing cold water on his face, Hector toweled off and twisted the handle, stepping back out into the rear portion of the Pan American Douglas DC9.

The fey, tall blond man originally slated to sit next to Haven Branch stepped into Hector, blocking his path. Hector scowled and moved to step around the man, but the stranger mirrored Hector's course correction, freshly intercepting him.

"Please, Mr. Lassiter, we don't have much time," the man said, his tone low and urgent. "My name is Terrence Hunt." He lowered his voice further, his gaze restlessly roaming around them. "I'm with the Central Intelligence Agency, Mr. Lassiter. You know, *CIA*. We know you're planning to rendezvous with Mr. Ian Fleming, and we think we know why."

Hunt looked over his shoulder again, making sure nobody was approaching. He said, "The man now sitting next to me, the Japanese, is a suspected member of a radical conservative movement in his homeland. A newly resurgent organization called The Black Dragon Club or *Kokuryū-Kurabu*. The woman, whom you know as Haven Branch, the woman who contrived to be seated next to you, is also not remotely what she probably appears to be to your eyes, not just some dishy, roundheels tourist. She's actually—"

Hector warned the man with his eyes.

Arching a dark eyebrow, Haven Branch said, "Gentlemen." A perfunctory smile, then she said, "So sorry to crowd you chaps, but the queue for the loo up front is rather epic just now."

"Very formidable, agreed." Hector smiled, gesturing at the door to the restroom. "Why we're both back here. Or call us egalitarians. Anyway, the commoners' facilities are all yours, Miss Branch."

Hector made a show of reaching for his Zippo as she squeezed past them. He said to the blond man, "That light you asked for, pal," Hector said.

Fortunately, the man indeed had some cigarettes in his pocket—his yellowed fingernails had tipped Hector he was a heavy smoker.

The man called Hunt cupped Hector's hand as the writer held his old lighter up to the man's Camel cigarette. Hector tolerated the stranger's touch. Once the alleged spy's cigarette was going, Hunt turned the lighter to better see it and then read aloud its engraved legend, "One True Sentence." He said, "It means something?"

"To me at least, sure," Hector said. He motioned with a hand to indicate the American agent should lead the way. After hearing Haven lock the lavatory door, they slowly set off toward the front of the plane.

The other man said softy, "We'll talk more, soon. Please plan to spend some time with me before we go to fetch our luggage, Mr. Lassiter. The men's room at the airport would be a good place to do that. It's a place certain others can't follow us again as she just did. Once there, I can fill you in completely. Until then, please believe that woman's not to be trusted, not for a second. And please believe she may even mean you lethal harm, Mr. Lassiter. Don't you dare doubt that is true. Are we clear on that much?"

Hector sized the man up, not fully certain. With an uneasy stomach, Hector nevertheless said, "Clear as crystal."

After settling into his seat, Hector instinctively fastened his seatbelt as the jet freshly bucked and rocked through waves of mounting turbulence. A bit worried for Haven, he glanced over his shoulder. She was making her way back up the aisle, holding tightly to seat backs either side to steady herself. As she neared Hector, the plane pitched hard to the left and Haven sprawled indecorously across the lap of the blond, self-proclaimed CIA agent.

Rising, she apologized, tucking her blouse back into her tailored skirt, then accepted Hector's hand as she further fought the plane's jostling. Haven settled in and deftly fastened her seat belt just as the plane took a stomach-dropping plunge.

Hector, nervous but determined to put up a brave front, said, "I'm sure they'll just climb a bit harder, go a bit *higher*—you know, rise above it all again, so to speak."

Surely enough, the nose of the jet was already arcing upward.

Hector chanced a glance over and saw the blond CIA agent was sweating, tugging determinedly at his tie and taking deep breaths.

The poor bastard certainly looked sick, and also—just possibly—terrified.

3

DEAD ON ARRIVAL

About an hour out from London Heathrow, the stewardesses began passing out damp towels and last refreshments.

As everyone else seemed intent on combating in-flight dehydration, Hector ordered a cup of piping black coffee and watched his fellow passengers stir back to wakefulness. It amazed him how many had managed to somehow sleep through the violent turbulence.

Having napped for about twenty minutes, Haven awakened looking sharp and focused, no trace whatever of a hangover. She was much woman, then, particularly when Hector calculated how prodigiously she'd out-drank him.

Haven excused herself to the restroom again and returned about ten minutes later, smelling of freshened, musky perfume and the minty aroma of toothpaste.

Settling in and accepting her own coffee—a morning wake-me-up polluted with cream and sugar—Haven nodded at the bulging seat flap close against his knees and said, "You finished your friend's book?"

"About thirty minutes ago," Hector said.

"And your thoughts? To use the advert writers' phrase, was it 'a corker'?"

He laughed and said, "It was very good indeed, maybe even Ian's best and strongest Bond book, although it ends on a sort of cliff-hanger. Not sure yet how I feel about that aspect. If Ian left it there, it would certainly be quite brave. But since I gather it's a fake-out of some kind because of subsequent 007 releases?" Hector shrugged. "Afraid I was kind of distracted in 1957 and 1958, so I missed this one when it was new and I haven't touched the follow-ups yet. You finished the Ambler?"

"Yes. And it was rather disappointing on the whole, I'll confess, just as I feared. I'd offer to trade, but I sense it would be a terribly uneven exchange from my end."

He pulled out the Fleming and handed it to her. "You take the Bond as a gift. That Ambler I actually read a few weeks ago." Hector, too, had found the book not quite up to par.

With a burst of mild static, the pilot interrupted them, warning of their impending landing and directing the airhostesses to begin prepping the cabin for final approach. Their captain asked all passengers return to their seats and buckle in, fearing more turbulence as they again sacrificed altitude.

Haven sipped more of her coffee, then asked, "Mr. James Bond's creator—he'll be meeting you at the airport, I suppose?"

Hector shook his head, signaling for a last refill of his own cup. "No, I have an accommodation in a very fine hotel before Ian and I fly out together to Japan. Putting up at the Dorchester, courtesy of an American magazine. One of the rare good perks of corresponding."

"Good indeed, but surely you're not going to simply hole up in that posh hotel, smashing though it is," Haven said.

"Wouldn't you like to get a little time on the town before heading to the East?"

Hector thought about that. He might like that very much— once he knew more about what Haven truly represented and if what he learned about her proved sufficiently reassuring. After all, according to the man he hardly knew, the alleged American spy across the aisle, Haven possibly intended to kill Hector.

But the more he'd thought about that ominous claim, the more ludicrous it seemed. What could possibly motivate this dusky, dishy Brit to mean him harm like that? What possible motive could result in this British-looker called Haven Branch wanting him dead?

Hector made an admittedly idiosyncratic but regular practice of cataloguing his enemies and keeping tabs on their whereabouts to the extent that was at all possible. Haven Branch didn't seem to line up with any old foes or lingering vendettas that made any sort of sense. She could have no discernible, logical link to the half-dozen or so of his monsters still lurking out there—the ones who'd indeed put Hector in the ground, given any reasonable shot at doing so.

"Dinner at the hotel would be on my current employer," he said, "but drinks out after could be wonderful, and maybe a bit of a walking tour after that would be good, too. Last time I was in England was during the waning days of the war. Too much of the city was still a pile of rubble, then. I'd guess that's all been put right by now?"

"*Put right* is one term for it," she said. A sad smile. "The last war's scars have been deftly obscured. But most of what was blown up or burned down was never really replaceable, you know. They just don't build them that way anymore."

He said, "I assume you were evacuated during the war?"

"No, I wasn't 'in country' at the time," she said. "My father was a kind of diplomat. We were in Japan, of all places, just before and after the war."

"You were very young then?"

"I suppose I was about nineteen or twenty, so not so terribly young," she said. "I loved Japan. I still do. I very much enjoyed going back after the war, even changed and wrecked as it was then. Even if the Japanese people had been regarded as some kind of enemy." She seemed to have trouble conceiving of how that could ever be so.

The freckle-faced stewardess, looking damnably and inexplicably fresh, began gently waking stubbornly sleeping passengers and making sure their seats were upright and belts fastened. She paused, frowned, then gently shook at the blond man seated across the aisle from Hector.

Terrence Hunt didn't respond. She shook him again, then said repeatedly, "Sir? *Sir*? Are you unwell?"

The stewardess—"Gwen," according to the metal tag pinned over her left breast—shook the man's shoulder a last time, then frowned once more and dared to touch the man's throat on the right side, just under the chin. She said too loudly, far too unthinkingly, "Oh, my *gosh*! I do believe he's *dead*!" Her shaking hand recoiled from the stranger's neck.

Frowning, Hector unfastened his seat belt and reached across the aisle, grabbing hold of Hunt's wrist. The still man was quite cold to the touch. No pulse at all.

The little Asian man seated next to the corpse immediately looked rather ill—pushing further toward his other, still-alive neighbor who was also shrinking away from the corpse.

Hector said softly to the stewardess, "Dead, yes, he is that thing, definitely. And he's been that way for quite a while, I think."

Hector let go of the dead man's wrist. The man's body was well on its way to assuming cabin temperature.

All of the passengers were at least briefly delayed in their disembarking as a result of Terrence Hunt's mysterious death. Because they had been the most-recently observed to interact with Hunt before he died, Hector and Haven were questioned last and longest.

Apart from admitting to offering the man a requested light, Hector had nothing useful to provide. He refrained from sharing the alleged spy's professed vocation, as well as the warning Hunt had given Hector about Haven.

Under the best of circumstances, Hector couldn't imagine that the strangeness of all that—let alone the fact it may all have been crazy talk, in the end—wouldn't result in anything other than further, longer entanglement with authorities.

As for Haven, she'd merely been pitched into the man's lap by the air turbulence, but surely that was hardly of consequence? Unless perhaps—as one of the airport security officials pointed out—the man had died from some communicable illness to which Haven might have been exposed through that robust, if fleeting, tactile contact.

But the dead man had not been coughing. Hunt had shown no sign of carrying a fever and he hadn't once reached for a handkerchief. He'd never asked for water to help wash down any pills, as Gwen, the sexy, ginger stewardess, testified.

Eventually, after leaving authorities information about where they might be reached during the coming hours, Hector and Haven were at last released to collect their luggage.

After lunch and a shower, Hector napped a bit in his sumptuous hotel bed, a restorative idyll that soothed the kinks in his back after the long flight spent almost exclusively sitting.

He showered again, then shaved and dressed for an evening about Westminster with Haven. He even elected to wear a black knit tie for their evening out, figuring any of the better English restaurants might be a bit fussier regarding such formalities than the eateries back home.

Hector sat in the hotel lounge, savoring a Perrier and waiting for Haven Branch to come and "collect him"—her phrase. She'd seemed quite pleased by the prospect of playing tour guide.

After ordering a second bottle of sparkling water—this one with an extra twist of lemon—Hector was startled to find his fleeting, former neighbor on the Pan Am flight from New York suddenly at his side. He caught himself instinctively reaching under his jacket for his Colt before remembering it was stashed in the gun vault in his home back in New Mexico.

He next considered the Perrier bottle sitting alongside his drinking glass—it might prove weapon enough in a pinch, Hector supposed. In the movies, bottles broke easily upon impact with heads. But that was just cinema hokum. In real life, hefted and swung, such bottles more typically shattered skulls, killing the one on the receiving end.

And even past sixty, Hector was willing to wager he had deciding height and weight on the little Japanese man if it came to any flavor of fair fight. He said to the stranger, "Please don't make me hurt you, pal."

The man's dark eyes widened. He was clearly startled by Hector's threat. "Hurt you?" His English was still rather faltering, but measurably better than on the plane. "No, not to hurt you. That's not the purpose I have. To protect you— that's what I'm trying to do, Mr. Lassiter."

"Very thoughtful, then," Hector said. "Who are you, exactly?"

The man held out a smallish hand in his approximation of a western handshake. "Hiroshi Takahashi."

Hector hesitated, bit his lip, then shook. His mitt engulfed Hiroshi's hand. He found himself throttling back on a natural tendency to apply some real pressure for a handshake that would be remembered, the kind of howdy-do he'd give some publisher or fellow Texan, back home.

"I'm Hector Lassiter, as you already seem to know." He flashed his less-than-friendly smile. "I'll let *you* know in a few minutes if I'm truly pleased to meet you, Hiroshi. Frankly, some troubling things have already been said about you."

"Almost certainly all of them are lies," the other man said. "The man who was killed, the man on the plane? He said something to you about me, yes?"

"That's right. He said you belong to a secret organization of some sort in your homeland. Didn't get the full fill before the luckless bastard turned tits up, but I gather the name translates into something roughly equivalent to 'The Black Dragon Club.'"

An emphatic headshake. "No. There is such a thing...we think there is. This Club is newer. It's a branch you could say, of an older club called the Black Dragon Society. That club was ended by your occupying authorities in 1946. Or it seemed it was ended. It is back now and inspiring other secret groups. All of them, we think, are dedicated to restoring the Emperor's surrendered status as a living deity—as a leader to be venerated."

The stranger's eyes grew earnest. "I swear to you, I'm not a member of that kind of a group. I am with the National Safety Forces. We are allies, then. And we—my people—are very worried about the Black Dragons. That is also because a writer like you, but one of my countrymen, a very important one, seems to be warming to the movement. But we believe a bigger, darker organization is in back of even that group that we *now* know as the Black Dragon Club."

Hector, palpably skeptical but not particularly concerned if he conveyed any doubt, said, "And who is this bigger, darker organization?"

"That's what I and my colleagues are trying to learn. It is something we believe may have come out of post-war Germany, but is now spreading its reach everywhere, and far more successfully than the Reich ever did."

"Ominous… You said some novelist has been caught up in this—" Hector almost attempted pronunciation of the Japanese version of the Black Dragon Club's name, but as a high school dropout who spoke several other languages, he told himself he had nothing to prove, and so went with the familiar. Course correcting, Hector said, "This writer you say is being courted by these Black Dragons—I'm trying to imagine myself doing something similar back home and coming up short. Who is this Japanese author, exactly?"

No hesitation: "A novelist of some renown, but known by his penname of Yukio Mishima."

Hector certainly knew that name. Hell, he'd also read in translation much of Mishima's works. The man was a quietly and stubbornly a contender for the Nobel Prize for Literature. Mishima's recent short story, "Patriotism," about a young couple making passionate love before committing graphically described ritual suicide together, still haunted Hector, particularly after what Hem's kid brother had resonantly described as Ernest Hemingway's equally recent "*seppuku* by shotgun." Mix in Ian's next planned Bond novel, and there seemed to be something decidedly *samurai* in the wind, presently.

But there was something else—a lunch with Mishima was already on Hector's Japanese appointment books. Too much there to be mere coincidence.

Hector once more hefted his Perrier bottle, again weighed it, but then used it to freshen his glass. "The dead man on the plane, who was he? Do you know?"

"You talked together by the bathroom door," the other man said quickly, toying with his inhaler. "Didn't the man tell you who he was?"

"Oh, he introduced himself, to be sure," Hector said carefully, "just the same as you did to me a few moments ago. I have only your word you're what you claim to be. The same can be said of that sorry son of a bitch who's headed to an icebox. You were sitting next to him during his last hours, and so you were certainly well-positioned to kill him." Hector smiled, studying the man. "Please try to see it from my point of view."

"But, *no*. The man on the plane who died was named Sebastian Keene. Mr. Lassiter, we believe Mr. Keene is with that darker organization I have told you about. You were an OSS agent, and working closely with a British spy. We know that. We know you worked with Mr. Ian Lancaster Fleming. You two came to Japan to try and get information regarding a weapon my country's government worked on as it raced to beat your country's atom bomb. We know all that."

Rubbing his jaw, Hector took a moment to reflect.

After a time, lighting a cigarette, he said, "You're saying your country was trying for the A-bomb, too?"

"No, not quite that," Hiroshi said. "The imperial government was after something quite different, Mr. Lassiter. Something…biological." He hesitated, looking rather ashamed at what his country had contemplated. "It was their aim to create a thing that could be spread through crop dusters. We—they—planned to have planes fly all over your country, dropping this thing on your farms, your crops. A thing that would have killed your farms, your animals. It would make everything it touched barren. No horse, no cow, pig, goat and chicken would ever make another. Your plants would all die. We—*they*—meant to starve your country into defeat. Is any of this ringing a bell, Mr. Lassiter?"

Hector took a deep and cleansing breath, finding his center. He shook his head, firmly. "Not a word of it. Honestly? It all sounds like a fantasy worthy of one of Ian's wild James Bond novels." Hector smiled, massaging his brazen lie. "Nah, it doesn't ring true to me, not one goddamn bit. Sorry."

A tepid smile. "Very sorry back, Mr. Lassiter, because I'm not sure I believe you. Not at all."

Hector smiled back, all menace. "I'm not sure that I care if you do." He opted for a change-up. "The woman sitting next to me on the plane—"

A knowing smile: "Ah, Miss Haven Branch…."

At least they agreed upon the name. That seemed something to draw at least *scant* promise from. "Yes, Haven. What's your take on Miss Branch?"

"*Take*? I don't really have any—*if* by *take* you mean an opinion of some kind. I'm told she's MI5." A half-smile. "That is to say, she is with British Military Intelligence, Section 5." A hopeful smile, anticipating understanding. "You know? The British Secret Service?"

The little man tried to make a joke, making a gun with his fingers. "Sort of like Agent 007 you're reading about," he said, feigning shots with his fingers at Hector's head, then at his heart. "Mr. Kiss Kiss Bang Bang?"

"Sure, just like Mr. Bond." Hector's head was spinning.

So who, if either, was *the* real spy—was it Terrence Hunt or was it Haven Branch?

Or was it maybe both?

Perhaps neither?

The little man pushed his glass a stool over and rose abruptly. "Speak of the devil and she will appear. Miss Branch can't see me here after the plane… Quickly—I know you are planning to meet with Mr. Mishima. Knowing what I've told you, I'd like you to question him on these things. Later, I will find you and we will talk about what you learn."

Listening, Hector glanced into the mirror—indeed, along came Haven, smashing in a long coat and sexy black crushed-velvet dress that accented her faint sunburn. He said quickly, "From *your* perspective, should I fear for myself from this woman?"

A confused smile. Hiroshi said, "You two are from allied countries. So what could you possibly have to fear, yes?"

With that lingering, sixty-four thousand dollar question left in a dying fall, Hiroshi swiftly took his leave.

Smiling, Haven slid off her coat, unveiling bare, still-bronzing shoulders and an enticing expanse of décolletage.

She deftly scooped up a menu Hector had asked for in order to preview and said, "Hullo there, Mr. Lassiter." A smashing smile and a kiss on the cheek, then Haven asked, "So Hector, what looks truly scrumptious?"

4

SAFE HAVEN?

Rather than pay hotel prices, even on someone else's tab, Haven convinced Hector they should venture out, wandering Soho in the rain to find their own fare.

Under a shared umbrella, Haven squeezed his arm tighter and recited a line of poetry: "When chill November's surly blast makes fields and forest bare...."

Hector smiled and said, "I will confess on that note that I love the rain, and autumn is my favorite season of all."

"The so-called season of the witch," Haven said, "and one to inspire poets."

"Inspire *and* depress, which is maybe too often the same thing," Hector said.

The wind tugged harder at the big umbrella, flinging a spray of rain under its cover, peppering their faces. He adjusted the angle of the umbrella and said, "We should settle on some place soon, before this thing gets turned inside out and we're left soaked to the bone."

Haven smiled and nodded at the Windmill Theatre. "Maybe there? Warm up while we muse over some *tableaux vivants*? Or perhaps you prefer the Colony Club instead? It's a haven for creative types, I've heard."

"That last place least of all," he said crossly. "I hope this won't disappoint you, but I really think I need to eat before we start crawling through all the places Soho is infamous in certain low quarters for offering. What do you say? Dinner before debauchery?"

"I'm starving too," she said, leaning into him. He fought another sudden and vicious tug at their umbrella.

They ended up in cozy little place sharing grilled sole and a couple of glasses of Pinot Gris. Over dinner, he said, "Did you sample any of Ian's latest?"

"The first three chapters," she said. "Oh, I'm hooked, to be sure. But I'd prefer to read something new of yours."

"That will have to wait for next spring," he said. "Although, if proofs catch up to me along the road, you're welcome to read those if you really care too. I'm typically sick of the next book by this point."

He smiled and said, "Warning, sorry trade secrets lay ahead. You see, by the time an author gets his proof copy in hand, he's already read the damn thing more times than can be counted. At least that's so the way that I work. Near the end of the process, you end up reading only what you *think* you wrote, not what's actually on the page. Even brazen typos get by you, and far too late in the sorry goddamn game."

She reached over and squeezed his hand. "Is that what they call an occupational hazard?"

"Real blessing-and-curse stuff, yes," he said. "What's your occupation, or are you maybe extravagantly well-off?"

She leaned closer. "If I confessed to the latter, would it change the way you think of me?"

"Well, I am a fulltime freelance writer, after all. Forever living by my wits and white knuckles."

A sad smile. "Sorry, but I'm afraid I haven't much prospect of becoming your patron, Hector. Not on a civil servant's salary."

Civil servant. Well, here it likely came, at last: Hector realized his fork was poised halfway to his mouth. She stroked a heavy wave of blue-black hair behind her ear. "Now comes his troubled blue eyes," she said.

"Reassure them—allay my troubled mind and eyes," he said, fingering the stem of his wine glass.

"Afraid that's not in the cards, either," she said. "Of course our meeting was no accident. You'll surely have gathered that by now."

A nod, slow and shallow. "Go on, it's usually best just to put it out there," he said. Hector certainly wasn't going to be finessed by a pretty face and body into simply volunteering what he thought he might know from others who'd spoken of her.

"To borrow a phrase from your author friend's growing oeuvre, I'm on her Majesty's Secret Service."

Hector rubbed his jaw. "That is to say, MI6?" He made a gun with thumb and forefinger. "Just like Bond, you're saying? Mr. Kiss Kiss Bang Bang?"

"No," Haven said, no more amused than Hector had been when Hiroshi Takahashi had attempted the same joking, 007 reference. "James Bond's MI6. I'm MI5. And unlike Commander Bond, I enjoy no license to kill," she said.

"Well, that much is a comfort," he said. "So why then are you spying on me? What on earth have I done to worry the British Secret Intelligence Service?" His faced darkened. "Or is this a favor for Mr. Hoover?"

She arched a black eyebrow. "You have some trouble with your FBI?"

"Find me an American author who doesn't," he said.

"I'm not sure that spying is the right word here," she said.

"Guardian Angel, perhaps?"

"Maybe closer," Haven said. "Still, you seem skeptical. Could it be you don't put much faith in female intelligence officers? Maybe you don't believe in women engaging in fieldwork? If that's so, I'm frankly disappointed."

Here he was, being taken for some sort of a misogynist, and not for the first time. In some ways, that seemed another so-called professional hazard tied to his writer's life. Thanks to Mickey Spillane, Fleming and some others, there seemed to be an assumption on the part of a segment of the reading public that male crime and thriller writers were inherently women-haters.

But Hector didn't regard himself as that sort, not a bit. Quite the contrary. It was men he rarely got on with, particularly over any extended period of time. His roster of enduring male friends was astonishingly short.

He said, "I actually married a female spy once, a woman named Duff Sexton. She was more properly OSS than I could ever lay claim to having been." Hector lifted the bottle of white wine and freshened their glasses. They were pacing the drinks far more responsibly than they had in the airport, or on the plane. "What are you protecting me from, Haven?"

"As I told you, that's not really quite right, either." She pulled out a Morland & Co. cigarette and Hector lit it.

"Please try to make it clear to me then," he said, clicking shut his Zippo.

She nodded, blowing a little smoke from the corner of her mouth over her bare shoulder. "Very well, here we go. We believe the notion of Mr. Fleming's next book taking place in Japan was suggested to Ian, a seed planted when Mr. Fleming was in Japan rather abruptly and unexpectedly three years ago and just preparing to leave. He was doing some travel pieces for the *London Times* with an eye toward publishing a later collection of the journalism between hard covers. I believe that book is scheduled for release soon."

Indeed: *Thrilling Cities*—Ian had spoken of the coming nonfiction collection to Hector.

He sipped more of his wine, mind racing. If Ian was being lured back to Japan for some dark reason, and this time with Hector calculatedly in tow? Hector had this terrible, sinking feeling taking hold.

Haven Branch deftly sawed off the limb upon which she had maneuvered them at his urging. "I see the angst again in your expression and those striking, pale blue eyes. You're pulling the threads together and hating what it probably all portends."

"*You* tell me what it *portends*, please." Once more, Hector wasn't going to be tricked or eased into offering up observations or admissions tied to that long-ago, secret trip he'd made into Japan just after the war on behalf of the OSS— the trip that had partly confounded his honeymoon with the aforementioned Duff.

"You're trying to establish that I really know some things," Haven said. "Very well. You mentioned one of your wives— Duff Sexton was her name. But your first wife was also an author, a woman named Brinke Devlin. Parenthetically—I really am a longtime fan of your novels, and of Miss Devlin's, too. At any rate, you've been enticed to come to Japan by the promise of claiming some of Brinke Devlin's allegedly long-lost writings."

Impulsively, Hector said, "Allegedly? You're saying it's a hoax?" God, he hoped that was not so. His heart was deeply set on wallowing in all those words of Brinke's he'd become convinced awaited him in Japan.

"I'm not certain about any of that," she said. "I'd suspect it's a ruse, yes. The timing just seems a little too coincidental and too good to be true, wouldn't you agree?"

"And why would they want to lure me back to Japan?"

"I suspect you well know the answer to that," she said. "But this probably isn't the place to have any more of this particular conversation. It's too quiet and we're in easy line of sight—all to the good for listening devices or spying lip readers. And, anyway, we have a friend from the plane seated just behind you. You know—the man who was originally seated next to you for the ride here before I got him moved. He's tried to disguise himself a bit, but poorly so, if you ask me."

Hector resisted the urge to turn and confirm all that. "And who is our friend from the plane? Any clue about that?"

"Nobody good, nor to be trusted. But again, we should talk someplace where it is less easy to eavesdrop."

"But we chose this place at random," he said. "I sincerely doubt there are any wires or microphones taped to the table bottom." He tapped the surface with his knuckles.

"There are such things as directional mikes," she said, "and there are those lip-readers I mentioned."

"Well, I've just about eaten my fill, anyway," he said. "Given where we're going, I suppose seafood will be a staple meal for the next week or thereabouts. We'll find another place."

"Lovely as I'm sure it is, your hotel room is clearly not to be trusted for this talk, either." A smile. "I am right in assuming you didn't choose your own lodging?"

"Here on another's nickel, as I've made clear more than once," he said. "That American magazine is indeed paying for my fancy digs. So I get your drift. The hotel is a known and pre-arranged destination and therefore my pretty room could be bugged to its lovely gills. I'll settle up and we'll find a more raucous joint." He checked his watch. "I also need to call Ian soon. Let him know I'm here now so we can settle our next travel plans."

"So you'll go ahead with your trip to Japan?"

"Certainly. I mean, I trust you'll be following, watching over me?"

"Following?" She reached over, her thumb stroking the dark hair on the back of his hand. "It would all be rather easier, and likely more pleasurable, if I wasn't simply skulking around the fringes and spying like that dreadful little man across the way."

"I'm certainly open to suggestions," he said. Hell, Hector was always open to those from an attractive woman. "What are you thinking?"

"I only have the most obvious notion," she said. "If we were to travel as a, well, as a sort of *couple*...? I mean, you *do* have a certain reputation to facilitate all that, after all."

"That is sadly so," he agreed carefully. "So you do realize all that that would imply?" A wolfish smile. "Or what it might *demand* in order to maintain tawdry illusions about me as lady's man? As you point out, I have a certain regrettable reputation to live down to."

"We were surely already headed that way, regardless of other circumstances, weren't we?" She gave him a knowing, decidedly carnal smile. "In my mind, I was already settled. But if you aren't interested...?" Her shoulders gave a sad shrug.

He turned his hand under hers, palm pressing to palm, his index finger on her pulse; he felt it quicken. He reached out with his other hand and traced the sleek line of her jaw with the side of that thumb. He said, "We'll go elsewhere, now. A place a bit more rowdy where we can talk more without worrying too terribly about being overheard."

"And after that?"

"After that, bugged or not, my hotel room should be perfectly fine for just about anything or everything *other* than talking, wouldn't *you* agree?"

The rain slightly abated and wind dying down, they decided to take in a set or two over drinks at Ronnie Scott's on Gerrard, before heading back to his hotel's bar for a nightcap.

After securing their table not far from the stage, Hector excused himself to make his overdue contact with Ian—the phone call that had taken on new urgency and purpose.

Several rings, then that voice—a smooth, cultured English accent delivered in a *bonhomie* baritone in which Hector could hear the wicked grin: "My favorite Texan," Ian said. "Dear chap, you're here at last and you're well?"

He imagined Ian sitting at his writing desk, likely. Ian, a creature of unwavering habit and firmly fixed rails, would be wearing a powder blue shirt and a black, spotted bowtie. He might even be sporting a suit coat, even in the comfort of his home, and even at this hour.

"Here, hale and hearty," Hector said. "But I'm also a bit flummoxed, just as you'll soon be, I'm going to wager." He gave Ian a quick fill on the past several hours, then said, "You still have connections, both sides of the ocean, right? Can you verify this woman's alleged associations?"

"I'm shocked she'd confess them to you if she's on the up-and-up, unless of course it was done under some kind of orders or official sanction," Ian said. "But, of course, yes, I can make some calls. I'll need an hour or so, perhaps."

"There's one more thing. I met two other gentlemen. One of them is now dead and under very suspicious circumstances. He'd claimed he was with the CIA. According to my other new friend that was a lie, as was the name I was given. Could you ask some questions about these two men from the plane, too?" He rattled off the names Terrence Hunt, Sebastian Keene and Hiroshi Takahashi.

Ian was palpably excited by the simple prospect of even a scintilla of possible intrigue underlying their looming trip to Japan. "Give me an hour, as I said. I also retain copious journalistic connections. So, better make that two hours, Hector. You can contrive to stay alive that much longer, yes?"

"At least for that long, sure. Two hours, it is." That meant enduring a lot of English jazz, unless they took their party elsewhere. Well, one just had to take the rough with the smooth, Hector consoled himself: He was no jazz fan.

The two authors said their goodbyes and Hector threaded his way through tables back to Haven in the raucous din of the Soho music club.

She smiled and said, "You reached your friend? Probably confided to him everything you know—or at least *think* that you may know—up to this point?"

Hector smiled, scooting his chair closer to hers and kissing her bare shoulder. "My friend is out presently," he said simply. "I'm to call back in a couple of hours. Why don't you tell me more about that man at the restaurant, the one from the plane whose seat you stole."

The music started up as a new band took the stage. She leaned into him, whispering into his ear so her mouth was blocked from view by his profile and her dark mane of hair—safely from the sight of any of those potential lip-readers she so seemed to fear might be watching.

Here and there, her lips feather-brushed his ear and throat.

She said, "Hector, have you ever heard of a Japanese-based secret society called *Kokuryūkai,* or 'The Black Dragon Society?'"

She didn't wait for him to answer, rushing ahead: "No? Well, it was founded by a man named Ryōhei Uchida...."

Two hours later, his head was filled with dark lore tied to the Black Dragon cabal and its sordid role in attempted trouble-making, even in post-Pearl Harbor America—everything from harassing fellow detainees at the FDR-driven Manzanar Interment Camp, to a flurry of FBI arrests of Dragon fifth columnists in Hector's beloved San Joaquin Valley.

Despite all the crazy thoughts running through his head after Haven's dark disclosures, on schedule, Hector made his way back to the payphone.

An eager Ian answered before the second ring this time: "It's confirmed Hector. She's very much what she claims to be. But more than that, they wouldn't tell me, which is slightly disquieting. I was not discouraged from going to Japan, but I could draw no more information about what might happen if we *should* go there. Your Japanese acquaintance from the airplane remains a mystery for the moment. As to Mr. Terrence Hunt slash Sebastian Keene? He appears to have been the latter, by birth. He had no American intelligence ties that I can find, or at least that my sources care to confirm. I do, however, know what killed him. That was a lethal dose of *takifugu*."

Hector swallowed hard, his head freshly spinning. "Well, that certainly sounds depressingly Japanese enough, whatever the hell it is."

"*It* is a fish, and yes, a Japanese fish to be sure," Ian confirmed. "A genus of the pufferfish, to be precise. When prepared by a master chef, it is *fugu*—a Japanese delicacy. But the fish is also remarkably, naturally toxic. It's positively packed full of tetrodotoxin. It seems if one is exposed to any of that stuff, one remains fully conscious whilst one's muscles become paralyzed."

Ian hesitated, probably for melodramatic effect, Hector figured, then continued with a taint of barely repressed relish, "Your throat passages constrict, Hector. You essentially paralyze and suffocate, all the while remaining alert and feeling it happen—quite a dreadful way to die, I think you'll agree. There's absolutely no cure. It seems a tiny puncture wound was found in Mr. Keene's inner, upper left arm. Presumably left there by a hypodermic or needle of some kind that likely was used to administer the fatal toxin."

Ian said, "This woman, Miss Branch—you'll take your leave of her this evening? I mean, you'll do that *now*, knowing what we know, won't you?" A slight pause, then, "Or, rather, what we *don't* know?"

There was just enough hesitation from Hector's end to provide its own answer.

Ian sighed and said, "I don't suppose you'll at least have your trusty old Colt tucked under the pillow tonight when you take that bewitching creature to your bed?"

"Peacemaker's back in New Mexico." Hector tried to make a joke of it: "So I suppose I'll just have to improvise with some *other* weapon—maybe that one I came into the world with. *If it should come to that.*"

Another sigh. Ian said, "Do survive the night, however you contrive to achieve that happy end, old friend. Tomorrow, we should meet up early and prepare our travel plans—the three of us, I assume."

Ian thought more about it, then said, "I'll come *your* way, if it's agreeable. That hotel they have you put up in manages exquisite scrambled eggs, and it does, after all, boast quite an excellent champagne stock. Let's resolve right now to put a memorable dent in Mr. Hefner's expense account reports. The stuff of legends. Lord knows, Mr. Bond has done more than his share to fatten Hugh's money bags of late."

Sometime after midnight, mounting thunder rumbled and shook the hotel windows. Hector awakened to crazy flashes of lightning splashing his room in strobing approximation of funhouse lighting.

Haven, tangled long and bare in his arms, sighed and snuggled closer, her legs twining with his. Her body positively radiated heat. Listening to the storm raging outside, Hector ran his fingers through her thick black hair, gradually giving himself back to sleep, all the while trying to convince himself of the validity of that old axiom regarding the critical importance of keeping one's friends close and one's (potential?) enemies still *closer*.

To that last point, he tried to reassure himself with the assertion that he surely couldn't get any closer to Haven than he presently found himself.

5

THE MAN WITH THE
GOLDEN TYPEWRITER

Ian arrived punctually at seven in the morning, tall and imperious. He was dressed in a conservative charcoal gray suit, pale blue shirt, and sporting his customary polka-dot bowtie.

However...

Hector was left unsettled and deeply depressed by the fact Ian looked so very much older than his years. He was leaning heavily on a cane and there was a new, faint gray tinge to his skin. His longish face was very deeply lined and gaunt; his eye sockets deeper than in memory. Ian's wavy, formerly brindle hair was brushed back from his high forehead and now nearly white, its limp contours brushing his shirt collar.

Yes, his younger friend looked very frail indeed in the wake of last year's heart attack.

It struck Hector that this trip to Japan was clearly ill-advised, and that was to put it in the most charitable of terms. If anything, Ian should be staying on a tight and doctor-supervised leash, Hector decided on the spot, rigorously minding his diet, absolutely ceasing his cigarette and alcohol indulgences and generally treating himself more in the manner of some fragile Ming vase.

But Ian would never stand for any of that mollycoddling of course, not any more than Hector's late-friend Hemingway was willing to accept such life-style restrictions when faced with grim intimations of his failing body.

Confronted with his raft of ailments and life-threatening conditions, Ernest had violently opted out rather than subside into some looming state of death-in-life, shuffling through his remaining days an increasing invalid.

The lanky Englishman shook Hector's hand, then said with a smile, "And you must be Haven." He kissed her on both cheeks, pulling her close, one hand patting her on the back, just above the coccyx. Haven tolerated Ian's liberties, then, smoothing out her pleated and dark charcoal skirt, she reassumed her seat.

Before Hector or Haven could demure, Ian took it upon himself to order up their breakfast: scrambled eggs *ala* James Bond, made to Ian's meticulous specifications, accompanied by a bottle of Taittinger.

They kept the ensuing breakfast conversation general and confined mostly to logistics of their coming travel. Ailing or not, Ian was his usual smooth and charming self, predictably preening and showing off for a fetching younger woman. Hector saw Haven was increasingly taken with his friend.

"We'll have two other journalists along," Ian said, smiling at her, "both male, I fear. So it will be your responsibility to feminize—that is to say, to *civilize*—the proceedings when and how you deem appropriate, my dear. That said, I *am* going there to research a James Bond novel, so there are certain necessary, if unseemly, destinations to which simple decorum and certain Japanese folkways will preclude your accompanying us when we venture into them, I fear. Sorry, my darling, but you'll occasionally be left to your own devices, here or there, perhaps even for a few hours now and again, though we'll try to keep those instances to the barest minimum, on my honor." He raised a trembling hand in pledge.

Haven managed a smile and said. "I'm sure you will do all of that. I'm to gather your wife isn't coming along then, Mr. Fleming?"

Hector hadn't had a chance to warn Haven of the long, unhappy and steadily unraveling of the tempestuous Fleming marriage so well underway.

At present point, despite some apparent, mutual and hard-to-fathom drive to seemingly hang in publicly—possibly just for the sake of their young son, Caspar, Hector supposed— Ann and Ian were in reality maintaining largely separate lives.

Indeed, Hector had heard rumors of some lover in Jamaica whom Ian had under wraps. He'd heard similar rumors of Ann indulging in a sustained affair of her own.

For his part, Ian said to Haven, "I fear Mrs. Fleming will not be along. No, not this time. I fear that I'll be decidedly stag in the exotic Orient, my dear."

After their Flemingesque—and potentially heart-damaging—breakfast of scrambled eggs and pink champagne, they headed upstairs to Hector's room, where the trio retreated to the rather spacious bathroom, turning up the taps to fox potential listening devices.

Sitting on the bathtub's side, Haven leveled her green-eyed gaze at Ian and said, "So exactly how much has your friend confided to you about me, and, well, about *everything*?"

Ian smiled, putting down the lid, then taking a seat on the toilet. Fingering the head of his cane, he said, "It's rather hard to know how to answer that since I can't be at all sure that I know everything Hector knows about this. Why don't we simply assume we're all in a posture of complete disclosure and you first confide what you and your MI5 compatriots know about why Hector and I might be being lured back to Japan together."

Haven shot Hector a glance. "Are you on board with this strategy for revelation?"

"Completely," Hector said, leaning back against the closed bathroom door and turning up the tap a shade harder as further precaution. "Even adamantly so."

"Very well," she said. "This begins with you two gentleman and your here-to-fore secret sortie on behalf of your mutual governments as part of what is now known, at least in our archives, as 'Operation Flea.'"

Ian and Hector were both startled by her admission. Hector started to speak, but stopped when Ian held up a cautionary hand.

Fleming still maintained shadowy connections to British intelligence, after all, Hector knew. The American author couldn't say the same of his relations with current U.S. intelligence organizations, although there was always that damned standing order from Patton's people, stubbornly still in place despite the fact old George himself was at last safely on the wrong side of the sod.

"Hector and I are under no liberty to speak about *anything* related to that time period, let alone any so-called 'Operation Flea,' if that was even something we had knowledge of, which I will say here and now, emphatically, that we *don't*."

Ian squared his shoulders and said, "Miss Branch, you know very well as I do, that the Official Secrets Act strictly prohibits—"

"*Please*," Haven said. "Please do spare me that charming yet clearly disingenuous denial and citing of the OSA, Mr. Fleming. I have, along with countless others in my organization, read the advance galleys of your forthcoming James Bond novel. The villain's ultimate scheme in your new book, to put it in the most charitable terms, can at *best* be described as an audaciously and thinly fictionalized treatment of the very sort of biological terrorism against the West that you and your dashing American friend here tried to help stave off in 1945."

Pointing a finger at Ian, she said, "When your next Bond novel, *On Her Majesty's Secret Service,* comes out next April Fool's Day—*if* it is even permitted to see the light of day, which, frankly Mr. Fleming, is a very open question at this moment, it will confirm for others in myriad intelligence services the world over—as well as many terrorist cell organizations—that long-standing whispers about your and Mr. Lassiter's involvement with a Japanese attempt at bioterrorism are *far* more than simple idle chatter in shadowy quarters of the intelligence world."

She leveled an accusing finger at the British thriller writer and said, "Interest in Operation Flea will reignite with a vengeance when your *novel* appears, and all variety of dark parties will rush to try and regain what was lost in 1945. The weapon Japan had in its grasp was years, if not *decades*, ahead of its time. Its destructive potential remains unmatched, even today. So it's a hotly desired property, as you can well imagine. Courtesy of your forthcoming novel, I fear that you and your American friend will soon find yourself in very hot and treacherous waters, indeed."

In popular and critical circles, Hector was known—much to his own rueful frustration—as "the man who lives what he writes and writes what he lives." He had increasingly used his life as fodder for his novels, and, more recently, even dared to make himself the actual occasional protagonist of his fictional works in a literary evocation of a kind of meta-fictional house of mirrors. It was a tactic that, lately, he increasingly regretted.

However, the assertion Ian had dared base a popular novel around their still highly-classified Japanese intelligence operation left Hector freshly startled and more than a bit angry at his friend.

In the moment, Hector could only rationalize that fact— if it was indeed founded in any kind of truth—by presuming ailing Ian must have convinced himself that he wouldn't live long enough to suffer the consequences of violating the United Kingdom's Official Secrets Act.

Still, before he could check himself, Hector blurted out at Ian, "You *really* wrote a novel about all that?"

Fleming's red-faced riposte: "Dear Lord, look who's talking, my dear, dear chap. You're hardly in a convincing position to come all-over outraged at the prospect of any of my fiction being rooted in fact."

Something thumped hard against Hector's back, jarring the bathroom door and nearly pitching him forward with its impact.

Hector frowned and was half-turning when chips of wood sprayed his face, nicking his cheek and forehead, drawing blood.

The shower tiles behind Haven exploded, peppering her in porcelain dust.

Someone had fired a shot through the bathroom door.

Haven reached under her skirt and said urgently, "Get down, Hector, do that now!"

She drew a Beretta from a holster bound around her shapely upper thigh and fired three times back through the bathroom door.

A slightly more distant, heavy thump followed.

Cautiously, Hector attempted to open the perforated door. Weight from the other side forced it open farther and faster in his face than he'd anticipated. The door very nearly smacked his already bloodied cheek.

A crouched Hiroshi Takahashi tumbled onto the bathroom tiles. In one hand he gripped a kind of radio or listening device. That was attached by a cord to a suction cup, which in turn was fastened to the splintered lavatory door. The device was also connected to earphones still affixed to the man's ears.

As Hiroshi sprawled onto the tile, Hector saw sharp metal stars projecting from the man's bleeding back. In his other hand, Hiroshi held a still-smoking gun—presumably the one that fired the single, errant shot through the bathroom door that had superficially wounded Hector and just missed killing Haven.

Further across the room, an even more grotesque figure lay sprawled and clawing spastically at the carpet with gloved fingers. The prone figure clutched at its back with its other, trembling hand. The stranger was clad head-to-toe in black—dark slacks, long-sleeved turtleneck shirt and a black ski mask.

Haven said, "Hector, quickly, get that one in here and on the tile before he bleeds all over the carpet!"

Grabbing the black-clad stranger by the ankles, Hector complied. He dragged the man face down into the bathroom, then dropped him untidily halfway across Hiroshi's corpse.

Haven, gun trained on the black clad man's head, reached down and tugged off his mask.

The stranger was likely in his mid-twenties, and clearly Asian. Haven gripped his jaw tightly and pressed her gun's barrel under his throat. She said, "You tell us who you work for or else—"

She let it drop, her threat hanging there, unfinished.

The young assassin stared up at her, eyes wide but unseeing, foam and spittle bubbling from the corners of his mouth. He'd bitten through some sort of suicide capsule—probably potassium cyanide, Hector figured.

Rising, Haven said urgently to Ian, "You better clear out, for now. We'll try and say any neighboring complainers were hearing gunshots on the television from some crime drama turned up too loud. I'll have my people dispatch a crew to come and clear the scene here. Hector and I will come to your home later this evening, Ian. Then we can resume this conversation."

Hector and Ian didn't question Haven's taking charge, nor did they balk at her suggested course of action: It all appeared to make cold enough sense in the bloody moment. Hector figured Haven had that thing Hem had so revered—so-called grace under pressure—in spades.

When Ian had gone and they were waiting outside the again-closed bathroom door, lingering to see if anyone would come knocking to inquire about overheard gunshots, Haven inquired, seemingly apropos of nothing: "Something I simply have to ask about your friend while I'm thinking on it, and on his infernal writings. Maybe it's just another myth. Are the stories true about Fleming actually having a golden typewriter?"

In 1952, about the time of the publication of his first Bond novel, Ian had indeed rewarded himself with the purchase of a customized, gold-plated, Royal Quiet Delux Portable typewriter. Hector distractedly confirmed as much for Haven.

She shook her head and said, "Do you have a gold typewriter like Ian's?"

"Christ, no," he said. "Not even silver or bronze. I favor off-the-shelf, portable Royals." For proof he pointed at the one sitting on his hotel room's writing desk. "Only Ian would have the audacity to write on a machine plated with gold. Jesus, if I had to write on such a contraption, I'd brood over every comma."

Hector turned his attention to the ruined bathroom door. Gesturing that direction, he said, "To more important matters—if someone beats your boys here, the bullet holes in that door are going to be damned hard to explain away."

Haven shrugged. "We'll simply say we had a row. I pushed and pushed and you punched the door in anger. Paint me as a bitch—it's a part I can easily play. And you have a certain reputation, as we both have acknowledged. So they would accept that. I'm sure. And I'm equally sure Mr. Hefner would understand when the repair bill came due—owing to that reputation of yours."

He was in no mood for joking. Hector said, "That man you shot through the door. Who is the hell is he? Any clue?"

"I expect we both know the likely answer to that. It will take some confirming, but my money is on the Black Dragons. I expect that man came to do the very thing he unexpectedly found our friend from the plane attempting—that is, trying to eavesdrop on us in there."

Probably that was quite so. Hector shook his head and took a seat at the foot of the bed. He thought about smoking a cigarette to calm his nerves, but memories of the way Ian looked discouraged him. He said, "Those pieces of metal he used to kill the man who was on the plane with us—what are those things? I've never seen anything like them."

"Japanese throwing stars," Haven said, at last re-holstering her gun after reloading, again showing quite a bit of leg in the process. "Those throwing stars tell their own story about the man I killed and of his probable origins. Or, rather that is to say, of his probable *affiliations*. Those metal stars are also called *shuriken*, which means, roughly, 'sword hidden in hand.' They're razor-edged, and in this case, likely coated in some sort of a poison, I'd wager."

"*Shuriken*. You speak Japanese, then?"

"I grew up there for the most part, remember? So, yes, I speak Japanese rather fluently."

She smiled and sat down next to Hector on the bed. She kissed him, slow and hard, taking the lead. Pulling away for just a moment, Haven said, "You know, I think we just stumbled upon my cover for you regarding your friends when we get to Japan. I'll be your chaps' official translator. It works for you?"

He'd already seen some first-hand proof she had a talent for tongues. He said, "Sure, it's a splendid idea."

6

GHOST OF A FLEA

Within twenty minutes of Ian's departure, several suspiciously fit-looking young men dressed in custodial garb bustled into Hector's hotel room.

The men seemed just this side of rough trade to Hector—a little too unpolished to make the grade as fully-fledged SIS. Yet, they were certainly efficient enough. They speedily tumbled the two corpses into a large, wheeled cloth container intended for transporting soiled bed sheets and used towels to the hotel laundry.

At the same time, another man set to work on eradicating a smattering of stray droplets of blood staining the carpet. He did that with a brush and some odorless cleaning agent in a spray bottle.

After covering the bodies with linens, his two mates helped themselves to a matching, unmarred bathroom door from an adjacent room that they deftly used to replace Hector's ruined door.

Watching them quickly sanitize the scene of the crime, expertly expunging all signs of carnage, Hector comforted himself at least Mr. Hefner wouldn't be receiving any bills for hotel room damages that might in turn trigger testy calls from *Playboy's* lawyers somewhere down his life's uneasy road.

After the murderous melee in his room, Hector decided it wasn't advisable to be out walking the streets, personally unarmed and exposed to another potential attack by parties still unknown. He therefore agreed to Haven's offer for "a company car" to transport them to Ian's home for the resumption of their travel and allied strategic planning.

Riding in the back of a tan Highline Console, a thick glass partition separating them from their driver—as well as from that man's ears, presumably—Haven said, "So, of course this is all about your and Ian's ties to the immediate aftermath of the last war and Japan's rather disingenuously named Army Epidemic Prevention Research Laboratory, commanded by Shiro Ishii. What eventually came to be known, rather notoriously, I suppose you'll agree, as Unit 731. Can we at least have that much out in the open now?"

Hector's stomach tightened. He'd been provided dark insight into human populations many times in his storied, blood-and-thunder life, but the things he'd heard, learned or actually observed regarding Unit 731 still made him shudder, *down deep*. All that could even now set the writer to grinding his teeth and wishing his nation's former Asian enemies in the deepest, tightest circles of Hell.

When it was a fully going concern, Unit 731 had been duplicitously declared a lumber mill by the Imperial Government in one of the iciest of wartime hoaxes.

In reality, Unit 731 was a clinic for the development of biological and chemical warfare, as well as still more horrific medical experiments and unthinkable, stomach-twisting endurance tests that used live human subjects, both "foreign and domestic."

When inquiring as to the success of some recent experiment or medical atrocity, the running joke among members of the Unit had reportedly been to ask, "How many logs fell?"

Hector tugged at his tie and said, "I'd rather not have to cover this sorry ground more than absolutely necessary, so we best just wait for Ian to be present for the rest, or don't you agree?"

Assessing him, then taking his hand in both of hers, Haven said, "Of course, darling. Just as you say. Anyway, the way you put it, it's the kind of question that answers itself. You've seen so many terrible things in your life. I've read your FBI file, of course. It took *some* time to do that, you know—it's terrifically dense, yet oddly compelling and even macabre—almost like reading one of your books. Coupled with your actual novels, I now have a piercing sense of the sublime sweep of your storied life. My God, it's no wonder you write the things you do."

Troubled by something she must have seen in his expression and sensing she was on uncertain ground, she hesitated, then changed the subject. One hand resting on his knee, she said, "I have a feeling that things between your friend and his wife aren't so terribly terrific."

At least a little grateful for the change in topic, Hector tipped his head back against the seat and closed his eyes. "I'm not sure they were ever good, much less *terrific*, for those two. Butterflies and deep-seated matrimonial fears are what gave birth to James Bond, you know. Ian wrote his first novel, *Casino Royale*, to try and take his mind off his looming wedding—a union I think he knew even then was a calamitous mistake."

Hector sighed and said, "Ann has *always* looked down on Ian's writing, often in the cruelest way, even as she's savored the considerable mad money it provides her. Her intellectual and supposedly more literary friends are always having a mean laugh at Ian's expense as they drink the fine wine and eat the caviar that Agent Bond has paid for." He shook his head, a sour frown on his face. "The sorry bastards."

An old, adjectival dig for such types that he associated with Hem seized his mind and he gave it voice: "*Pilot fish*."

"He could leave her," Haven said. "By all accounts, Ian's got a kind of mistress in Jamaica, where the Bond books are written once a year."

"If his health wasn't so poor, Ian might really do that. *If* he and his wife didn't have a child together." Hector shook his head and said, "That old, bloody and sorry word, *if*."

He looked over his shoulder and said, "I suppose your man at the wheel is attuned to the possibility—hell, the strong *probability*—we're being followed?"

"Yes, and we are most certainly being spied on—those cars in front and in back—but by people from *our* side," Haven said. "That also of course makes it easier to spot tails from the opposition, particularly when you're traveling in numbers as we are now. I'd wager there's no exaggeration in my saying that at this moment Hector Lassiter, you're probably the safest you've been since you left your bed in New Mexico so many days ago."

As if to underscore Hector's confidences to Haven about the tempestuous Fleming marriage, they arrived at Sevenhampton to find Ann off to visit the lefty politician Hugh Gaitskell, her current lover.

Ann's affair; Ian's affair? Life was too short to suffer in the yoke of such a befouled union. Hector simply couldn't fathom sticking it out in a sham marriage, not even for the sake of a child.

As dinner hour loomed, Ian looked extremely tired and even more drawn than at breakfast. Hector thought again of how his younger, yet craggy and haggard-looking friend must not have truly recovered from the heart attack he'd survived several months back.

Yet the near stub of a Morland dangled from Ian's cigarette holder, presently. Countless others littered an ashtray. Hector wondered to himself exactly which coffin nail of the day this one constituted.

In Ian's novels, the indestructible and perpetually thirty-five*ish* James Bond was attributed with smoking some impossible number of handmade Turkish-blend cigarettes each day. Hector sometimes feared Ian had a compulsion to match his fictional beast's impossible-to-sustain nicotine indulgence.

He'd heard before the heart attack struck so few months ago, that Ian was actually averaging something like sixty cigarettes a day.

Even in his youth, other than during a couple of terrible, white-knuckle emergency room vigils, Hector couldn't remember smoking more than twenty cigarettes in a single day, but he all too well remembered feeling like hell after hitting *that* sorry mark.

Once more, Hector impulsively resisted the notion to smoke. Maybe this trip to Japan and Ian's cautionary example would finally break him of the damned habit forever, he told himself. He hoped so.

He'd stopped before, here and there, after all—given it up entirely and cold turkey more than once, though doing so mostly for the presumed love of—or lust after—the right wrong woman passing through his life at some ultimately fleeting interval.

Closing and locking the front door behind them, Ian said, "I should confess at the outset Miss Branch's colleagues were by here a bit ago with all kinds of Bondian or Q Branch-style gadgets and this place has now been declared happily and emphatically to be a bug-free zone."

With that assurance, Ian smiled and said, "And now it's officially the martini hour. Indulging in the cocktails to come is compulsory, even if you're still on Her Majesty's clock, Miss Branch." He handed her a drink and said, "This is called a Vesper, after the hour."

Hector accepted his drink, always having enjoyed traditional vodka martinis, long before Fleming's Bond had popularized them.

For his part, Hector despised gin; he also idiosyncratically and instinctively distrusted those who imbibed it as a cocktail of preference—but Ian's gin-and-vodka-hybrid version of the martini was one of his own creation and a good bit off the well-beaten, Gordon's path.

Hector also more typically preferred olives in his drink rather than Ian's proscribed, large slice of lemon peel.

Still, no bartender in the world made the cocktail quite as Ian did when he presumed to play mixologist, and how many more times might *that* happen with Ian in such a frail state?

That was the trouble with being over sixty, Hector thought, and it was far from his first time doing so. It was the same with *everything*, these days, wasn't it? Increasingly, he found himself simultaneously chiding and warning himself, typically along the sorry lines of:

Best enjoy this, old pal—savor it. Is this the last dance? Probably that is so. Knowing that, you best make it last longer.

Or:

Is this *your last time seeing Paris? Better hit all the old haunts again, just in case....*

Is this the last, calamitously desirable fine young lady you'll be granted?

Is this *one your last novel?*

Will you live to write this *particular story, all the way to 'The End'?*

No.... Better write faster, because life is a promise nobody keeps.

Ian twisted the cap tighter on the bottle of Kina Lillet, then sat down in a leather chair by the fire with his own drink. "No further issues at the hotel, I take it?"

He nodded at the ceiling. With a certain bitter irony, he said, "I'm alone for the evening—*all* evening I'm fairly certain, and for the night in full, as Caspar is staying over elsewhere, too. I'm already packed for the Orient, so you're welcome to stay here in a guest room for the evening, Hector. Safety in numbers and all that." A dark smile of inquiry and commiseration: "Or perhaps us being together is simply too much convenience for the enemy?"

Ian turned, smiling sadly at Haven. "Afraid I can't extend the same offer to you, my dear. If Anne returned and found a beautiful younger woman under this roof, even one attached firmly to a good friend like Hector? I fear it's just unseemly enough for some of Ann's near always-present and remora-like friends to ratchet up the friction I too often endure."

"I'll think seriously on the offer of lodging," Hector said. It actually made a certain sort of sense: It wouldn't be hard to have his luggage collected and brought over by Haven's people. And anyway, the bathroom and entryway of his hotel room now carried unpleasant enough memories, despite all the work done to erase the killings that had happened mere hours ago.

There was that other factor, too: It would give Ian and Hector time alone to plot, to talk and to plan without Haven potentially spying on them.

Ian stared into his drink—to his credit, he was nursing the cocktail he shouldn't be touching, not at all—and said, "So where to start, Hector?"

Crossing one long shapely leg over the other and leaning forward—her elbows crossed, deepening the valley between her breasts—Haven said, "How about with October 15, 1945, when, under the guise of visiting journalists, you chaps went to Japan in a clandestine effort to recover critical, microfilmed materials. That strip of film my people believe detailed a potentially devastating biological organism that would result in complete cattle and livestock infertility. The thing that was planned to be delivered via fleas encased in special, porcelain bombs."

Hector and Ian shared a long, searching look.

The English author at last said, "Indeed. Why don't we start just there?"

Strictly speaking, Hector and Ian were casually acquainted prior to their first shared trip to Japan—it was simply that neither had any grasp of the other's peculiar role in relation to their nations' respective, national intelligence programs in the early going.

Hector's ties to the OSS were particularly well hidden and obscured by design, as his official, *public* role as a war correspondent strictly forbade the very activities and weapons predicated by his responsibilities for the Office of Strategic Services.

Once they were officially paired for their shared mission into Japan, the two "journalists" got on like crazy, treating their strange sortie into the freshly vanquished "Land of the Rising Sun" as a kind of drunken and woman-deflowering, would-be spies' holiday.

Their so-called mission was decidedly outré, after all.

An American crime novelist and sometimes journalist—coupled with a British journalist-turned-Naval attaché—were being sent over to quietly meet a Japanese poet.

This was being done in an effort to liberate a scrap of precious microfilm created by self-recriminatory Japanese scientists after being clandestinely ferreted out of the sinister headquarters of Unit 731.

That smuggling out had all been undertaken under direst of risks, as well as the very noses of Russians eager to lay claim to the fabled, infertility-carrying pests for potential use against the Kremlin's wartime allies.

As Ian presumed to tell the tale to Haven, Hector half-listened, more firmly moving in the country of his memory regarding that strange and boozy, long-ago idyll—Ian's half-heard words stirring recollections of their strange Japanese nights and days.

The one who delivered the microfilm to them was indeed a poet, a gentle appearing man named Mitsuharu Kaneko.

But Kaneko possessed real steel and cunning, belying his seemingly benign occupation as composer of verse.

Throughout the war, quietly and steadfastly, Kaneko had bravely penned *reams* of anti-war poetry.

When his beloved son at last reached dreaded draft age, the calculating poet had made his boy inhale damaging smoke so he would fall ill with apparent asthma, so he would be spared conscription and saved from certain-to-prove fatal combat as the tides of war turned so decidedly against Imperial Japan.

Through channels never adequately explained to Ian or Hector, the poet had somehow come to possess the precious, deadly microfilm carrying all of the unspeakable fruits of Shiro Ishii and Unit 731's monstrous germ warfare program— in particular, the Russian- and Red-Chinese coveted "flea bomb."

The microfilm contained the secrets of the infertility virus that had already been successfully test-detonated in its early and less potent forms with devastating results in China.

The weapon had since been honed with an eye toward use against the West, it had been said.

But America beat Japan to the most devastating of all punches, avenging Pearl Harbor and all the lives lost since December 1941 with its own unspeakable new weapon that would cast a pall over the world forever more.

With a snap of his fingers, Truman ordered the first atom bomb dropped on Hiroshima, then, just three days later, the second such bomb was turned loose over Nagasaki.

Japan, and its emperor, crumbled, nearly at a stroke.

Not so terribly long after, with Japan safely surrendered, there was a special writer's dinner arranged, one with journalists, novelists and poets—scribes from the East and the West—united for a kind of literary formalizing of the peace. There, Hector and Ian supped on exotic Japanese fare and drank far too many flasks of belly-warming sake.

At some point after their dinner, very much in the company of Ian and Hector, the poet Kaneko ostensibly rose to relieve himself.

The microfilm had been secreted in the spine of a collection of poems by Kaneko gifted to Hector in the restaurant's restroom.

Ian started to object, but the poet raised a hand. He said softly, "My dearest Ian, please *don't*. We both know in our hearts Britain is all but a spent force in this near dark world. For better or worse, the United States and Russia are clearly the next great powers. Given that reality, the choice is obvious for me and for those whom I represent tonight. You're too wise and worldly to argue these facts. Your government can request the thing from his." The poet then nodded at Hector.

To that point, everything was going perfectly to plan—except, perhaps, from Ian's patriotic perspective.

The three men of letters, more than slightly drunk, were headed back to rejoin their fellow writers when they overheard harsh words uttered in Japanese. The obvious threats came from the dining room.

Uncomprehending, yet knowing *that* tone, looking to the poet for understanding, Hector and Ian were surprised when Kaneko reached into Hector's suit coat pocket and reclaimed his gifted book of poetry.

Looking frantically around, he seized on a curving Japanese sword that hung on the wall.

The poet drew the samurai sword from its scabbard. Using his shirttails, he wiped the top of the blade clean of its protective film of corrosion-curbing *choji* oil. He wrapped the precious microfilm around the blade, re-sheathed and then hung the sword just as several masked, Japanese men came upon them, toting guns.

The writers raised their hands. The masked men searched them meticulously, all the while hurling questions at the Japanese poet.

Unsatisfied in their search and impromptu interrogations, the armed men led the writers out into the chilly courtyard—sans shoes—and proceeded to search them all for a second time as they stood in the cold night air, shivering.

Still frustrated, the armed men were about to search the restaurant again when a scrappy and fairly drunk Japanese novelist lost his temper and charged one of the armed men, setting off a bloody brawl resulting in most of the participants—Hector and Ian included—being hauled off for still more questioning, first by Japanese police, and then by American occupation authorities.

When Hector and Ian were at last free and returned to the restaurant, they found it was shuttered.

Undeterred, they broke into the establishment in the early morning hours, only to find all of its antique Japanese weaponry that served as décor—including that particular samurai sword—had been removed under standing U.S. orders, confiscated as a by-product of the evening's earlier raid and all of it presumed destroyed immediately upon discovery.

At that moment, the microfilm, along with their secret mission to Japan, became a frustrating but firmly-closed chapter in their secret intelligence lives, at least so far as Hector, Ian and their respective governments were concerned.

Haven took it all in then said, "So you maintain the microfilm absolutely was lost with the sword? You didn't even try to make further inquiries?"

Ian, his back clearly up, said, "Oh, we and others tried, do trust in that. But we weren't exactly *katana* aficionados, dear." He smiled and said, "That is, of course, the real name for—"

"For a Japanese samurai sword, yes I know," Haven finished for him.

"Well then perhaps you *also* know the occupying government nearly immediately banned such swords and even the art of crafting them for many years," Ian said. "The swords—some of them quite precious and valuable—were collected and destroyed in vast numbers in the immediate aftermath of Japan's surrender. It was simply very bad timing for our side. So yes, we presumed and I think most probably rightly so, that the microfilm—perhaps blessedly for this sad old world—perished along with the sword in question."

Haven sat back in her chair, glowering. "What do you two *really* think happened?"

Hector and Ian exchanged a look. "Just what I've finished telling you," the British novelist said, sounding ever-so-slightly exasperated. "The sword was confiscated and, with the microfilm, was most probably lost to all. When we soon return to Japan, if others hope to find it otherwise, I can all but promise you they'll be doomed to bitter disappointment."

Hector rose and stretched. He presumed to mix himself another martini, this one on the rocks and made without a single drop of gin—three plump and skewered olives would have made it perfect.

His back still to Ian and Haven, he said, "I've decided I will stay the night. Haven, if you could see to having your people with their special expertise have my bags collected

and brought round—hopefully without anyone following—
it would be more than a boon." *Boon?* As he said it, Hector
realized the more he was here in England, the more he found
himself falling into a temptation to lapse into some Texas
version of English idiom. That somehow reminded him of
something else:

He turned and said to Ian, "This next Bond of yours, do
you have some galleys around here, a proof copy I might read
this evening?"

Ian blushed a bit and said, "Bear in mind it is indeed a
proof copy. And on that note, do please let me know if you
see any typos or other issues. There's still some barest fraction
of time to fix them, you see." Ian covered a sudden yawn that
wasn't to be denied, then said, a tad redundantly, "And I'm
frankly exhausted. Time for bed, at least for me. You can see
to answering the door to claim your things when they arrive,
I trust?"

"Certainly," Hector said. "Get some rest, buddy."

With Ian safely away, he rose to escort Haven to the door.
They kissed at the threshold, passionately. "That's so you'll
think hard on what you're denying yourself tonight," she said,
eyes glistening. "We could have had this night in that grand
hotel bed. Don't you two go out wandering the streets for
tarts—at least grant me that."

Hector just smiled. "You pack, prepare…because
that's just what I'll be doing. It'll be an early evening trip
to the airport tomorrow and then a long bit of travel. Those
facts, alone, assure there'll be no debauchery, not for me
tonight."

He looked up at the ceiling and shook his head. "I'm as
shocked as you to be alone down here for the next few hours,

by the way. His health is clearly terrible. Ian would never abandon me like this in the hard-charging old days."

"So what do you really do alone tonight?" Her palm drifted to his cheek. He turned a bit to lightly kiss the pulse at her wrist.

Hector said, "I suppose I'm going to spend the evening with a single glass of wine I will heroically endeavor to stretch out, and, I hope, in the company of a good book by a friend who, I'm afraid, has me very worried about him."

It was Hector's long habit to awaken in the early morning to write.

But upon this English dawn, he instead rose to resume reading Ian's next Bond thriller, *On Her Majesty's Secret Service*.

He completed his reading about ten a.m., terribly shaken by the novel's startling end that stirred old ghosts and Hector's memory of the piercing loss of his beloved Brinke Devlin.

Given the circumstances of Brinke's death and that of a particular character in Ian's forthcoming book—all of that coupled with Fleming's shameless raiding of the purpose of their clandestine trip to Japan in 1945—Hector was left wondering if Ian had consciously dared to evoke Brinke's death to inform the tragic, startling climax to his new Bond novel.

It would constitute a kind of bitter—even unforgivable—betrayal in Hector's mind if ever proven true.

Starving, bedeviled with such questions and terrible memories, Hector showered, dressed, and then went in search of Ian.

7

THE LAST MISSION?

Hector grudgingly offered to make breakfast to Ian's usual, heart-mauling specifications.

As he did that, Ian—looking a bit stronger if florid-faced and stiffly formal in another of his endless wardrobe of pale blue cotton shirts and spotted black bowties—sipped his coffee and said, "Did you have a chance to sample the next Bond? Do feel free to lie and say you've not gotten to it yet, even if you in fact did, assuming you might indeed have read it in full and found that you loathed it."

"I finished it this morning," Hector said. "It cost me sleep, buddy—I mean that in the best sense." Ian was clearly elated. He stirred the eggs with a spatula and continued, "I've not read them all, so I'm a little outside the overall continuity, but it was quite wonderful Ian, along with *From Russia*, a favorite. The bit where he escapes the villain's lair and skies down that mountainside into the little sporting village—that part I loved the best, I think."

Ian said, "I sense an implied *except* lurking in there."

Hector shrugged. "I loved it all except for that ending. The climax absolutely shredded me, buddy. Left me gutted.

That was very, very tough for me to read, you know." One word—actually a name—hung unsaid between them: "Brinke."

A deep and pained sigh. "Ah, *yes*. I was terribly thoughtless in that sense, Hector, Lord knows that's so. Should bloody well have warned you. I'd forgotten how terribly close to home that ending would strike for you, of all readers. It was an absolutely necessary plot development, one I knew I had to undertake even before I put down the first sentence introducing my girl—or rather Bond's...his latest, bird-with-a-wing-down *inamorata*. But clearly I'd forgotten some particular, painful aspects of your biography, old friend. Things that even you didn't put down on the page yourself until many years after the fact, evidently because they clearly pained you so. I'm so dreadfully sorry I didn't think of that before allowing you to read that damned galley. It was an appalling lapse on my part. Can you ever forgive me?"

Given the way Ian smoothly put all of that, Hector decided Brinke's terrible fate in 1925 quite possibly hadn't informed the dark and wrenching ending Fleming had chosen for the climax of his next Bond thriller. And, either way, it was an ending the artist in Hector recognized as the right and necessary one for Ian's novel.

Hector scraped scrambled eggs onto two plates and then sat down across from Ian. After freshening his cup of coffee from a stainless steel flask, Hector said, "The overall plot, is of course, precisely what Haven said—a clear reach-back to Operation Flea. Sorry to say, but I agree with the lady. I'd frankly be shocked if your government doesn't suppress your novel."

A diffident hand wave. "My health is obviously quite poor," Ian said. "I'm not much longer for this world, and we both know that's true." Ian now held up a pre-empting hand this time.

He said, not looking Hector in the eye, "Cleaner living might add scant time, but not an iota to the quality of this wretched half-life I now endure, Hector. You know me probably as well as it's possible for another man to pierce the infernal veil. So it will not come as news to you when I say I've always had one foot not wanting to leave the cradle, and the other in a hurry to get to the grave. It makes a rather painful splits of one's life."

A frosty smile, then he amended, "It's also not easy on one's dearest friends, I fear. But rest assured, I by no means intend to leave this life the so-called easy way. I'll not do it all at a bloody sitting, with a rope, or with a firearm like our friend Hemingway. There's a line from your countryman, Jack London, which I'm adopting as my life's last new motto: 'I shall not waste my days in trying to prolong them. I will use my time.'"

Hector had no good response to any of that so he said—and he knew he did so rather lamely—"How are your eggs?"

"Same as perfect," Ian said. "You've nearly mastered the recipe." For his friend's dying heart's sake, he had skimped on some stipulated butter.

"All of that aside," Hector said, "the shadow of censorship of your new novel under your country's Official Secrets Act still stands, at least from my perspective. Your villain Blofeld in the book, his scheme, it really is Operation Flea, writ large."

Ian waved a hand. "But still, to the common man on the street, it would be seen as almost a science fiction conceit, as far-fetched as all those loathsome critics said my plot was for *Moonraker*," Ian said. "My God, my editor of this next book insisted I spend *paragraphs* explaining what the term 'biological warfare' even means for the benefit of the 'general reader' whatever sorry creature that is. And, anyway, the government needs me for this last little mission of Red Indians and I'm risking what's left of my health playing ball with MI6. I'm not precisely yearning to exhaust myself, grinning, gripping and bowing my way across Japan and doing so mostly in stocking feet, you know."

"Then why go at all, Ian?"

"On the one hand, because I mean to reward some old friends in this novel I'm going over to research. Also to punish some enemies, via print. You see, my very dear Hector, I've learned my lessons from the man who lives what he writes and writes what he lives. What's that line you deployed recently in *The Times* interview announcing our coming, shared travel? Oh yes, '*Roman à clef.* Just a sexier way of saying revenge.' That was really quite wonderful."

Ian then lowered his voice and said sadly, "On the other hand, I'm going back, indeed, to try and make a last effort to recover the microfilm for *my* government. It's why I really want you along with me. I think we both need to complete that mission at which we failed so calamitously seventeen years ago. In the old days, of course, you know I had my own commando team, 30 Assault Unit—my own 'Red Indians'— who existed precisely to go into the enemy's camp and seize such documents and intelligence as those festering from the Unit 761 project. Maybe it was hubris to think I could do much the same myself in 1945. Either way, it's unfinished business, and I would loathe to live long enough to see that infertility pest unleashed against England or America. I'm sure you feel just the same." A thin smile. "You know how I adore my eggs and bacon, and they quite require an inexhaustible crop of chickens and pigs."

Certainly, Hector wouldn't want to see his homeland rendered a wasteland by some Frankenstein's flea. He dashed a little more salt and pepper on his eggs and said, "You were in Japan for your travel pieces, when, about 1960?"

"In fifty-nine," Ian corrected. "I was there for the same purpose, secretly. And, again, it proved abortive. You see, I purposely adjusted my *Thrilling City's* itinerary expressly to get some time in Japan to renew the hunt. I was led to believe the singular samurai sword had been located, and so, perhaps with it, the microfilm. I'd rather hoped you'd accompany me that time, but you demurred for some reason I still can't fathom."

Hector almost lost his temper at that. He took a breath, then said, "Maybe I didn't adequately explain at the time. I had loose ends of my own to attend to. Other old, bad business needed handling. It, too, was real life and death stuff. I had to go to Cuba and patch things up with Hem, while also closing out old poisonous business that threatened Ernest and I in that year. Just after all that, an old friend of sorts surfaced. She was terminally ill. I saw her through to her end, and after *that*, I candidly just wasn't good for much of anything for a few months. All of that also undid some other, more pleasant life plans I'd just begun to set in motion with a young woman in Los Angeles. So, yes, my time and efforts were spoken for. I'm sorry I couldn't come along to play Red Indians again with you that round, buddy. Just no time for spies, not in that sorry goddamn year."

Ian nodded slowly, clearly attuned to Hector's mounting anger. "I am sorry. I didn't know the particulars, of course. Anyway, the 1959 trip was an absolute bust. Just a result of hopeful intelligence, in the end—the most treacherous kind of dope, of course."

"Always the case," Hector said neutrally.

"Like you, I had…*plans*… Thought I'd go back in the next year to renew the search, but then my goddamn heart blew, and after…?" A desolate shrug.

Hector relented a bit, his voice going easier. "So tell me, what makes this time different from the last one, buddy? You really think we have some shot at recovery?"

"I really think we do this time," Ian said, rallying a shade. "My source this round—unlike in fifty-nine—is none other than our old friend the poet, Mitsuharu Kaneko. I therefore trust we have a real opportunity here, Hector. Based on all the interest and intrigue—not to mention the mounting body count we've amassed before we've even left for Japan—I gather others think that to be true, too."

Hector said, "You come by the spy trade honestly enough I suppose, but writers as spies in general? I frankly don't see it."

Ian wasn't having *that*. "You have formidable and proven skills in the area of espionage, Hector," he said, "as do I. And, anyway, as writers, we're hardly unusual in being recruited for this sort of thing. Authors and journalists are paid to ask questions, to observe. We travel widely and do so often to gather information for our books. We're publicly identified as snoops from the get-go, to resort to an Americanism. Hemingway, Dahl, Graham Greene, Le Carré and Maugham—all spies, if of varying strips. And I could go on. The fact is, writers have been spies for as long as there have been writers."

Brinke Devlin, too, had done a bit of intelligence work in her travels in the early 1920s, by all accounts.

Hector confided then to Ian about Brinke's supposedly recovered writings awaiting him in Japan. "I'll likely have to split off from you to check on all that when we're over there," Hector said. "I know you have your own must-do itinerary for the next Bond."

Ian said, "We'll see if we can't work it out so we stay together, and for the distance. And anyway, this business of Brinke's writings has the scent of a trap or a trick, if you ask me. How better to entice you to Japan than by dangling such a dandy carrot as Miss Devlin's allegedly lost writings? Simply wouldn't do for you to go into the lion's den alone. So we'll see if we can't manage to do that one together, too—work it in our travel planning. We should do that right now, don't you think? Work out our schedule to the nth-detail? After all, we must be at the airport at Heathrow by eight tonight."

"What about your other tagalongs? Your other writer friends?"

"Already there, and firmly *in situ*," Ian said. "Japan is their home and workplace. I simply had to delay my original departure for movie promotion reasons." Ian made a funny face. "I had my doubts about the film, particularly its star, who is not the Bond I saw in my mind's eye, but that is changing now. The film came out well enough in the end. For better or worse, that strapping Glaswegian is now the public's image of Bond."

"One thing I don't quite understand, Ian. If Haven is working for MI5, and you're acting on behalf of your intelligence services, how is it you haven't been working in concert with her from the start? Seems to me you'd already be partnered."

"This is old business, at least as it started for me," Ian said. "Some chums I worked with in our original, 1945 escapade are still firmly in saddle at MI6—men grown gray in service to Her Majesty. I'm indeed operating under that organization's auspices, this time. Your present lady friend is MI5. They're not the same thing, you see, not at all. While MI5 has certain farther-reaching powers, they are, in the end, mostly domestic.

When it comes to MI6, well, the entire bloody world is our—I mean *their*—devil's playground. I gather the reason for our not being in concert is just the usual left-hand right-hand nonsense."

Wincing, Hector said, "Then this has all the hallmarks of a potential civil war when it comes time to lay claim to the microfilm, as only one can actually have it. I know it's all Britain in the end from your perspective, but you know how these things go when turf is tested. I know how it would go to pieces if the FBI and CIA were attempting to work hand-in-glove toward receivership of some single intelligence scrap, let alone something as volatile as this alleged doomsday weapon. It would explode bureaucratically, then it would descend into some sort of petty but lethal inter-agency bloodbath, I reckon. On that note, remember the CIA is indeed keyed into this, as well. If we should lay claim to this strip of film, and *if* we should have three parties demanding personal possession of this goddamn scourge?" Hector raised his eyebrows as if to say, *Well, what* then, *Ian?*

His English friend sighed. "Please, dear boy. One crisis at a time, Hector. Worry is a dividend paid to disaster before it is due."

"I don't suppose you can arrange for some sort of weapons of our own once we reach Japan," Hector said. "I'm feeling positively naked without my Colt. As you've pointed out, we've not even left London and we're already racking up a body count."

Another tepid smile. Ian set to work fixing a fresh Morland to the end of his cigarette holder. "There, I can at least provide you with some solace," Ian said. "Clandestine arrangements have been made through channels for some proper tactical support. And, yes, even some armament technical support once we reach Japan. But that's really all I can say about any of that for the moment."

"That's all still pretty cryptic."

"But nothing in there to fear, Hector. It's the good sort of intrigue, the sort that gets the tired old blood singing again, yes?" Ian lit up his cigarette and blew a single smoke ring. "Anyway, we're not completely at our enemies' mercy. Like any good scorpion, we're not lacking for some sting."

Ian hefted his walking stick, then suddenly twisted its handle. Roughly six inches of razor-edged, stainless steel snapped from its end.

A sword cane. Delighted, Ian said, "Have you ever seen the like?"

Hector had been on the receiving end of just such a weapon in 1920s Paris but held his tongue. He reached out to touch its stained, slightly yellowish tip, remarking, "I think your blade needs a brisk cleaning, Ian."

"Don't touch it, for God's sake, Hector!"

Ian quickly pulled the end of the sword cane safely from Hector's reach.

Ian said sharply, "That's curare staining the tip, for Christ's sake."

8

NO LEG TO STAND ON

Another airport, another evening departure and yet another interminable international flight. This one was broken up, just a bit, by a brief pit stop in Helsinki.

Hector was sandwiched between Ian and Haven for the duration of both flights. Their neighbor to Ian's right, completing a row of four, was a fit-looking young Brit in perhaps his early- to mid-thirties, Hector guessed. He also assumed—and he was fairly certain rightly so—the youngish and too-athletic English stranger wasn't just some fellow traveler in the innocent sense. It was, Hector decided, really just a question of which intelligence organization—or what other shadowy, less-than-government sanctioned coalition—whose interests the stranger served.

There was one improvement, at least, regarding this over-the-ocean flight when measured against Hector's recent Atlantic passage: nobody was pronounced dead upon arrival, not this time.

Ian, leaning hard on what Hector couldn't regard as other than Ian's sword cane since he'd learned its true nature, surveyed the concourse with a grimace. "I would have expected to have been met straight away by Dick and Tiger," he said. "They're usually the punctual sorts."

Dick was journalist Richard Joseph "Dikko" Hughes, a robust and balding Australian with a florid face that was fueled by copious drink. Hughes was a noted foreign correspondent for the *Sunday Times*. He was also known to his phalanx of journalist friends as "His Eminence Cardinal Hughes," an impertinent bit of nicknaming that had started during the war in North Africa, according to Ian.

Tiger, whose given name was Torao Saito, was another journalist and Fleming friend who worked for the Asahi Shimbun newspaper group, covering aviation when he was not engrossed in the editing of the sprawling annual edition of *This is Japan*.

Just as Ian lamented their evidently having somehow missed connecting with their local guides, there came a harsh call out to Ian across the concourse. "My God, it's goddamn Fleming—there's the insufferable bloke, at last! *There's* the profligate prodigal son, returned to Mother Japan and there's not a naked, knife-wielding white or Asian girl in sight to bid welcome to the daft British bastard who invented Mr. James Bond!"

The two Eastern-based journalists waved and made their way through the crowd. That attention and the imposing Hughes' bonhomie bluster also brought them a flurry of press attention—Ian at last having been identified to the lurking Japanese media who'd so far missed spotting the tired-looking old British tourist.

Ian greeted Hughes as "Your Grace" amidst hearty black slaps, then the imposing Aussie gripped Hector's hand and said in a stubbornly enduring accent, "You stick with me, my Yankee son—I'll see you safely through this passage of Japanese hissing and scraping you're going to endure the next two weeks. I know Japan like the back of me hand and every glorious inch of me expansive, naked body. You're another mystery writer, am I right?"

"Crime writer, if you need a label," Hector corrected, a little coolly, still taking the gruff stranger's measure. "Or maybe I'm just a novelist who writes about crime."

"Mystery writer" was a lukewarm term that invariably set Hector to grinding his teeth. It was most often, by design, all too clear in his novels who the villain was, after all. It was the dire dance between the "hero" and the "villain" that nearly always drove Hector's narratives, not some silly goddamn puzzle or contrived whodunit spun to keep the blue-hairs engaged and feeling good about their own presumed cleverness.

"A fair and important distinction," Hughes said, redeeming himself. "I expect I'll love your books, Lassiter. Always enjoy a good thriller or crime story. You know, I formed the Baritsu Society—the first Sherlockian reading club in all of bloody Japan? Yoshida Shigeru—you know, the former prime minister—he's quietly a member of me club. Maybe we could arrange for you to speak to my society before you dart back west? What say you to that? Yeah?"

"*Maybe*," Hector said, sincerely hoping not.

To the good, Hughes and Saito's efforts that deftly sped Ian through customs also oiled the passage for Hector and Haven once it was known they were part of the 007 creator's suddenly boisterous and somewhat profane entourage.

For his part, Ian put forth the weathered, bon vivant's face expected of him, making quips, flashing smiles and giving good quotes to the local newsmen before being whisked off by the two journalists.

As they moved through the airport, they were briefly delayed by a Japanese man on crutches struggling to mount an escalator. The young man, perhaps twenty but surely no older than twenty-five, had a badly burned and scarred face. He was also clearly still trying to master use of an artificial leg.

Shifting his suitcase to his left hand, Hector offered a steadying right to assist the young man in his treacherous passage down the escalator. At the bottom, the author saw the stranger safely off and onto solid footing that elicited a slight head bow and a throaty "*Doumo arigatou*" in gratitude.

A private car had been arranged for Ian and company, but the unexpected addition of Haven exceeded its capacity. Rather than leave her alone, Hector elected to hang back with Haven. They were left standing at the curb with their bags, awaiting their own cab.

As they stood curbside while a valet went in search of an available ride, Hector looked around for any potential spies other than the comely one at his side. Nobody stood out, but then given the way that Hector—who topped off at a lean six-feet, two inches—found himself towering over virtually everyone in his midst, he realized it wouldn't be particularly hard to keep tabs on him, even in a bustling Tokyo crowd.

Haven squeezed his arm, turning him to face her and said, "I almost forgot." She took his hand and slid a gold band on the third finger of his left hand. "Decorum is quite important in this country, Hector."

She showed him the diamond ring and wedding band she now wore on her left hand. "Please don't lose that ring, mister—it's her Majesty's property so I'll be needing it back. Until we clear Japanese airspace, I'll be Haven Lassiter, if that's acceptable to you. It will just make things so much easier, particularly in terms of shared lodging, as we move in country."

Hector admired the diamond ring on her hand—it made him look extraordinarily generous, not to mention quite wealthy—and said, "Sounds like very solid strategy, Mrs. Lassiter. You may also be the first woman to actually take my last name, even fleetingly."

Brinke had stood on Devlin. Subsequent wives also opted to retain their maiden names. But that was okay, really; Hector wasn't terribly crazy about the name Lassiter, himself.

She smiled and said, "At least it makes the monogramming of towels that much easier." She bit her lip and said, "This wait for a taxi is ridiculous. I'm going to see if I can't find us a ride."

Hector watched her go, at last giving in and reaching for a virgin pack of Pall Malls—the last unopened pack of cigarettes he'd brought over from America. When it was gone, he vowed to himself, he'd not buy another.

Watching the crowd as he fumbled with the cellophane of his cigarette pack, Hector saw the wounded Asian man whom he'd helped down the escalator, moving a bit more easily through the crowd of a sudden.

And—*very strange, this*—the young man's right pants leg now flapped *emptily* in the sultry breeze.

The artificial limb was no longer suspended there.

How very odd, Hector thought. *Where in hell had the damned thing gotten to?*

Prosthetic limbs were quite expensive so far as Hector knew, and so not the kind of thing one would simply discard or perhaps forget in some airport restroom.

Puzzled, Hector shook his head, then frustrated by the light wind, he turned in the other direction to shield his match from the gusty, balmy breeze. The flint of his vintage, engraved Zippo had proven itself exhausted as he prepared to board the final flight from Helsinki to Japan.

As he moved in this new direction, the hairs rose on the back of his neck.

It was a terrible, grotesque and sinister sight that greeted him.

An artificial leg leaned against a concrete pillar, not two feet from where Hector was now standing.

Instinctively, Hector kicked the artificial limb away, hitting it hard with his toe and sending it spiraling and skittering across the sidewalk, off the curb and under the front end of an idling, late-model Hino Contessa.

Still fearing for the loss of his limbs or life, Hector rolled behind another stout pillar for protection. He simultaneously felt the heat and blast of the resulting explosion before the sound of the munitions-packed artificial limb set his ears to ringing.

Screams and the smell of blasting powder.

The scent of fire and spilled gasoline poisoned the air.

Sprawled half across his battered and well-traveled leather suitcase, Hector looked around, quite dazed and his vision slightly blurred. He felt arms around his torso, then hands at his face.

As she leaned in close to search his eyes, he read Haven's lips more than heard her desperate, single question: "Are you hurt?"

He couldn't hear his own voice as he snarled back, "Forget about me, damn it! That boy from inside, the one on crutches—he did this thing! He only has one leg, so get after him now because he can't possibly get far! Go after that man right *now*!" Hector shoved Haven away from him, pointing in the direction he'd seen the bastard last headed.

Frowning, Haven turned and ran off after the maimed young Japanese man just as Hector ordered.

9

TOMORROW NEVER LIES

Long ago during their first trip to Japan, while discoursing on the subject of kidney stones of all prosaic but miserable maladies, Ian had remarked, "Pain is a private address. Only those who have been that way before know the unlisted number."

Hector's palms were scuffed and his knuckles barked from being slammed against the pavement. His back ached and his forehead and right cheek were bruised. One knee was swollen and throbbing. Hector thought he certainly knew pain's present address, at least on this sorry day.

But it was his ears he most feared for—rather more specifically, he was scared for his future hearing. Gradually, sound was returning to him as Japanese medics fussed over him while local police hurled questions at him he wouldn't have been able to answer anyway because they were put to him in urgent Japanese.

But, even if his hearing returned to him in full, Hector stewed about longer term woes like tinnitus—the medical term for an infernal, perpetual ringing in the ears that had recently driven an exasperated actor friend to suicide after incurring the condition in the wake of a botched special effects explosion some years ago on a film set.

The condition had steadily worsened in the intervening years, slowly driving the poor bastard mad, then, inevitably to self-murder. Like Hem, his friend had reached for a shotgun to bring back some sought-for sense of serenity.

When Haven returned, pulling aside police and talking to them in what Hector took to be more Japanese, things began to change in a slightly more hopeful way. He was beginning to make out familiar sounds he could recognize and could *just* make sense of.

The purr of a car's engine was somehow now improbably delicious, almost as appealing as that of a never-before-encountered species of Japanese bird's trilling song issuing from a tree limb high above.

Hector was eventually loaded into an ambulance and transported to a close-by hospital for more testing and light treatment of his myriad scrapes and cuts.

At the medical center, an English-speaking doctor assured Hector, who could intelligibly hear the man's words at last, that he didn't think there would be long-term effects from the explosion, although he conceded to being more than a bit concerned about the potential for a mild concussion. He urged Hector to avoid any strenuous activity or the imbibing of alcohol for at least twenty-four hours.

The novelist was legally required to exit the hospital in wheelchair much to his chagrin.

Japanese paparazzi flashed away under the canopy of the emergency room entrance as Hector was wheeled to a waiting cab in the manner of some aging, ailing American invalid. Thank God he wouldn't be able to read the resulting local headlines. *And please, God,* he told himself, *don't let the bloody wire services back home pick up any of this!*

Once in the taxi, he at last got off a single burning question to Haven. He snarled, "*Tell* me you found the bastard who did this. You did do that, didn't you?"

Fortunately, nobody had died in the bombing. Hector's conscience had been spared any luckless bystanders blown to rags or their insides left jellied by the blast's potentially lethal initial concussion or its resulting shockwave.

The car under which the false leg had actually exploded had been unoccupied, as had another car left flattened when the initial blast flipped the blue Hino Contessa end-over-end, landing squarely on the Fiat parked behind. Both cars burned, then exploded as their fuel tanks were compromised, one after the other.

Sure, nobody innocent had died, but Hector of course wanted the man who did all this to pay, and to so *dearly.* The sons of bitches had clearly meant to kill him, after all.

"I found him and I didn't," Haven said carefully, a hand resting familiarly on Hector's thigh as they were driven through Tokyo to their hotel. "Yes, I did just that. But he was quite dead when I came upon him, darling. Frothing at the mouth, just like the other in your hotel room. More cyanide, I expect. I'll know more tomorrow about that when tests come back." She shook her head. "Whoever is in back of these people, he pulls their strings like a puppet master. They actually kill themselves for this person."

So it was another dead-end, so to speak. Hector said, "Any idea who or why? Who the hell commands the kind of power to drive these assassins to suicide after taking their best, lethal shot?"

Hector had once faced a kind of suicide cult before, long ago in Paris, so he had some biases in that direction.

Haven solemnly shook her head side-to-side, glistening black hair brushing the collar of her coat. "Not a clue yet. Not a one, I'm sorry to say. But that said, suicide *is* a prime constituent of the Japanese character, of its culture. It's hardly a cult thing, you know."

His next lodging place was Tokyo's newest and most posh—the Hotel Okura Tokyo, opened just a few months before and already a sensation.

Haven saw to their check-in and the moving of their bags to a Western-style room: Given his current aches and pains, Hector firmly dismissed the prospect of "sleeping same as on the goddamn floor" as he put it, despite Haven's urgings to go native. Standing firm, Hector directed her to secure a non-traditional Japanese room at whatever cost.

Having done that, a still rather shaky Hector detoured two floors up to check on Ian.

As Tiger ushered him into the first of several spacious Fleming suites Hector would encounter over the ensuing couple of weeks, he was again much relieved to find his hearing further improving. Hector could easily enough make out Fleming lecturing, though the subject was that of an increasingly favorite, grim topic—that of decay and of death.

Ian implored someone—Hector presumed it to be Dikko Hughes—"Please don't lecture me so, dammit. I'd stay home in piss-water England and take all that from She-Who-Must-Be-Obeyed if I wanted to hear more of this pointless, hair tearing and handwringing blather about embracing or making do with a half-life. The Iron Crab took his best pass at me last year and missed with his major claw. Inevitably, the Crab will return, and the next time, he will likely succeed. Therefore, in the interval, I mean to enjoy myself to as close to full as I can still manage with my battered vessel. Just living, in and of itself, is really nothing, at any rate. Surely you agree. Most people are unconscious up to seventeen years of age. They are dreaming until twenty-five or so, awake to perhaps the age of thirty-nine, all but mad after the age of forty, and the ones who did it right are properly dead before or soon after the age of sixty."

Ian waved a disgusted hand and added, "From that perspective, we hardly really live at all, and all four of us, as we embark on this particular, uncertain trip into the borderlands of the undiscovered country that is the East, have already long ago passed from the zone of living well and true."

Ian turned as he saw Hector. Smiling, he rose on shaking legs and rushed to embrace the American novelist. "My God, it's been on the news and it took forever to get Haven on the phone to assure us you weren't killed. You are truly well, then?"

"Alive at least, obviously," Hector said, awkwardly accepting Ian's hug. "Or as much as that can be said of anyone our age." He felt obligated to make that little dig at Ian's unrelenting fatalism. He then added, "But I'm more than a bit banged up." He patted Ian's back and said, "In the end, I'm mostly okay."

Ian said, "Who was it who did this? It simply can't be permitted to stand."

"Well, on that note, some invalid from the airport was immediately responsible," Hector said. "That Japanese youth with a missing leg I helped on the escalator, do you remember him? He left his fake limb standing next to me outside the airport. It was stuffed full with plastic explosives, maybe TNT.

Something bad, anyway. It was probably detonated, whatever it was, by some kind of radio signal."

Freshly red-faced from a first round of room service sake, Dikko said, "Dear God, things like that simply don't happen here." The corners of his mouth turned down. "And so it will make the world press, of course. And where is Miss Branch right now, if I might quickly ask of you?"

"She's seeing to our accommodations and settling in. We're two floors down." Hector saw that there was a third man in Fleming's rather luxurious suite—this one saturnine and sixty*ish*. The man wore thick glasses with horn rims. He had a prominent jaw that made him look argumentative, even in his momentary silence. His thinning silver hair was slicked straight back. The stranger wore English tweeds and a striped bow tie. Ian said, "Burton, I'd like you to meet—"

The stranger quickly held up a hand, finger to his lips, signaling for silence all around. He led them into Ian's bathroom, closed the door, then turned the water faucets all the way up.

Hector, frowning, said, "Why the hell are we all in the bathroom together?"

The man called Burton said, "Because I haven't had time to get my people over here to comb the place yet, to ferret out listening devices or the like."

Smiling uncertainly, Ian said, "This is our equipper and fixer, so to speak, courtesy of MI6's tourism department, because Britain, sad to say, has no official station here in Japan these years. Hector, do please say hullo to Alec Burton."

The elder Brit shook Hector's hand, already sizing him up. He presumed to spread open Hector's sport coat, then placed his hands on either side of the writer's tender torso. He raised a quizzical eyebrow as Hector winced. "Are your ribs hurting? I'll take more care if that is so."

"Ribs are sore, but no need to mollycoddle me," Hector said, not certain where this was heading. He raised an eyebrow. "But why touch me at all?"

Burton said, "I see you wear your jacket cut very loose and large. Presumably you do that for concealing a gun back home. One of some considerable size one must deduce. Unless, of course, your tailor is habitually the worse for drink?"

Actually, Hector mostly bought his suits off-the-rack: they tended to take a lot of wear and tear, after all. Take today's ensemble, for example. Feeling a bit of a blush, Hector said, "Peacemaker, that's what I sometimes carry back home. Sorry, that is to say I favor a—"

First a dour expression from Burton brought Hector up short. A tone of civilized disdain ensued: "That is to say, a single action Colt, model year 1874, yes? Real cowboy and Indian stuff. Extraordinarily long barrel and all but utterly impractical in a shoulder holster as you seem inclined to carry your frontier museum piece. I suppose you do that in some sort of jerry-rigged Berns-Martin, split-front, spring-retention holster?" A sniff and near sneer. "Don't bother confirming it so, my dear fellow. It's clear that's the case and, just as clearly, you're an antiquarian sentimentalist. You're afforded merely six shots, then you have to individually eject the spent cartridges with a built-in rod before you can reload. In the hands of even a mildly competent marksman, even the most tepid automatic would outshoot you to hell and back mere instants after you've spent your six. You wouldn't survive an exchange with even me. I'm frankly stunned you've endured this long, sir."

Now Hector was close to fuming. Ian saw that and raised a finger to his lips, winking, as if to say, *Do settle down and listen, dear boy. You really must choose your battles.*

The British weapons master rummaged through a metallic suitcase and pulled out a Walther PPK 7.65 mm and a Chic Gaylord holster he handed to Hector with what seemed palpable regret.

"Ian is now carrying this one's twin," said Burton. "And, yes, it's the Bond gun. Please don't lose it, and for God's sake, certainly don't get caught carrying it. It goes without saying Her Majesty's government will steadfastly deny any knowledge or involvement with you possessing that weapon, much less having provided it to you. If caught, you're quite on your own, is that understood?"

A furrowed brow, then he added: "Paradoxically, I would also strongly discourage its actual use, as leaving a further trail of corpses here in Japan is hardly going to go unnoticed or unpunished by local authorities. Having said that, given the bulky cowboy gun you favor back home, are you going to need instruction in use of this infinitely more sophisticated and refined firearm, Mr. Lasher?"

"Lassiter," Hector corrected, "and no, thank you, I know how to use an automatic. It wouldn't even be my first time handling this particular model."

That was quite true. Some foolish, James Bond-infatuated publicist had made Hector pose with just such a gun a year or so back for a blessedly rejected dust jacket photo. But after the modeling shoot, Hector hadn't been able to resist venturing behind the shutterbug's studio to blow to smithereens a carton of empty Coca-Cola bottles in an effort to see how Mr. James Bond's already-legendary gun truly performed.

The gun expert thrust several clips into either of Hector's jacket pockets. "I'll leave it to you to better sort out the concealment of these," Burton said.

The stodgy Brit turned back to his bag of tricks, showing Hector his back. Still facing away, Burton said, "I'm told you're a smoker, so a cigarette lighter won't be an eyebrow raiser, will it?"

"Quite the contrary, in fact," Hector said. "It would prove quite useful just now. My Zippo's flint has had it for the moment, so I could use a temporary replacement until—"

"No, you don't understand," Burton said.

Hector raised his eyebrows. "I don't understand what?"

"You don't understand that this isn't what it appears to be." The Englishman held up the lighter—it was much narrower and far more vertical than Hector's cherished Zippo. "You only get to use this Ronson a single time, Mr. Lasher. It's not a lighter, of course. This is more akin to a flamethrower. Across a distance of six feet or thereabouts, it should prove frightfully effective. At very least, it will create immediate and disfiguring burns. At its best, it will permanently blind or perhaps even kill an assailant. The happier news is, if caught having deployed this particular instrument, you might be able to fob off its lethal or disfiguring results as some manner of production defect. Let the hapless manufacturer carry the sorry water for the wicked outcome, yes?" A nasty if hopeful grin.

Hector warily accepted the cigarette lighter, weighing it in his palm. "You're sure it's safe to actually carry? Seems a little like lugging around a live bomb."

"Provided it's not struck by a bullet or compromised by an exploding artificial leg?" Was that a twinkle of amusement in the Brit's cold, gray eye? He said, "Oh, I expect it's safe enough to carry about. At least until its actuator is depressed. Once that happens, you'd best have a target acquired."

Burton reached back into his bag of tricks and said, "Right, then. You've acknowledged you are a smoker. I'm told you favor Pall Malls. I'm afraid that's rather too difficult to manage at short notice."

He held up what appeared to be a virgin pack of Morlands. As Hector reached, the man took a quick step back. "No! Don't simply go around bumbling with things you know nothing about! This just happens to be a quite literal explosive device you will carry around on your person. This item does require very special handling."

His head spinning, Hector said, "That thing is a bomb?"

"In a word," Burton confirmed. "It contains two chemicals in discrete glass containers hidden inside. Contrary to the cigarette pack boasts, this one is very crushable. You do that, breaking the glass and allowing the vials' contents to comingle. Then you throw it and run like all hell. It's a tad unpredictable in terms of detonation time, I confess— anything from nearly instantaneous to under two or three seconds. It has an absolutely lethal range of perhaps six feet. If you're still within twelve feet when she blows, you'll likely incur serious damage."

Hector nodded his understanding and carefully accepted the pack that he slid with the lighter into his jacket pocket alongside the ammunition clips. He determined he would be sparing in his packing of the cigarette bomb, if he dared carry it at all. He said, "So, is that everything?"

"Just one more item," Burton said. "I've noted you're right-handed."

"That's right," Hector confirmed.

"Then please give me your left arm."

Scowling, Hector did that. Burton pushed back Hector's sleeves and eyed his trusty old Timex, *tsk-tsking*. "How quaint. I suspect we can do rather better than that." He removed Hector's watch and actually presumed to toss it into a wastepaper basket sitting next to the hotel's rather spacious writing table.

"Here you go now," he said slipping a new band around Hector's wrist. "A Rolex Submariner 6538 on a nylon strap—modified, of course. The stem has been reengineered and made into something a bit more useful." Burton tugged at that stem, drawing out a thin length of tensile steel wire that emerged with a sinister hiss.

"A garrote," Burton said, rather unnecessarily. "Apparently, this idea of building one into a watch is a KGB inspiration. But even if that bit of apocrypha is proven one day to be accurate, I assure you we've more than improved upon the concept."

Hector eyed the deadly watch. Unlike the gifted lighter or explosive cigarette pack, it at least fulfilled its apparent primary function by actually keeping time.

Shaking Ian's hand, Burton said, "Please do be diligent in returning all issued items in something close to their original condition, yes?"

"Of course," Ian said on Hector's behalf. "As always. I hate to think we'll even be bothered to entertain their use."

The expression that elicited from Burton—even for such an accomplished writer as Hector—was *ineffable*.

Once the man had left the room with his deadly, metallic suitcase, Hector dipped a hand into the wastepaper basket and retrieved his Timex. He slid his customary watch into his pocket along with the deadly lighter. "What a mean little son of a bitch that character is," he said sourly.

"Yes, and then some more," Ian agreed. "But now we have guns thanks to the little bastard, so one simply must take the rough with the smooth." Ian hesitated, then gripped Hector's arm. "The fellows and I have been talking—yes, Dikko and Tiger know all about why we are really here. One question stemming from all that, Hector. When this bomb went off at the airport—where exactly *was* Haven Branch?"

"Not so close by at all," Hector said bluntly, his mind instantly starting to gnaw at it, probably just as Ian and Hughes intended. "She was trying to find us a cab." He fingered the deadly lighter in his pocket. He said softly, "You have your doubts about Haven now? You don't trust her?"

"That might still be putting it too strongly," Ian said. "In you, I have no doubts. The same can be said of Dikko and Tiger. I certainly know my own heart and head, all too bloody well, of course." Ian paused and said, "I'm just asking you to be judicious when trusting in or confiding to Miss Branch until something of moment occurs in which she can, to use an American phrase, *prove out* as completely trustworthy."

Hector looked from Ian to the two journalists.

Ian pressed on. "No, don't be like that, Hector. Please don't go and get your back up. The stakes are unbelievably high and we know next to nothing about her save what she's told us. Well, *almost* nothing. Tiger and Dikko have done some digging you see, and their initial inquiries have prompted more areas to explore, I fear."

"You have to explain that," Hector said. "You have to do that right now."

"I can't. *We* can't, not yet. There are just…we'll call them implications and insinuations. It's all rather frustratingly like stroking smoke, at least for the moment."

Ian raised his eyebrows, searching Hector's face. "Neither of us is a child, and we've both known our share of betrayals. We've broken sacred vows of our own. We've done so, time and again, I'd daresay. Hector, friends and lovers too frequently betray, as you well know. Even family, our very blood, disappoints, sometimes most bitterly of all. Promises are more often than not made with every intention of being broken when it eventually becomes efficacious to do so, quite heedless of any of the potential consequences. Surely you must agree that only the unwritten or yet to happen is to be trusted, Hector. Because it can make no promises, only tomorrow never lies."

10

TRUST DIES. MISTRUST BLOSSOMS

Haven hugged him as he closed and secured their hotel room's door. She kissed his cheek and said, "You should probably lay down and rest for a while. It's not that long ago since you were nearly blown to rags and jam."

A hand to his forehead, as if checking for a temperature, she said, "Remember what they said about your poor head."

Hector shook that head. "Ringing in my ears is gone and there's no nausea. I wouldn't want to play eighteen holes of golf or to try and land a marlin, but I'm feeling sound enough to move around the room, here and now."

"In that case..." Taking his hand, Haven led him to the window. The sun was almost down and Tokyo was transforming into a sea of pulsing neon. It looked a little like New York City if all of the Big Apple was illuminated in the same busy and blinding manner as Times Square.

Haven said, "Quite a view, isn't it? A view to kill for?"

An odd way to put it, he thought. Hector stood behind her, hands on her shoulders, considering the riot of light.

You didn't even have to read Japanese to know what most of it was pushing—a cataclysm of American goods advertising

Kodak and Coke and a hundred other brands from back home. It was less than twenty years since Japan's surrender, and the conquered country was already well on its way to the sorriest form of Western commercialization.

"The problem with a room with a view is that view usually becomes its own problem," Hector said. His lips lightly grazed the soft black down at the back of her neck.

Haven whispered softly, "Please, don't be cynical, not tonight, darling. If you are feeling up to it, what's the plan for our first evening in Japan?"

"I'm thinking just you and me tonight, if you don't terribly mind," he said. "Ian's quite jet-lagged. Given his damaged heart, I really don't want to press. He already feels some tragic need to play at being James Bond every time he has any kind of audience at all, so I'm just relieved he's being somewhat sensible tonight."

"And the other two—Dikko and Tiger?"

"They live here. It's just home to them and so no special night in that sense."

Disappointment in her voice: "Will we have room service dinner then? At least perhaps take a little walk through the downtown after, Hector? But only if you're truly up to that."

Hector was tempted to say something brash and full of bravado, perhaps something like, "Screw room service, kid. Show me the goddamn town."

But his scuffed hands hurt a bit more, now. Just a few hours after the blast, more aches and pains were settling in and asserting themselves. His battered cheek and knee throbbed with fresh urgency.

And, at least in this room and freshly armed, Hector enjoyed certain advantages in safekeeping he wouldn't have out there on the bustling, Tokyo streets.

This night, having come so close to death, Hector felt something he couldn't remember ever experiencing and certainly not with such vivid unease. For perhaps the first time in his life since the befouled trench lines of the Great War, Hector felt utterly and terrifyingly *vulnerable*.

Nobody stays tough after forty. Wasn't that another Fleming axiom?

"Room service, definitely," he said. "Then a safe and quiet night in that big bed, please." A smile. "Not necessarily to *sleep*, mind you, not at first, anyway. But I really do need to give myself a bit of an easier night after this bloody day. Candidly? I've seen firsthand a time or two the insidious, long-term results that can come from ignoring a head injury. The sorry prospects after doing that are pretty sobering."

Irresistibly, he thought of Hem: Ernest stood as the textbook example of inventing myriad ways *not* to behave after sustaining the latest in what ultimately had proven to be a lamentable and likely to have proven collectively lethal series of personality-altering blows to the head.

Hector was never less than conscious of the fact his hands and brain were his primary instruments as a writer. Those parts of himself, at least, he tended to look after.

"Sounds like a plan then," she said. "Will you trust me to choose your night's fare?"

"Completely and utterly, I trust you to do just that," Hector said, very aware of every trace of irony in his answer, but careful not to let any of that awareness seep into his voice or posture, possibly tipping her to his growing skepticism of her alliances.

Though he craved a real drink with his meal—particularly since he'd been infected by his comrades with a stubborn sense of doubt regarding his enticing bedmate—he resisted the urge even for sake, instead settling for green tea.

While Haven was a bit more daring with her dinner order, she kept it simple and pleasing for Hector, ordering him *misho* soup, *tempura* and rice, and some *kuzumochi* for dessert.

Before setting down to savor her seafood, she'd taken the trouble to dim the lights in order to better see the bustling, whirl and flickering rush of neon laid out before them. Chopsticks poised for a bite, Haven said pointedly, "It's not remotely the country you remember, is it?"

"Not by a long shot, no it is not," Hector said softly, putting down his fork. He turned slowly—a rued concession to his aches and pains—in order to better survey all the light and commerce as he sipped more of his tea. "It was all but laid waste then, of course. It was still just 1945, after all. But, then, London was in ruins, too, courtesy of that other Axis partner."

"The Germans," Haven said, unnecessarily.

"Yeah, them."

"You spent most of World War II in France, didn't you?"

"Mostly, that's so," he said. "Paris and Lyon stayed largely intact. Those were my primary locations at the time. It was only the occupiers of those places that left much to be desired."

Pointing with her chopsticks she said, "You know, of course, that a lot of people out there right now probably still feel that way about you Americans."

"And about you British," Hector said, watching to see how she would take that.

A shrug and a smile. "And us British, of course," she repeated, "yes. Lord knows, our tentacles around the East once gripped infinitely tighter." She sipped her ginseng tea, then said, "Maybe, after this mission and when we're both off the clock, to use Ian's phrase, we could go to Hong Kong. It's a *good* blend of East and West. It's rather more its own place, in a peculiar, but a *good* way."

"Something definitely to think about," he said.

She moved to refill his tea and he held up a hand. "Thanks, but no, darlin'. I have a feeling that stuff could cost me sleep taken in any significant quantities, particularly at this hour."

She smiled sadly and said, "You look like you're in real pain."

"Just getting sorer as the night gets on," he said. "Aspirin and sleep will probably do me wonders. It's like the aftermath of the car accident, you know? You feel it all much more a day or two after the actual event." *Because tomorrow never lies*, he thought, haunted by the phrase Ian had placed in his head.

"Your wife—Brinke I mean—and her writings, where are they exactly? Here, or...?"

"Nothing so straightforward or so easy to reach," Hector said, smiling at his first wife's memory. "Other than New York, Paris and maybe Rome, Brinke wasn't really one for the more obvious tourist places. She was more the pure explorer. Brinke liked to get to all the best places before the rest of the world knew their names. It's quite possible she never set foot in this city. To answer your question, her belongings are said to be in a little place called Beppu. Do you know it?"

Haven seemed genuinely fascinated, leaning across the table to take his hand. "I absolutely do *not*. Oh, I've heard of it, sure—it actually is a kind of tourist spot, at least these days. But I've never come closing to visiting there. I know next to nothing about this region, not in any real depth."

The candlelight danced in her dark eyes and burnished her black hair. Once again, Hector was reminded of how much this woman resembled Brinke.

He had a sudden, urgent sense he'd need to watch himself if he somehow succeeded in getting around his mounting aches and pains in order to make love with her this night. The risk of his mind drifting, of his imagining that Haven was in fact Brinke rather than herself—of maybe even calling Haven by the wrong name in a moment of passion—seemed treacherously high.

He realized his index finger was tapping the diamond adorning Haven's left hand. What was the title of Ian's earlier Bond book, the one inspired by some long-ago jeweler's advert copy that had stuck in Ian's quirky mind?

Oh, yes, *Diamonds Are Forever*. Diamonds endured, certainly that was true. Far more perishable were those loved ones who drove such eternal stones' acquisition.

He closed his eyes, trying to visualize Brinke's diamond ring and its mated golden band. For several years after her death and before eventually remarrying, he had worn them on a chain around his neck. Now they were back home in that vault in New Mexico, stored alongside the venerable old six-shooter the British weapons master had so soundly disparaged just scant hours ago.

Hector did some math, calculating from the year of Brinke's murder. My God, had so much time really passed in this life without her? In long-ago Cuba, the night of the day of her death, it had seemed inconceivable he would endure the week without Brinke.

The first night he'd returned home alone to Bone Key, he'd slowly, deliberately emptied the Peacemaker of live cartridges and tossed them into his backyard in the dark, fearing he'd put the gun to his own head or against the roof of his mouth, otherwise.

Tonight Hector piercingly felt his age. My God, what was he doing with this stunning, possibly duplicitous, other black-haired and black-eyed beauty—one some twenty or more years his junior?

The same old honey trap.

An axiom suddenly came to him, one of unknown provenance: *The chains of habit are too weak to be felt, until they're too strong to be broken.*

Not granted access to his thoughts, Haven, mellow and settling into a sensual languor, stroked his hand. "At least you're in Japan at its most beautiful time of the year," she said. "Fall days here are comfortable and clear. The nights are rather cold, but the colors in the gardens and of the trees more than make up for that."

Hector couldn't say the topiary even remotely interested him.

And weather? That was just something that happened or typically had to be endured.

He rose and said, "Still hungry, or shall we…?" He nodded at the waiting bed. At some point when he hadn't seen it occur, Haven had invitingly turned down the sheets.

She said, "You're sure you just don't want to down a handful of aspirin and sleeping pills and then plunge into oblivion? Just the bruises and cuts I can see now look like they'd be terribly uncomfortable."

A smile. "I'd certainly like to try for something more than simple sleep."

"Thank God." Smiling back, she excused herself as he gathered their plates to set them out in the hallway. "Give me five minutes," she said.

After checking the locks, he turned to find Haven framed in the window, a sexy silhouette against all that frantic backlighting of downtown Tokyo. She was nude with the exception of a black garter belt, sheer black stockings and her wicked black stilettos.

Hector walked toward her, slowly untying his black knit tie. He dragged it loose from under his shirt collar, wrapping a bit of either end around each fist. He lowered the tie behind her head and then raised it under her bare bottom, pulling her up onto tiptoes and then against himself as he kissed her, fiercely.

This, he assured himself, must surely be the proper *improper* way to keep a potential enemy *closer*.

He walked backward as she guided him to the bed, kicking off her heels along the way. She unbuttoned and gently pushed his white cotton shirt over his shoulders, gasping softly at the sorry sight of his bruised torso. It was his first time seeing his body in several hours and he was equally appalled by the sorry mottled state of his chest and arms. He expected that still painful knee wouldn't look much better.

After she finished undressing him, Haven kissed her way down his torso and then spent some time down there as he gathered her long, loosely worn black hair in his fingers. "I like it that you don't wear your hair up or do all those dubious things to it that women seem driven to try these days," he said, his voice raw.

Current hair fashions reminded him more of 1950s American cars, all sweep and fins—regrettable architectural arrangements facilitated by too-many cans of hairspray.

"I love your hair lose and natural." He said it raw-voiced, increasingly fearing he might peak in this way, before he could make her feel wonderful, too.

He urged him up to him and she kissed his mouth, then she eased him back on the bed.

"Life's too short to take that much trouble with something as silly as hair," Haven said. As he started to shift on the bed, she shook her head firmly and said, "No, please, just lay on your back. After all, that side of you is the only part that isn't all freshly beaten up. I'll do most of the work, I promise. It's doctor's orders, after all—nothing strenuous now, not for you. Tonight calls strictly for TLC."

Straddling Hector, she really did proceed to make love to him, taking charge and quite fiercely at some points. Her uninhibited exertions against his bruised body made this particular act of love all the more piercing for its edgy mix of pleasure and dull pain.

In the low light, with her much longer hair and curvier body, Haven blessedly did not in fact conjure the vivid memories of Brinke he had dreaded. There was something much more exotic about Haven's looks, something a bit foreign and even feline.

If he was forced to make a comparison to anyone in this moment, he supposed Haven most resembled present-day Natalie Wood—there was something quite similar there in her wide, dark almond-shaped eyes and wide, sultry mouth.

Haven's animal aggression, her dark good looks and her erotic near-nudity—not to mention the perhaps lethal threat she might pose against him even as she rocked against Hector with a sexy snarl teasing her lips—it was all too much, at last.

When he did climax, Hector did so quite recklessly, still deep inside her, some part of him half-hoping something might come of it.

Haven screamed, peaking with him, collapsing spent and sweat-slicked across him, the weight and pressure of her breasts setting Hector's bruised chest to a soft, emphatic pulse of dull aching.

They fell asleep just like that, still one.

It was the oddest dream. He was there, nude in bed with Haven, still a tangle of limbs and bed sheets, but he was also dressed and at the table by the window, sipping sake and smiling at Brinke whose black hair was now much longer than he had ever seen her wear it in life—every bit as long as Haven's and then some more, just teasing her tailbone.

His first wife was obviously nude under a short silk Japanese dressing gown. He remembered seeing that gown on many a Key West morning and evening, the same as a lifetime ago.

"She's quite beautiful," Brinke said, considering Haven and that Hector on the bed.

"She's also potentially quite some kind of trouble," Hector said, considering the same tableau.

Brinke smiled and sipped her warm, Japanese rice wine. "What woman worth anything can't the same be said of? You know, given less than half a chance, I'd share her with you, if I was still capable. Maybe I'd even take her from you. What do you think about that?"

"I'd prefer the first option, if only for old and tawdrier times' sake," he said. "But seriously, some friends think she might mean me real harm, darling. They suspect that she means to be, well, you could say she's angling to be the *death* of me, if they're remotely right."

His late-wife's look grew more serious as she took his hand. "You know we all have to die someday. Even you, Hector. In some ways, it gets very lonely this side, waiting for you to at last arrive home."

Brinke took another long assessment of Haven, sprawled nude and inviting on the bed. She said to him, "And, anyway, surely there are worse ways to go?"

11

CONFESSIONS OF A MASK

In concession to Ian's stubborn, probably misdiagnosed "jet lag"—compounded by Hector's lingering stiffness from his injuries—the four writers and Haven decided to remain another day in Tokyo before setting out on Ian's barnstorming tour of The Land of the Rising Sun.

They had finalized a series of points of interest, all of them Ian's picks of course, and macabre fodder for his new Bond novel. Each site had been carefully selected by Ian because it embodied at least one of the "terrifying manifestations of the horrific Japan."

Ian now had the notion of ending their shared travels in Beppu.

There, with Ian by his side, Hector would at last claim Brinke Devlin's long lost writings, if they really existed.

While Ian lazed about the hotel under the watchful, slightly drunken eyes of Dikko and Tiger, Hector at last dared to venture out in daylight for a bit of sightseeing with Haven. He also asked her along for that brief lunch with his fellow writer that had been arranged at the insistence of their shared Japanese publisher.

This was to be his conversation over *sashimi* and *sake* with Yukio Mishima, the well-regarded Japanese novelist and sometimes actor who was supposedly becoming harrowingly radicalized as he entered his early middle age.

But before that lunch, as they walked arm and arm through the Rikugien gardens—Haven's favorite in all of Tokyo, she had confided—Hector was watchful for any threat, making certain she clung to his left arm in case he might need to draw his much smaller but allegedly deadlier new automatic.

He'd kept the Walther's existence hidden from Haven so far. He'd slept with the PPK under his pillow—a habit dating back to his far bulkier Colt—and he'd put on the holster and quickly covered it with his jacket while his lover dressed in the adjacent room.

But so far, there was no hint of menace. It was simply a bright, clear autumn day in Japan.

Strolling slowly with linked arms through the gardens, she said, "This truly is the best time of year to see all this, Hector. Better still, you're seeing the city before all the stuff that they'll do for the 1964 Olympics changes things even more, and almost certainly for the worst."

Smiling and shaking his head, Hector remembered Gertrude Stein long ago wringing her hands over the probable dire impacts of a now long-forgotten Paris-set Olympics games.

Those eternal circles of history repeating, again.

They stood for a time on the curve of the graceful yet solid Togetsukyo Bridge, taking in the view. The bridge rather reminded Hector of a stone seesaw balanced on a boulder. Standing at just the proper angle on the un-railed crossing, one could evade sight of the skyscrapers and imagine oneself far from civilization, possibly standing somehow outside time itself.

"It's really quite beautiful," Hector agreed. "If it was just a bit warmer, it'd be a good place to sit down for a few hours with a notebook and a pen. Seems a fine place for writing but only for writing about gentle, good things."

Of course that was not the kind of writing typically associated with Hector Lassiter.

After a couple of hours of further traipsing of the winding paths of the park, they at last caught a cab and headed into the Foreign Correspondents Club for their scheduled lunch with the writer who had been born Kimitake Hiraoka.

Hector took Haven's hand and said, "You'll translate for me?"

"Surely, if need be," Haven said. "But I really don't think it will be required. I've seen him interviewed on TV several times. Mishima speaks quite fluent English. And so once again, I'm *really* looking forward to just sitting back and being a fly on my lover-writer's wall."

Yukio Mishima's brushy black hair was close-cropped; his eyebrows quite bushy. He wasn't at all tall, but years of bodybuilding and sword handling had put real muscle on the writer, most of it concentrated in his upper torso.

Mishima seemed more initially imposing than maybe he really was—some of his presence had already dimmed now that he was sitting next to much taller Hector.

The Japanese novelist wore casual western-style clothes— dark slacks, loafers and a dark blue sweater over a white shirt, open at the collar.

As Haven had promised, he spoke English quite well, even eloquently, and despite some misgivings about the man's politics and personal life—Yukio Mishima was long married and had a couple of children, but the writer was widely reputed to be a closeted homosexual—Hector found himself charmed by his Asian peer.

Over a traditional Japanese lunch and more green tea, Mishima shared his frustration with Hector regarding the self-imposed "mask" Japan still presented to the world in the wake of the most recent war.

Commanding Hector's blue eyes with his own intense, nearly unblinking dark-eyed gaze, Mishima confided, "I think we Japanese still have quite a brutal side, and it's only thinly hidden now. It's been hidden far too long since the war, and it now looks for expression. But it's not good or healthy to have denied it for so long as we have. When it comes out, it will come as an explosion, and I think that explosion is much closer than many of us care to imagine."

Mishima paused to tap off the ash of a cigarette, thinking some more, then he added, "I don't like that Japanese culture is now represented only by the flower arrangement, by this false-face notion of a peaceful culture. We still have a strong warrior's mentality, and it's just barely cloaked." A funny smile, then Mishima added, "At least that's so in some of us. A rare few, maybe. I suppose I feel driven to transcend the currents of history. After all, I come from a samurai ancestry. I revel in its culture in which beauty and death are very much linked."

"You really should meet my friend, Ian," Hector found himself saying.

"You mean Ian Fleming," Mishima said. He made his fingers into a mockery of a gun and said, "Mr. Kiss Kiss Bang Bang? Licensed to kill?"

Mishima laughed along with Hector. "Actually, I would like to meet that man and as an actor, after a sorts, I'm looking forward to seeing the film, *Doctor No*. Fleming fascinates me, and in many ways. I read one of his Bonds, the one about Russia, many years ago in English. He's far more writer than most of your Western critics give him credit for. Anthony Boucher just clearly doesn't get the man." A wry smile. "But then Boucher is an idiot."

Hector smiled and said, "I agree, and your next flask is on me for certain. I'll confess that Boucher's a kind of bête noire of mine. He doesn't really *get me*, either."

Another, much harsher laugh. The Japanese novelist said, "What do critics ever know? They're all now savaging my new novel, *Utsukushii hoshi* or *Beautiful Star*, some even as we speak, I expect. True, it's almost science fiction and so unlike most of what I've done before now. But it was the book I had to write. I can't give them the same book over and over, even if it would help sales. Do you know what I mean?"

Hector smiled in commiseration and reached across to light a fresh cigarette for Mishima, using his newly re-flinted Zippo. He again resisted the urge to get out a smoke of his own.

As he lit the other author's cigarette, Hector said, "As popular writers, we endure vogues. Ups and downs we can do much too little to control."

"Just so," Mishima agreed. He presumed to take the lighter from Hector's hand and to read the engraved inscription there. "A gift from Hemingway? I heard you were friends. I know that line about the true sentence is one most-associated with Hemingway."

"That's right," Hector said. "I suppose not a day's gone by since last July I haven't thought of poor Hem. Maybe the *critic* Edmund "Bunny" Wilson said it best somehow, despite his day job. Hearing of Ernest's death was like having one of the pillars of the world suddenly and terribly collapse, Wilson wrote."

"But surely Hemingway was right to do what he did, taking his own life," Mishima said unhesitatingly. "Admittedly, I may have certain biases in this area—" another funny smile "—but from *my* perspective, Hemingway's only mistake was in not dying when he was young and beautiful and at the top of his game as a writer. Tell me, if you can confirm it: Is it true his mother dressed Hemingway in dresses when he was young?"

"I've seen the pictures to prove it," Hector said. "And Hem told me about all that more than once." Hector sighed and said, "Hem may be the only man I've ever met who, I believe, truly *hated* his mother."

Mishima's face grew dark. "My grandmother raised me for many years. She did something similar. My father was so concerned about my 'feminization' that he destroyed many of my early writings, thinking them a kind of symptom. He thought writing unmanly." He rubbed his jaw and said, "Did your father approve of you becoming a writer?"

"I hardly knew my father," Hector said candidly, suddenly almost feeling the actual weight of Haven's gaze.

It was the first time he'd shared the story with another man. Hector wasn't sure what it meant that he felt compelled to do so with this particular person. Yet, he pressed on: "I actually shot my father, just after he killed my mother. He caught her with another man. I winged my father and nearly cost him an arm. But the state eventually executed him for mother's murder. I was raised by my grandfather. The old man was cordially dubious about the craft of writing as a means to make a living, but to Beau's credit—I *guess*—he certainly didn't try to stop my trying."

The Japanese author, who many felt would claim a Nobel Prize any year now, leaned back in his chair, contemplating the fleeting fire at the end of his cigarette. It was some Japanese brand that seemed to burn faster than its Western counterparts.

Mishima at last said, "It's been a crazy interval in my career these past few months, so I should perhaps be forgiven some of my thinking if it offends or concerns you in some way. I no sooner got back from a world tour with my wife than I was sued for libel—a very unusual thing to have happen here in Japan. I was sued by a politician offended by my novel, *After the Banquet*. Was this man, this *politician*, thinly disguised in my novel?" Mishima smiled. "Yes, he was. But then you of all authors know something of the risks of using real people in fiction.

"Next, an extremist political group took offense at one of my short stories. They issued a death threat and promised they would burn down my house, preferably with my family and I still inside. This was no hollow or idle threat, my friend. I had to have a bodyguard for the past year, just in case they followed through. It's only lately I can feel safe going out by myself like this, not looking over my shoulder all the time."

That last sentiment certainly resonated with Hector given certain current circumstances of his own.

Mishima reached over and shook Hector's downturned hand, letting the touch linger after the shake was over. Mishima's much smaller hand came to rest on the back of Hector's bigger, hairier mitt. It was an unusual gesture coming from another man and evoked more thoughts of certain rumors about Mishima's sexuality. Hector let it happen though.

The Japanese writer searched his eyes and said, "Sometimes I think the fools forget we're merely myth-makers. In the end, what real harm can we do anyone? You would agree?"

At a loss for any worthy words, Hector just smiled noncommittally.

Mishima ended the lingering, intimate touch and sat back in his chair again, his cigarette in one hand, his cup of tea in the other. "And the days are getting shorter. Within a year or two, I'll be forty-five and will have to make a plan for my life."

Mishima's glowered, his thick, bushy brows knitting closer. "When a man reaches the age of forty, he has no chance to die beautifully. No matter how he tries, he will die in an ugly way. So he has to force himself to live from that point on. It is undeniable, yes?"

Now Yukio Mishima really reminded Hector of Ian Fleming. It seemed a shame the two peculiar, egocentric and fatalistic writers couldn't meet and commiserate about decay and death over raw fish, just as Hector was doing with Mishima.

That very morning, quoting Raymond Chandler, Fleming had groused, "Lust ages men but keeps women young."

The Japanese author abruptly pointed at Hector's scabbed and bruised hands and said, "Speaking of threats and enemies, what's behind what happened yesterday to you at the airport? It's all in the news, as I'm sure you know. It frankly sounds more like the kind of thing that would have happened to me—that is if those threatening me had had any real guts to act."

Hector shrugged and said, "I honestly wish you could tell me what all that might mean. I'm really just here to sight-see and to write about Ian pretty much doing the same."

Outside the club, after a goodbye and a firm dry handshake with Mishima—when it was again just the two of them and Hector was weighing hailing them a cab—Haven reached over and caressed his un-bruised cheek.

She said, "You look very troubled darling, what's wrong? Are you not feeling well?"

He shook his head and sighed. "Just reflecting on our lunch and all of the gloomy talk that went with it. Honest to God, am I the only writer on earth who doesn't want to die, *not ever?*"

Haven smiled and hugged him close. "Certainly stay alive as long as you can, my darling Hector. The novelty and charm of you hasn't nearly worn off for me and I have all manner of carnal designs for you back at the hotel and elsewhere across this grand country. Even now, I'm thinking we should go somewhere naughty together soon, perhaps we should do that right this instant."

"Sounds like a stellar idea," Hector said. "But first, I think I need a drink—a proper, strong and Western-style cocktail. Tell me, my lovely Haven, where in God's name in Tokyo can a man get a potently-made double bourbon on the rocks?"

On the way in search of a bar that might serve some drink equal to that of Hector's dreams, Haven talked him into a film after promising it was *the* scandalous talk of Tokyo—a new genre of filmmaking dubbed "eroduction" and a piece of cinema that only ran a little under half-an-hour.

Reluctantly, Hector complied. What, after all, was half-an-hour?

In the end, the Japanese stag film called *Flesh Market* really did nothing for Hector more than heighten his desire for that stiff Western-style drink.

Haven eventually led him to *Golden Gai*, or "Golden Town," a cramped and bohemian little sector of shops and bars that seemed somehow a world away from the neon flash of Tokyo proper.

They found a hole in the wall joint that seated maybe a dozen diners, tops, and Hector at last got his stiff, American-style drink. He also finally permitted himself a blessed cigarette.

Watching him, Haven smiled and shook her head. "You're already homesick, I think."

Hector blew a long, thin stream of smoke, mulling her observation. That cigarette—he already thought he could have skipped it. Another sign, maybe, he was closer to changing his way of living…no mean feat past sixty.

He shook his head and tapped off a little ash. He said, "Not like you mean. For one thing, I'm still rather shaken up by that whole Cuban Missile Crisis interval. I suspect we all came closer to Armageddon than we ever want to know. America doesn't feel all that safe to me, these days. Kennedy is a worry. He's clearly too young and callow for the office. For another thing, I've always been a traveler, but I suppose Europe isn't all that terribly far from America once you tick off the language differences. Lacking the language, lacking the map in my head, and clearly being somebody's target over here? It's just not shaping up to be a sightseeing lark, this passage, you know? It's a little too much like living in an Ambler novel, or maybe one of Graham Greene's so-called *dark* entertainments."

Looking a bit sad and disappointed, she said, "I so wish it was different, but I understand what you're saying, of course. It's all undeniably the way it is—the world feels like it rests on the knife's edge. More and more, that seems so. Ideally, we'd get this thing with Ian and the microfilm handled sooner rather than later and then—or at least one would expect—the pressure on you would quickly drop off."

Hector didn't see how that could come to be—not unless he and Ian called some kind of conference for the world press to say they'd recovered the key to manufacturing an unspeakable biological weapon, but then turned it over to the British or the American governments.

Hector heard Ian in his head delivering this imaginary press conference, cigarette smoke trailing as he spoke with his hands: "So, there you see, ladies and gentleman—Hector and I have *nothing* more to provide the espionage community and so now we're off to seek some nubile naked Japanese pearl divers and to savor other, most robust treasures of the Orient."

Following his second double bourbon, Hector finally felt a pleasant numbing sensation setting in. Sensing the change— Haven seemed terribly attentive and attuned to him, Hector thought, almost cloyingly so—she smiled and said, "Your blood sugar issues aside, will you trust me on one thing and try some Japanese whiskey?"

Hector almost laughed. "Holy Jesus, there is such a thing?"

Smiling, holding up a finger, Haven ordered in Japanese. Hector thought he caught a brand name. He repeated, "Suntory?"

"Suntory Old Whiskey," she confirmed. "They modulate their handling of the whiskey in relation to the changes of the seasons."

"Really? That sounds complicated."

"But well worth the efforts," she said. "You'll see."

To his surprise, Hector found he quite liked the Japanese whiskey. He was something of a single malt *aficionado*—even a kind of whisky snob, probably.

Hell, Hector figured even his fellow whisky-phile, good old Jimmy Hanrahan, would grudgingly approve of this Japanese stuff.

Haven tapped his glass with hers and said, "You like?"

"I like very much."

"It's your turn for the toast," she said.

He'd taken some trouble to learn a few key phrases from Tiger. He said, "*Kampai.*"

"That's charming, *if* ever-so slightly mispronounced," Haven said, stroking his leg slowly under the bar, out of sight of their server. Her hand drifted elsewhere. Husky voiced, she whispered in his ear, "Where'd you learn that?"

Before he could answer, he felt something sharp and hard poke his right kidney. Haven was suddenly sitting up straighter.

There was a mirror behind the bar. Two smallish men in dove-gray trench coats and matching gray porkpie hats stood behind them. Both also wore white surgical masks that hooked behind their ears, covering more of their faces.

Hector assumed the other man, just like the one behind him, had a gun pressed to Haven's spine.

The one standing behind Hector said, "You will get up very slowly, and then you will walk out quietly with us, your hands in your pockets." His English was disarmingly assured.

Nodding at the bartender, the masked man said something in Japanese, then nodded toward the front of the establishment where a third man, one dressed the same way and also masked, stood glaring back at them.

Haven said to Hector, "He just told the bartender to relax and to do nothing, or else that man at the door will pitch a hand grenade in here, killing everyone and likely burning down the entire block."

Hector said to Haven, "Who are these fools? Do you have any ideas?"

Before she could answer, the man behind Hector said, "Shut up, both of you, or I'll kill you right now. Don't you put me to some test, Mr. Lassiter. Nor you, Miss Branch."

12

A HIDDEN CLAW

Remarkably, their would-be captors didn't search them or even pat down Hector to discover his gun. On the other hand, he couldn't have done much with it anyway, not after his hands were jerked behind his back and secured there with some kind of surgical rubber cord that all but robbed the circulation from his fingers.

Haven's hands, too, were lashed behind her back. They pitched her purse onto the floorboard of a waiting car, then forced Hector into the back seat, stretched out on his back. Haven was slung face down across his chest, her weight and its impact sparking fresh pain from his earlier bumps and bruises.

She said softly, scared-eyed, "I'm *so* sorry, Hector. I was a perfect fool to have us go wandering around like bloody tourists when all this is boiling around you. This is my fault, *all* my fault."

"I said to shut up," warned the man who spoke English. "No more words, or I'll shoot this woman in the leg and leave her to slowly bleed out in front of you, Mr. Lassiter. She is frankly of no practical use to us. It's *you* we mean to talk to. Be clear on this—it's only you we need. It's important you both understand this woman of yours is merely a means to an end, and we will act accordingly. You should do the same if you would spare her further suffering."

Riding in grim silence, smelling her fear-born perspiration mixed with his own, Hector tried to calculate and memorize distances and the turns they took in case he got some chance to try and navigate them in reverse in the course of an eventual escape.

That seemed a very remote possibility, however—his mental exercises just something inchoately arrived at to keep him distracted from whatever dark outcome might loom for the two of them.

All the light went out just as the car began to slow and then stopped—Hector assumed they'd entered an underground garage of sorts. He estimated they'd traveled less than two miles, but there had been a fair number of turns before arriving.

As they hauled him out of the car after Haven, while seeking to get a better grip on his rangy body, one of the men at last felt the hard piece of metal under his arm and grunted.

The Walther was immediately taken from his shoulder holster and shoved into the pocket of the man who spoke English.

So much for that possible tool of escape.

That said, he still had his deadly lighter and his garrote watch. Given any chance at all, he'd use them, Hector promised himself.

That was *if* he could ever get his hands free to do so.

Pinned behind his back and with Haven's weight fully on his chest, Hector hadn't been able to work at the rubber bonds on his wrists as they were being driven.

As he stood up, Hector began to turn his hands, the surgical rubber tubing tearing painfully at his hairy wrists but already intimating some promising new slack.

Shuffling a few steps ahead of Haven and her escort, Hector was shoved through a connecting door from the garage into a larger empty room—this one with bare concrete walls and a slightly pitched concrete floor that sported a center drain just visible in the low light.

This space looked old and appeared to have survived innumerable earthquakes: troubling cracks speaking to the region's sorry seismic history spread across the floor, ceilings and walls like spiders' webs.

Seething, Hector watched helplessly as two of the masked men shoved Haven through yet another door. A shouted order in English before that door was slammed shut: "Strip! Take off every stitch of clothing, you white bitch!"

Haven clearly resisted: Screams and the sounds of tearing fabric ensued, then muffled cries just before the door firmly closed, followed by a torturous silence.

Moving toward that door, Hector was stopped when his own PPK's barrel was shoved up tight against his back. A curt voice said simply, convincingly, "No."

A single chair was positioned in the middle of the main room. Its legs appeared to have been fastened to the floor with metal plates and screws. The man holding Hector's gun pointed for the author to take a seat there.

Furious, still hoping for some window for escape or counterattack that would allow him to help Haven, Hector moved cautiously to the chair, taking a last, hard look around at the three men guarding him, then he sat down.

A strap was quickly pulled from the bottom of the chair—thrown over his thighs and then fastened soundly with a metal clasp.

Hector took a closer look and saw his lap strap was a simply a repurposed seatbelt salvaged from a car. The thick nylon would resist cutting, even if Hector had a knife. The metal clasp, designed to hold its grasp even under the forces of high-speed collisions, would also hold tight under these far less taxing circumstances—it would do that at least until its chrome release button was pressed.

Hector's legs began to tremble.

He'd found himself in chairs like this one a time or two, but he'd been younger then—under forty or still close enough to it to be much "tougher" than he felt now.

Trussed up and guarded by not-so-long-ago enemies infamous for their pitiless treatment of captive allies, foes dreaded because of their facility for cold-hearted, meticulously implemented torture—and, of course, thinking of Haven in the next room, the poor darling stripped bare and subjected to God only knew what to motivate her unfortunate lover—Hector now felt anything but formidable.

Two other men left then, opening the door and going into the adjoining room where the others had taken Haven.

Hector thought he heard soft calls for help as the door opened, but it immediately closed after them, returning to near silence the larger, colder room in which he sat strapped to his chair.

The man who still held Hector's gun stood in front of the author, watching him while stealing covetous, admiring glances at the Walther. Evidently, it was the first one of those that the masked man had held; he was clearly confounded by the gun's slide-mounted safety.

But the fool was standing on the perfect side of his hostage's chair—at least that was so from Hector's perspective. As the man fiddled with the gun, trying to grasp its operation,

Hector twisted and pulled at the surgical rubber hose binding his arms at the wrist.

He simultaneously rubbed the hose against the rough edge of the stout wooden chair, sloughing off not just layers of skin, but of rubber, as well.

The door to the other room where Haven was being held briefly opened and a strange figure—rather perversely barefoot on the cold concrete—padded into the room as the door once more closed behind.

This time, there were no audible cries from Haven. Hector took that as a very bad sign.

Hector said to the strange figure now standing in front of him—"If you hurt her—"

"Hush!" A muffled, harsh voice said it in Japanese-inflected English.

The figure before him was truly grotesque—draped in a shapeless black silk kimono that hung very loosely, for the moment obscuring any hint of a silhouette that might have given Hector at least a sense of gender or even simple physical size.

The person in the kimono might have been very thin or quite fat.

The tent-like kimono itself was emblazoned with a golden, writhing dragon.

It was the mask the stranger wore, however, that was most striking thing about the calculated disguise.

This wasn't some simple surgical mask fashioned from fabric that hooked behind the ears such as their kidnappers had worn.

This face-covering was a real Japanese *Noh* mask of the kind Hector had glimpsed in shop windows while play-acting *gaijin* tourist with Haven.

The mustard-hued Japanese *Noh* mask was a horribly grinning *Hannya*, resembling a devil or demon's face, replete with fangs and two long horns thrusting out of either side of the head.

The muffled voice said, "You will talk only in answer to questions. Your answers, in turn, will have a direct bearing on the fate of your friend in the next room. If, that is, she is indeed of actual importance to you. It has been said true friends are best known in *first hardships*, and I sense this is just such a hardship for the two of you. It may be the first of many such trials. Almost assuredly that is so if you prove foolishly stubborn."

"She is my friend," Hector said, "but I have nothing I can possibly say or do to—"

A slight nod from the masked head drew Hector up short. The man who held Hector's gun slid it back in his pocket, then turned and raised a stiffening hand. With the cutting edge of that hand, the man struck Hector hard across the back of the neck.

Hector felt his body briefly go numb from the point of impact downward, then a terrible burning sensation exploded inside his head. He saw cascades of fireworks in the low light. Hector shook his head and blinked, struggling to clear his blurring vision.

"Excuses and stalling efforts are not how this encounter will be permitted to proceed, Mr. Lassiter," the stranger in the devil's mask hissed in English. "This is how things are going to move forward." There was a slight, sibilant emphasis on the *ss* in Hector's surname that resulted in it coming across as something closer to *Lasshiter*.

"There is a microphone hanging from the ceiling above you," the masked stranger said. "I'm quite fond of devices like that and so have installed many of them in the various places in which you have been spending time since reaching Japan. I therefore have heard and already know many things. I have been a kind of fly on the wall for myriad conversations that you have had with your other friends, particularly with Mr. Fleming. So understand that I know very well why you are both here, and I of course know what your real quest is. It is one I share, obviously. And I will see my will done, at any bloody cost to you.

"Now, as I have said about your woman friend in the next room," the voice continued, "I mean to test the depth of your friendship toward her, this night. I mean to earn your loyalty and friendship—your obedience in fulfilling my aims—by assessing the actual depth of your commitment to your friend in the next room. You see, I believe that a true friend is known or found in adversity, rather like gold is proven in fire. Your friend will therefore suffer each time I put a question to you and find the answer unsatisfactory or untrustworthy. I need merely give a short order into that microphone above us, and the next in a series of already planned and very excruciating procedures involving cutting instruments will be inflicted upon Miss Haven Branch's comely person. This process will continue to her ongoing disfigurement and even her eventual death if you do not cooperate. Now, *do* we understand each other, Mr. Lassiter? Are we most *clear*?"

The rubber tying his hands was nearly chewed through as a result of frenzied friction with the chair back's splintered, distressed edge. There was just enough give to his elastic bonds now that circulation was returning and with it, some useful control of Hector's blood-starved fingers.

Hector tried to stall for the precious few seconds he'd need to free his hands. He said thickly, pretending to be more groggy from the blow than was actually the case, "If you truly have

Fleming's hotel room bugged, then you know that we have no idea where the thing everyone seems to want is hidden. Ian has already tapped out once coming over here, looking. He did that just a couple of years ago, on the same so-called quest. There's simply no reason to believe this attempt won't prove any less fruitless."

A harsh laugh. "We haven't heard *everything*, sadly. Your friends had a visitor, recently. Occasionally you have thwarted our eavesdropping, through luck or calculation. You and Fleming were paid a visit by someone called Burton. Who is that man? What was said when he took you all into the bathroom and turned up the faucet taps? Is he the one who gave you that German gun? What precisely was said in that little room, away from my many invisible ears, Mr. Lassiter?"

Invisible ears? Christ, it was very much starting to feel like he'd staggered into some Fu Manchu potboiler.

Blessedly, just at that moment, the rubber cord around his wrists at last parted. Hector managed to catch the severed rubber tubing in one numbed palm before it could hit the floor and so reveal he was no longer bound.

Buying just a few more vital second to get his hands in useful working condition—they were throbbing painfully with the sudden, unimpeded return of blood at last flowing from wrist to fingertips—Hector thought about it, then decided to state the obvious:

"Burton is some kind of British agent, I guess you'd say. Probably SIS but not of the field agent sort. You're right about this much—he gave me the Walther. He's a kind of quartermaster or guns supplier, that's all. It was all hardware talk and that's truly it. He's not part of any of this beyond seeing we had a little firepower for protection."

Hector looked around the gloomy room and nodded at the masked man in front of him. "Not that it's done us much good, obviously. Witness our sad current circumstances. Now, who the hell exactly are *you?*"

Another headshake, this one more emphatic. Something was said in Japanese, then in translation: "*Nō aru taka wa tsume wo kakusu.* The talented hawk hides it claws, Mr. Lassiter."

Hector smiled and said, "Indeed." As he spoke, he reached around suddenly and depressed the button on the seat belt binding him to his chair. Even as Hector lunged to his feet, the man with the surgical mask reached for Hector's gun, fumbling with it again as he tried unsuccessfully to pull the trigger while the safety was still engaged. Once again frustrated by the gun's mechanism, he quickly cast it aside, then assumed a judo or karate position.

Hector thought, *Jesus Christ, really?*

Remembering the paralyzing blow the man had dealt him with that single, modulated chop to the back of the neck, Hector decided not to risk further contact with the man if he could evade it. Instead, Hector calculatedly cocked a fist in an almost cartoonish telegraphing of an intended punch.

As the man readied to parry Hector's expected roundhouse, the writer instead kicked the man hard between the legs. It wasn't a "cricket" move of course, but it was crudely and devastatingly effective against the smaller martial arts expert.

There was a soft, spastic gasp as the man clutched at his groin and dropped to his knees, robbed of all wind, his overtaxed nervous system telegraphing a freight train of pain signals to his beleaguered brain.

Hector quickly slid around behind the man and drew the slim cord of wire from his modified Rolex. He wrapped it twice around the man's neck, then pulled it wickedly taut, strangling the stranger.

A soft cry of fear and motion to his right: The robed figure in the devil's mask was dashing toward the door of the room where Haven was being held. Hector didn't wait to confirm the his more immediate foe's death, instead slamming his perhaps already strangled opponent's face hard against concrete floor twice, then kicking the man once in the temple. He was sure that abuse had almost certainly killed the man if the garrote hadn't already done the job.

Hector scooped up his Walther and got off a single shot into the closing metal door. There came the sound of a ricochet, first against metal and then pavement.

When he reached that door, Hector found it was locked from the other side. He shot the knob twice, then kicked off what was left. Throwing open the door and rolling to one side in expectation of a returned shot, the author was instead met with frightening silence.

Hector carefully leaned around the jamb once more, very quickly, and saw Haven was alone in the room, nude and sprawled on the cold and cracked floor. She was already bruising from what appeared to have been a savage series of blows or kicks.

Even as he registered all that, Hector heard distant, retreating footsteps on concrete stairs. Tempted as he was to follow, he instead crouched down close to Haven and said carefully and urgently, fully expecting the worst, "Haven, honey—are you still with me?"

She stirred and groaned. Hector cast his gaze around, saw her discarded clothes.

Another groan. He reached for her overcoat and wrapped it carefully around her, warming her. He said, "Stay with me now, darlin'. Don't you dare pass out! It's all over now. I'll see you get help. I swear I'll see to that."

13

DOUBLE AGENT/DOUBLE CROSS?

Haven was groggy from the assault. Nude under her coat, she was already showing bruising to rival Hector's equally nasty contusions from his own series of bumps and bruises resulting from the airport explosion.

He tried again to talk Haven into a visit to a hospital, but she stood firm: "There'd be inquiries and they likely would assume you did it to me—some kind of stupid *gaijin* domestic row," she said thickly. "Anyway, it's not my first beating, and so you know, that's *all* that was done to me back there. They shamed me by taking all my clothes, then they went to work on me with their fists and feet. Oh, they certainly threatened the other, and they might even have gotten around to raping me in due course, but thanks to you that didn't happen."

She took his hand and squeezed it hard. "Thank you so much for saving me, Hector. There simply aren't worthy words. Thank God for you."

Hector stubbornly persisted in his arguments for professional care as they sat at the back of a commuter bus, whispering urgently to one another. He said "Darlin', please understand that if a rib should be broken, and if that splintered bone should then find an organ—"

"No," she insisted, cutting him off. "I'd know. It looks much worse than it is, though maybe not as bad as it feels just now. I just need some time to regroup, that's all. I need a hot bath and some pain pills. Then, like you after the explosion and your injuries, I just need some rest." She managed a little smile. "I need your TLC in return for what I gave you earlier."

Her face was remarkably undamaged, at least—her bruises confined to her torso and upper thighs that her overcoat quite fortunately covered. Her other clothes—some of them likely torn beyond possibility of mending, Hector had folded and was carrying under one arm.

When the bus at last reached their hotel, he rose and helped Haven to unsteady feet. She leaned hard on him as they made their way through the lobby and into an elevator that left haven feeling quite queasy. Then, as Hector all but carried her, they at last meandered down the longish common corridor and into their room.

There, Hector drew her a hot bath, then helped Haven off with her coat and held her hand as, naked, she gingerly lowered herself into the hot water.

He handed Haven a glass of drinking water and three aspirins, then excused himself for a moment. Haven called out to his back, "You're not actually leaving me?"

"Just using the phone to call upstairs," he said. "Have to make sure Ian and the others aren't trussed up in some damned underground bunker themselves."

Ian answered on the second ring. He said angrily, "My God, where have you two been, Hector? Your literary lunch stretched into dinner and then some. You've left me fretting terribly, frankly. Even Dikko was getting worried."

Hector gave a brief, near breathless run down of their kidnapping to an increasingly horrified Ian. He ended with, "Let's plan on all meeting up for a nightcap and strategy session in the bar. It's harder to bug every square inch of that place at least, but we need to be sure *we* pick the table and don't let some conniving bastard window dress the thing with a nice tapped candle or dainty flower arrangement or the like, yes? Oh, and Ian, on that further, cautionary note, it's probably best to figure your room is wired ten ways from Tuesday. Probably best to assume that our rooms' phones are tapped, too."

It was still two hours until their scheduled rendezvous over drinks. They were lying in bed, Hector dressed and Haven stretched out naked under the sheets, but holding comfortingly to one another, watching all those crazy lights coming on again, one-by-one outside their room's panoramic picture window that opened onto downtown Tokyo.

"They did to me only what you saw—what you *see*—that's really all, darling," she said again quite unnecessarily from Hector's perspective. Yet it seemed important to Haven to reiterate to him nothing sexual had been done to her.

She paused, then said with a little tone of anger creeping into her otherwise tired voice, "You really should have told me about your gun. *And* about that deadly watch. At least they might have given me a little more piece of mind going into that horrid room with those men. I thought we were unarmed goners." A beat. "I fully expected to die, you know."

Hector sighed. "For all the good the first of those gadgets really did, perhaps I *should* have told you. But there was just never enough time for any of that. Or, rather, the subject just hadn't come up yet. I'm sure it would have, and quite likely sooner rather than later. Living in close quarters as we've been, you were going to see me dressing or undressing eventually. You would have seen the holster and gun."

She smiled and kissed his throat. "Or at very least I'd perhaps have felt it during the next passionate hug." She paused, then said, "The person in the devil's mask who ran past me—who do you think that was?"

"No damned clue," Hector said. "Certainly not government, not dressed like some Shiwan Khan knock-off or Saturday matinee villain. Even the voice is a hard call for me. Could have been male or female. No, that person—man or woman, because again, there was simply no telling what truly lay under that big old robe—that *person*," he resumed, "is something not official. They are clearly something *else*. Only that much I'm sure about."

Haven gave a little shiver.

He said, "I can turn up the heat or get another blanket. After a beating like that, I'm afraid it's not unusual to run a fever. Your body is in shock—sending out an all hands-on-deck signal to all your innards."

She shook her head and held him tighter. "Please, don't move, because this is very nice, just like this. Quite comforting. And *fever*? You're like my doctor. Come to think of it, your file said you were a medic between the wars. I'm right about that, aren't I?"

"Just after the so-called Great War," he confirmed. "So, *yeah*, I've got some modest skills in that direction."

"Hopefully, we won't need them more than we have today."

"Hopefully we will not," he echoed softly. "Listen, since you're clearly not up to the bar, I can have Tiger or Dikko watch over you while Ian and I—"

"No, I want to come along," she said. "I'll be okay. I've got another hour to lay here and recover and savor snuggling up tight with you. Just let me have that for a time more, please?" She searched his eyes. "You *will* grant me that gift, yes?"

In the end, Haven was not in fact yet ready for any trip downstairs as she had hoped. Hector left her in the bathtub with a fresh round of aspirin tablets and a generous tumbler of her favored Japanese whiskey over ice. He crossed his fingers the rather risky mix wouldn't pass her out and result in an accidental drowning. To that fearful end, Hector promised himself he'd keep his time downstairs very short.

He also left Haven with his Walther for protection before setting off for his rendezvous at the bar.

Ian, Dikko and Tiger were nursing cocktails at a table in the corner. When they saw Hector, they rose and moved to another available table, taking their drinks with them.

"Can't be too careful now, as you've made all too clear," Dikko said to Hector. "Just be sure and speak clearly into the center of that water lily there in the bowl between us, my Yankee friend." His voice rose, slurring a little, and Dikko said, "We do that for the benefit of any of the cocksuckers maybe panting and hanging on our words in some little cramped sweaty cabinet hidden off the lobby, you goddamn poofter voyeurs!"

Grinning, Dikko picked up the centerpiece, then, with infinite care because he was fairly smashed, he carried the floral arrangement to the bar where he deposited it with dismissive flourish.

As the Australian journalist weaved his way back to them, Hector checked and saw the trio of writers was hewing to sake this evening—Ian, particularly, seemed to be an enthusiastic convert to the stuff.

For his part, Hector ordered another double bourbon. At his companions' urging, he gave a fuller account of the dire brush he and Haven had endured just a few hours before.

Ian said, "This villain hiding behind that *Noh* mask sounds absolutely ludicrous, rather like something Cyril Connolly would say he might expect of me in my cups, but even *I* wouldn't jump those rails, not on my weakest day as a writer. And you've been very circumspect about the gender of this masked villain. You think it might actually have been a woman?"

"Just possibly," Hector said. "I'm coming around to that more recently as I reflect and remember. But only because I got a look at the body in motion, in profile. The silk kimono was clinging to curves a bit more when in fast motion. I think there were breasts under there…possibly even substantial ones."

Tiger said carefully, leading Hector, "And this masked, barefoot person ran back into the very room where you then found the buxom Haven, quite naked and so also barefoot, obviously, sprawled on the floor. You only heard some unknown number of footsteps pounding away. Can you possibly say how many feet were fleeing?"

Hector immediately grasped Tiger's insinuation, of course—that dark theory must already have been thrashed around by the three journalists—or the three paid professional cynics as Hector now regarded the reporters.

"She really could have arranged her own beating first," Ian said carefully. "Then, naked under the robes, hidden in that mask but tellingly barefoot, she might have come out to confront you, torturing you with the notion of her own torture presumably underway just through that metal door."

It could have happened that way, Hector supposed.

It was possible, perhaps even plausible.

And the retreating figure in the mask had moved in this funny, pained way—almost gingerly.

Perhaps he or she had been moving in agony from a freshly-suffered assault that had left one tender and stiffening with increasing pain?

Even as he started to entertain the notion, Hector instinctively pushed it away.

No, this was clearly *insane*.

Haven had suffered a beating and been threatened with even worse at this mysterious, masked man or woman's hands, just as Hector had been threatened.

At the same time, the seeds of doubt had again been planted by his colleagues and they were already spreading their infernal roots.

Hector said, "Why do you all insist upon thinking Haven is some kind of enemy?"

"Because she's already a proven and self-proclaimed spy, and rather an accomplished operative, one would conclude from her term of service with MI5," Dikko said. His Australian accent was becoming still broader and perhaps even a shade more bellicose as a result of all the drink.

"But why do you suspect her now, apart from coincidences and odd bits of timing and the like?" Hector searched each man's face. "Why this sudden surge of fresh suspicion?"

Dikko plunked down his flask of sake and pointed a finger at Hector. "Because, you dense Yankee bloke, tonight's kidnapping comes straight off the heels of our expressing a compelling need for her to 'prove out.' That was a call for proof that could have been overheard in Ian's bugged room. Taking a beating for you contrives to serve that very purpose. Wouldn't you agree to that, at least in principle?" He arched his eyebrows, then said, "But there's much more, old boy."

Dikko Hughes suddenly stopped there, possibly realizing even through the mists of all the spirits that the bigger and more devastating revelation shouldn't come from his lips.

With a sigh, Ian tugged at his bowtie, then looked around to make sure there was still no sign of Haven's approach. He shook his head and said, "It's almost certainly like this, Hector," he said. "Information has now come through about her. Information about Haven's, well, let's call them her unfortunate *antecedents*."

Hector squeezed the bridge of his nose. "Define that please."

"In this case, I mean her parentage," Ian said, carefully. "Haven has a dubious pedigree, to say the least. But in this context, and faced with our present set of circumstances, all that also seems downright calamitous, if not outright sinister. It also seems Haven's own agency is actively investigating her, and with some real haste, all of a sudden. Your lady friend is a hair's breadth from being ordered out of the field and back to England until this internal inquiry is complete. It happens MI6 is *also* now looking into Miss Branch and her possible affiliation with certain parties in the East. At the moment, rightly or wrongly, she's in very real and official jeopardy."

Hector mumbled, "Antecedents, pedigrees and parentage… *Affiliations*. What the hell is this all really about, Ian?"

The English thriller writer presumed to order Hector a second drink. As Ian was doing that, Hector found himself lighting up another cigarette—what would prove to be the first of several over the next twenty minutes of misery and dark revelations.

When the waitress had left them alone again, Ian said softly, "Hector, have you ever heard of a Scotsman named William Francis Forbes-Semphill?"

Hector shrugged. "Christ, no." He thought more about it to be certain, then said again, "Hell, no. Who the hell was he?"

"Who the hell *is* he would be more precise," Ian said. "The man, I'm afraid, still lives, but obscurely now, hiding from the possibility of his true and traitorous nature being revealed."

"And again I ask," Hector said, "Who is this Scot? And he's Haven's father, you said?"

"He is a Scottish Lord," Tiger piped in. "He was an aeronautical engineer, a pilot, sometimes diplomat, a recipient of the Air Force Cross and also of the Order of the Polar Star. He was stationed over here and fell in love with Japan— perilously so, from Ian's government's perspective, and, by extension, your country's, as well. *My* country came to love him back, I suppose you might say. He was honored as a 3rd Class of Commander in the Order of the Rising Sun, among other honors bestowed upon him by Japan."

Ian's voice suddenly ran to ice as he cut in: "But he also betrayed many British intelligence secrets to Imperial Japan. He did that over many decades, including the war years. Eventually he was found out."

"How did this betrayal not come out?" Hector said, "It should have been all the news, just like Burgess and Maclean.

Sounds like you're saying this fella is still moving around Britain and suffering no consequences for his betrayal."

"Essentially, that's all too accurate," Ian said. "And it is terribly unfortunate that it is so. But you know how these things sometimes come about. Candidly? Churchill rather protected this man because of the way it would have damaged him politically if the man's treachery became widely known. It was almost criminal negligence that allowed this scoundrel to betray Britain for as long as he did. Much, if not all, of the blame for that could justifiably fall at Winston's doorstep."

Hector tapped his ash and took another deep drink, his mind racing over all that. He said, "And Haven is his daughter? How exactly is that? I have to think that your government investigates its potential secret agents to within an inch of their great-, great-grandmothers' dowdy lives. How did it miss *this* damning alleged connection?"

"Well, as one might expect," Ian said, "efforts were made on the part of nearly all parties most immediately involved to obscure Miss Branch's parentage, at least to most of the world. The 19th Lord Semphill arrived in Japan in 1921. Haven, the illegitimate issue of an affair that began soon after his arrival here, was born in 1922. Her parents-of-record contrived to have Haven actually delivered in England to secure her British citizenship. You know—to make England her legal country of origin, of course. But most of her young life was spent here, in and around Tokyo."

Ian began to prep another cigarette. He said, "It's my belief that as a result, Haven's cultural and patriotic identification is wholly with Japan—certainly infinitely more so than with Britain. She is very much her birth father's daughter and managed to spend considerable time with him, more than sufficient to bond with him, so to speak. She shared enough time to acquire his interests and deep and abiding sentiments toward Japan. She assumed her father's twisted patriotic loyalties. Her father began spying and passing information on to Tiger's government in the 1920s and continued to do so well into the 1940s. It's firmly believed now the daughter has resumed her birth father's odious spying for Japan. It's believed she's a double-agent."

Hector extinguished his cigarette and promptly got another going. "You confessed that your man Churchill covered *this* man's tracks with a backhoe because it was politically expeditious for him to do so. To spare himself embarrassment. That's just *wonderful*."

"Not just Churchill," Ian chimed in, getting defensive. "This man has connections to the Royal Family, too. But now, at least, he's ostracized in the circles that matter most to him."

Hector rolled his eyes and said, feigning an English accent, "*Ouch*. I do so hope that bloody hurts him, and how."

Ian had little patience for Hector's sarcasm. "Oh, do come along now, Hector. We're both men of the world and hardly vestal virgins by anyone's standards. Only the good can be *really* bad. Only the believer can effectively blaspheme."

"You're sure Haven is this traitor's child? You're really sure?"

"Quite certain," Ian said. "There's no doubt whatever about any of that."

Hector took that in. "And the notion is she's some sort of double-agent for Japan?"

"Or at least for someone or some organization faithful to Japan," Dikko said, "yes, that's the belief. A downright certainty, actually. Maybe it's the Black Dragons, maybe it's something else."

"And that someone or something wants the Flea Bomb back for Mother Japan," Hector said. He considered his nearly drained second drink, then looked to the bar and nodded his assent for a third. It was too much liquor of course—*far* too much with his blood-sugar issues. But this one last time he wanted to be numb as he used to get during the good old days of this twenties and thirties, when one didn't care or even think about any potential for consequences from an over-indulgence; like it was in his prime when he could rebound so much more quickly from the dulling wonders of liquor.

Dikko said, "Is it also conceivable that she injected that Japanese fish poison into the bloke who died on the plane? Might she have done that when she was pitched into his arms by the air turbulence, using that rough ride as cover to get close and give the sorry bloke the lethal shot?"

"Of course it's not impossible," Hector said dubiously, yet letting himself toy with the idea. He quickly ran through every dark thing that happened since the bar in Idlewild and assessed Haven's possibility for having a *sub rosa* role in any of all that.

The results left him at once chilled and conflicted.

Enough of this, he argued with himself. *The terror—the real poison—of course, comes in your not knowing.* Well, there was something he could do about that, and right now. Hector ground out his fresh cigarette and stood.

Ian scowled. "Where are you going?"

"Heading upstairs to confront her, of course," Hector said. "I'm not pussy-footing around this anymore. I'm tired of being threatened and I'm too impatient to live looking over my shoulder constantly for the next two weeks."

Ian started to rise to follow but Hector held up a hand. "Best I do it alone."

Ian squinted at Hector's left arm. "You are at least carrying your Walther?"

"But of course," Hector lied.

God willing, Haven wouldn't turn the German automatic lose on him this night if backed into a corner by the confrontation to come.

He rapped twice on the door. When that elicited no answer, he keyed himself into the room.

He said softly, "Haven?"

Silence, again.

The lights were on low and the bed was remade. Haven's suitcase was gone, but her musky scent lingered like a specter.

On the table by the big window lay the Walther PPK, resting alongside a single pink Japanese rose. Under both of those was a slip of paper.

Hector tugged loose the note with a sense of fascination and dread: How many times had his future turned on the words left on a sheet of paper by a lover in full flight? All of that really started with Brinke in Paris on a long-ago February night, he supposed.

Hector pulled out a chair by the window that afforded its dazzling view of downtown Tokyo. He turned the chair around to catch the light of the city—the most garish of light to read by—and sat down. He pulled on his glasses and, bracing for it, he began to read:

My darling Hector:
    My invisible ears really are everywhere.
    So now you know how it is.
    Like Mishima, I abhor what has become of Japan.
    I dread what lies ahead for my country of choice under
    its continued neutering by the West.

We'll never have our own nuclear bomb of course, but we can have *this*—this "weapon" that we created and can use to shape our destiny. We can use this "weapon" to resume our position as a world power and sovereign nation. Japan's ingenuity created this thing, and Japan should benefit from that effort, however dubious and destructive all that might seem to you.

With you, Hector, I'm truly quite taken, my darling. Please know that becoming your lover was my idea, and my desired outcome, and it was not done under any orders or for any devious purposes.

We'll meet again, of that I'm fairly certain.

Please, darling, when we do next cross paths, just stand clear and don't make me do something to you that I would hate.

In the end, you really don't have a dog in this fight, to use an American term.

I firmly believe that Japan would never reduce America, much less the United Kingdom, to some desert, except under conditions of total combat, but I don't think either side would allow that to happen again—not for several generations to come, at least. (China or North Korea, admittedly, might be a different matter.)

I truly have relished showing you at least a little of the country that I love and willingly would die serving, even if that death should come at your hand.

Know, too, my love, I would still kill you to see Japan free and back on its proper, imperial path.

Ever yours,
Haven

Well, well.

Hector looked the note over again. He let it sink in—all its passionate revelations and threats—then he set it on fire with his Zippo and left its remains to smolder in an ashtray.

He made his way back downstairs, finding his friends still there in the bar.

Hector's chair was empty and his nearly untouched, third double bourbon still sat there, now sweating a bit. He slid back into his seat and took a deep drink, very aware of his friends' eyes studying him.

It seemed it was Ian's to at last ask: "Well, where *is* she, Hector? What happened, for God's sake?" He looked around, then said, eyes narrowing, "Is there some tidying up to be seen too?" A grizzled and arched eyebrow.

Hector was appalled that Ian's mind had gone to *that* place. Sourly, he sipped his drink, then shook his head.

"She was already gone when I got up there, so no, there's nothing to clean up after," Hector said, voice going to gravel.

He took another deep drink, then added, "The bitch has fled."

PART 2

"…AND THE JOURNEY ITSELF HOME"

1

INTO JAPAN

That morning, sipping what Hector found to be extremely unsatisfactory coffee while waiting for the hotel shuttle that would ferry them to the train station, Dikko shared with Hector the gist of the letter Ian had written months before, a wrenching epistle laying out Ian's dreamed itinerary of the queer sites of Japan that might "fire" his "depleted muse."

It seemed Ian first wanted to spend a couple of days in Tokyo, just as they had been doing—"acclimatizing," as he put it. Then Ian wished to hop on a "luxurious modern train" and race southward.

Ian also wanted to see pearl girls diving and to experience a Japanese hot bath.

Most of all, Ian very much desired to see a live volcano where his villain could potentially lure depressed Japanese into committing suicide—a key plot point of his projected next James Bond novel.

Hector listened drowsily. He was starved for real rest; it had taken him a while to fall asleep, and only after calling down to room service and asking the sheets that still smelled of Haven be changed.

Then he had spent several uneasy hours dreaming of Brinke and Haven until he received his six a.m. wake up call.

Reading his mind, Dikko studied him with red-rimmed eyes, then said, "We win them, and we lose them, old boy. Women, I mean. So don't sing the weeps too much. There's always another one waiting in the wings. At least it's my experience that's so for the dashing sorts like you."

"Until there simply aren't anymore who are interested," Hector countered.

And dashing?

Please.

Their waiter was suddenly there, bowing and excusing himself for interrupting, then noting Mr. Hector Lassiter had an urgent phone call awaiting him. The phone in question was sitting atop the bar, in clear view of the room, so Hector didn't fear this particular incoming call was some sort of ruse calculated to isolate him.

Walking to the bar and scooping up the receiver, he half expected it to be Haven on the other end. In fact, some part of him hoped that was the case. He said, "Lassiter speaking."

No woman on the other end: instead it was a man with a *basso*, European accent.

The voice said, "I feel compelled to give you a sporting chance to survive your trip to Japan, Mr. Lassiter. Because of your brash actions, you've already stripped from me, and from yourself of course, the very delectable and sensuous Miss Branch. This could have been a very easy and satisfying escapade for you, if you'd only enjoyed her company and let matters unfold as they inevitably must. But now I fear it may have to become bloody between us."

Hector tried to place the accent's point of origin:

German? *No.*

Hungarian? Just *possibly.* Yes, he really thought the latter.

He said cheerily to the stranger, "Let's please not run off half-cocked and threatening, not straight from the gates, old pal. To start with, who the hell are you? Your accent sounds Hungarian."

A soft snort: "It hardly matters—accents, I mean. There are the places we're born, or where we are raised, and then there are the places we love and the homes of our choosing. I think of Haven Branch, of course, as I say that. Japan is her country of choice. Hungary is, I must confess, a dreadful place, at least from my perspective. So, like Miss Branch, I've selected Japan as the home of my spirit. I will tell you my real name because it so long dormant and because I have not used it in a very, *very* long time. I was indeed born in Hungary, on May 28, 1908, so I'm a few years younger than you, Mr. Lassiter."

He noted Dikko watching him carefully from across the bar. Hector supposed something now showed in his face, alerting Hughes to the tension he now felt. Hector said to the voice, "You promised me a name, friend."

"Ah, yes, a silly name for you to give to your spy and journalist friends so they can dig and dig into it, but toward no revelation. I will tell you now, because after all, what in the end, is a mere name? How easy is it, after all, to bury a mere name?"

"Then share yours, already."

"I was born Ernák Szász Bulcsú. Shall I spell any of that out for you, Mr. Lassiter?"

"Where are we going with this, Mr. Bulcsú?"

"I told you that is no longer a name I answer to."

"So what do you go by now? I'd surely like to get it right—at least have something polite to call you by. What name are you known by these days?"

"Sharing that would of course not do at all. I've built a very fine life for myself here in Japan and at no small expense and effort. I certainly have no intention of spoiling any of that, Mr. Lassiter. This is what is important; this is what you must take away from this conversation. Very simply, I need you to stand aside, or better still, to recover and then hand over to me the Operation Flea microfilm as soon as you have it in hand. If you do not do that, then I will systematically begin to kill everyone who matters even the slightest to you, Mr. Lassiter."

The voice grew silkier, more menacing: "Not just the obvious ones, like your current three motley friends, will suffer. No, I will reach back into your life, Mr. Hector Lassiter. I will, one-by-one, eliminate every one of your dearest and darling ones—from best friends to fleeting sweethearts. People you care about, some of them very much, will die. Let me give you just two examples. My first proposed target is a certain Irish policeman based in someplace called Cleveland, Ohio. The second is a beautiful young Latina currently living in Los Angeles, California. You are already aware of the Black Dragon's activities and presence in your own country, so you surely must see this is no idle threat. I can quite easily reach these people of yours. I can have them dispatched in well under an hour. A phone call just like this one is all that is needed to set that in motion. Do I make myself perfectly clear, Mr. Lassiter? Have we an understanding now?"

Jimmy Hanrahan and Alicia Vicente were the man's threatened first victims. Hector's blood was boiling. This mystery man had just signed his own death warrant. Even if it was eventually proven to have been an idle threat or utter nonsense, Hector vowed to himself to kill this man simply for putting such bloody threats out there into the world.

"I hear you," Hector said. "It's very clear to me what must happen." He again promised himself he'd spend his remaining time in Japan first finding this man, then killing him and those around him, just as systematically as this man had vowed to slay Hector's darlings.

And he would kill Haven Branch, too, if she was somehow proven to indeed be part of this mystery man's machine.

But Hector said for now, smiling so it would come across in his voice, "How will I find you in order to turn over this piece of property if I somehow come across it?"

"I'll find you, of course," the man once called Bulcsú said. "Just as I have ears everywhere—though not all of them as enticing as our friend Miss Branch's, to be sure—I also have eyes nearly everywhere. You do well not to forget that. In the future, Mr. Lassiter, I advise you to assume that every word of yours, and every action you contemplate, is almost certainly well known to me." A pause, then, "How is your current bourbon, by the way?"

"Delicious."

"I'm *so* glad. It could have had special ingredients, you know. All it would take is another phone call and that next drink might kill any of you four men. Just know it could happen if you push things in a direction unpleasing to me."

The stranger's tone changed a bit; Hector could now hear the smile back in the man's voice as he said this next: "You're an author, of course, so I leave you with this last warning in verse, Mr. Lassiter. It comes from the man I think to be Japan's greatest writer, Matsuo Basho. I think of this haiku of his as one that well describes the situation you'll find yourself in, if you dare

even *contemplate* thwarting my will. In English, and depending
on the translator, it goes something like this Mr. Lassiter:

> *Sick on my journey*
> *only my dreams will wander*
> *these desolate moors*

A little chuckle, then the voice said, "*Viszontlátásra*, or
rather, *Goodbye*, Mr. Lassiter. Goodbye for *now*."

The connection was severed before Hector could respond.

Seething, he returned to his seat. Ian and Tiger were in
the bar now, sitting alongside Dikko and also studying Hector
with burning eyes.

Frowning Ian said, "You look like the devil."

"Possibly because I just spoke to the son of a bitch," Hector
said. "Seems that man on the phone was the true villain of this
misadventure. At least I think that is so. He claims it to be true."

Hector searched his fellow writers' eyes. He said, "Do any
of you know of a prominent Hungarian who has taken up
residence in Japan?"

The train in which they left Tokyo was indeed modern,
even sumptuous.

Watching the Japanese countryside slide by their window,
Hector further filled in Ian and his journalist friends about his
threat-filled phone call.

Tiger and Dikko promised to have their sources
immediately investigate the name Ernák Szász Bulcsú. Fleming
said he would set his SIS sources to the same task.

Hector just smiled and shook his head. "Probably not really worth the effort in the end," he said.

"Why?" Ian put a hand on Hector's arm. He asked, "Why not worth the effort?"

"Partly because he gave it up so readily, and partly because I think this man, whoever he is, also has a mean sense of humor," Hector said. "I think he's sneering at us. Consider those initials: E.S.B. They should resonate for you, of all men, Ian."

Tiger and Dikko were clearly turning the letters "E", "S" and "B" over in their minds.

Dikko at last shrugged and said, "Jesus, I'm dry."

Tiger said, "This means nothing to me."

But Ian clearly got it. He said, "E.S.B. are the same initials as the head of James Bond's current bête noire, SPECTRE." Ian said softly, "E.S.B.—Ernst Stavro Blofeld." The English thriller writer let go of Hector's arm and stared out at the passing scene, yet clearly not really seeing any of it. "That birth date he gave you for himself, Hector—that's *my* birthday. Yes, clearly this fiend is having us on."

"The search I really need you fellas to press for," Hector said, "is the one I mentioned back at the bar. You need to have your people identify every Hungarian now living in Japan. Seems to me that can't be a terribly long list. He's probably been here for some time. Maybe he came over soon after the last war."

As he said that, he noticed Ian scratching furiously away in a small notebook, the one he used to keep notes for his novels—to scribble down bits of possible dialogue or scraps of description that might flash through his mind in stray moments.

Hector made out what he took to be a theme Ian must consider of possible use for his Bond novel, one that again

made him think of Haven. Ian posed the thought as a question
to himself:

"How many of one's own nationals want to live in another
country," he wrote, "and how many of that country want
to live in yours? What threat does the latter pose when the
number is far greater?"

For one strange, sensually charged week, Hector found
himself virtually embalmed in Ian Fleming's idiosyncratic,
Bondian world.

They saw sumo wrestling matches and Shinto shrines. Some
of them brushed bits with geishas and visited some very snazzy
houses of ill repute where other, more private bits brushed.

At the same time, Ian was vehement about avoiding
traditional teas, *Noh* plays or anything remotely smacking of
what he regarded to be the typical and tame Japanese tourist fare.

Ian was very much focused on Samurai tradition and
what he, at least, saw as a national obsession with suicide and
violence.

But there was something quite disturbing to Hector in Ian's
explicit, desperate drive to try and experience Japan through
007's eyes—that impossible to achieve, much less to *sustain*—
heightened appreciation of all things sensual and deadly.

Late one afternoon, Ian positively nonplussed Dikko by
presuming to caress the shoulder of an underdressed and fetching
little Japanese pearl diver as she surfaced. The intimate contact
startled the girl and shattered all Japanese social contracts.

But Ian insisted it was necessary for him as an author to
know *exactly* how the wet flesh of a young Japanese woman
felt in order to accurately describe it for his readers.

A bit after that, alone at another bar and sipping sake, Dikko Hughes, once again very much in his cups, confided to Hector his mounting concerns for Ian. "He looks like hell, of course, more so now that we're at full gallop. He views his heart as a time bomb, and perhaps he does that with a firm foundation. Hell, it's all but certainly so, based on his breathing and his color. He's aged terribly since I last saw him here in Japan. He looks at least ten years older, the poor bastard. I'm painfully aware of the skull beneath the skin when I look at him, now. Death in the face, don't you know. Ghastly stuff. *If* he actually survives this trip, and *if* he gets a book out of it, I expect it will be our friend's last."

A long pause. "Honestly? He's already confided to me he means to leave Bond for dead at the end of this next novel. I take that as a grave sign, no pun intended."

"Really?" That was news to Hector, and disquieting enough.

"It's so cruel, really," Dikko said. "The money and fame are at last arriving and only now, when it's all but too late for his enjoyment or comfort. I asked Ian last night how it was to have this Bond movie doing so well back in the U.K., and another already in production—to know the big money is coming just down the line. He said to me, looking very exhausted indeed as he did so, 'Ashes, dear boy… Ashes.'"

Hector was tired of fretting over his own age, and growing all-too fatigued at worrying after ailing Ian.

He was tired of hectoring Fleming to forego that next drink, to taper off still more on his incessant smoking.

Hector was also tired of worrying about Haven's current whereabouts and the possibility he might find himself ranged against her in some final, perhaps even deadly confrontation. He found that he now carefully inspected every vaguely

Western-looking woman he saw, trying to decide if she might be Haven in disguise.

Dikko made a gesture with his hand and said, "Hush for now. Ian comes yonder."

For all their talk of his failing health, and despite the fact Ian seemed to be leaning a bit harder on his cane as he fought the motion of their latest "modern" train, Fleming seemed almost ebullient as he took a seat alongside Hector. Tiger sat down next to the English thriller writer.

Smiling and starting to work on preparing a new cigarette, Ian said, "That conniving bastard may hide behind phony birthdates and joke names, but he can't obscure his accent, by God. As my dear Texan here hazarded, there are indeed damned few Hungarians living in Japan—very damned few." A sardonic grin. "To be a Hungarian in Japan, to borrow a turn of phrase from my *other* dear writer friend, Mr. Raymond Chandler, is to be just about as conspicuous as a fig leaf on a fan dancer."

Hector said, "Is that your way of saying you have a lead on this son of a bitch, buddy?"

"On an identity, yes, I believe I do, and perhaps even on a location," Ian said. "I believe the man you spoke with is Béla Gustav Herczog—at least that's the name he came over to Japan with. He did that after the First World War, a conflict he managed to survive while so many of his countrymen did not. Very little is known about his background before then. He had a brief stint as a journalist before and during WWI— yes, Béla Herczog is another one of *us*, I fear, Hector—by *us* I mean a writer, and, like us, a sometimes spy. In his case, Herczog was spying for the Russians, it was suspected. And, anyway, he no longer uses that name. He arrived in Japan about 1921 and soon after opened a health institute that he continues to operate.

Hector arched his eyebrows. "A health institute? *Really?*"

"That's right," Ian said. "Did you know that Hungary has the largest thermal lake in the world? It also boasts the most extensive thermal water cave system. Most of those are sufficiently hot to scald one to the bone, but some of them there are actually suitable for bathing, or at least they can be regulated artificially to be so. Our man's family had some experience operating just such a therapeutic bath service before the Great War back in Hungary. Mr. Herczog used that knowledge to locate a similar, temperate thermal water pool near Beppu."

Ian smiled to see the reaction that place's name elicited from Hector. Ian said, "Yes, Hector—it would seem all roads lead there, just where your lady's lost writings also are said to languish. Now, it seems that rather like Hungary, Beppu is positively lousy with noted geothermal hot spots. The most significant of them are called the Eight Hells of Beppu."

Hector could see how very much his English friend relished that exotic name for the hot spots—it was exactly the kind of macabre local color that was always very much up Ian's peculiar alley. Hector just smiled and shook his head, awaiting more from the British journalist-turned-thriller writer.

Ian continued, "Anyway, Mr. Herczog bought his mud, sulfur and sand pools and set himself up as a kind of latter-day Dr. Kellogg, one presumes."

Dikko interjected, "But the most recent war, old boy— surely Herczog must have suffered some issues as a result of all that." He jacked a big thumb at Hector and said, "After all, his country locked up even its innocent, longtime Jap citizens, the wretched buggers. Roosevelt did that just on the off-chance they might be fifth columnists."

Ian shook his head. "Not so in this case. Because Herczog was viewed as stateless and long regarded as intensely loyal to Japan, our fellow evaded internment or repatriation. Apart from the deprivations and dangers anyone would experience living in a country under wide and sustained bombardment, life for our Hungarian expatriate in Japan went on largely as normal during the war years."

"The same could be said of several *gaijin* expatriates living here during the war," Tiger said. "It's not widely known, but some non-Japanese did live out the conflict years here in relative freedom, it's true."

Hector said, "You said this man doesn't even use the name Béla Whatever anymore"

"*Herczog*, and exactly," Ian said. "Now he's gone utterly native and is known now as Doctor Fumio Oshiro. He's all but a recluse, so his appearance doesn't stand much risk of giving the lie to his new Asian name. I've decided we can adjust our schedules slightly once we reach Beppu. I think we'll agree we need to see this man's health operation there, up close. I for one, look *forward* to the experience and could perhaps even benefit from a hot sulfur bath. Certainly after your beating, you must surely feel much the same, Hector."

Hector said softly to his fellow author, "Aren't you the one who always says it's better to travel hopefully than to arrive?"

Ian waved that away. "Just a turn of phrase. And, anyway, that one is hardly original to me, dear boy. It's just received wisdom, and you know what a slippery and disappointing slope that sort of thing can be. Better that we learn by doing, experiencing. Humans are sensory creatures, and none of them more so than the writing kind."

2

COMPANY MAN

Three more days of bone-tiring but distinctly Ian Fleming-style, idiosyncratic sightseeing had passed and their next promised stop was the one that had originally brought Hector to Japan—Beppu, where he might finally lay hands on Brinke's writing.

And now, so much more hung in the balance regarding that visit.

The nearer they came to the place, the more intense Hector's dreams of Brinke became—alternately erotic and emotionally wrenching.

It was almost as if Brinke had nocturnally insinuated herself back into his life as a real and living presence, but one only available to him in dreams. There they shared delicious bouts in bed followed by long, lingering meals and deep conversations, his imagination providing all-too realistic Brinke Devlin-style banter and cutting—though always charmingly put—insights that left him awakening to the daily piercing reality of her terrible absence from his waking life.

Every night he had her again in his life; every morning he freshly mourned Brinke's loss.

He supposed he was therefore coming to savor that nocturnal contact—far preferring time with this delectable succubus to the strange tourist life and dirty intrigue that bedeviled him by day as he moved through Japan with Ian and company.

At some point, Hector realized he was beginning to eye bottles of sleeping pills with intent.

Even now, Ian and his journalist buddies were off to some strange new destination, something about a training camp for something called *Ninja*.

Hector had begged off from this "gallivant," as Ian termed it, opting instead to spend some time alone in the bar with tea that was a damp echo of his preferred but unavailable coffee made to his Cuban-strong specifications. At least he still had a notebook and a pen.

He'd neglected his own writing for too long, a dangerous thing because it too easily could become a habit to procrastinate in the forging of the prose that paid for his maverick lifestyle.

Looking up from his notebook as he searched his mind for the right next word to describe a pretty Asian young woman he was writing into his current story, Hector saw that a man was making his way across the bar.

The stranger was a Westerner. He was also tall, with darkish, gray-flecked hair.

That suit and something in the man's bearing made Hector think, *CIA.*

Hector once again caught his hand drifting under his suit jacket toward his gun, because, after all, he *could* be wrong.

A wave and a smile. From several feet away, the man— evidently for the benefit of the room and maybe to stay that tellingly straying hand—called out, "Mr. Lassiter, I *thought* I recognized you! Sam Denkins—you know from Columbia

Pictures? We met last April at that wrap party in the Pacific Dining Car?"

Hector grinned and played along, calling out, "Good ol' Sam! It's indeed a small world, after all." He put out a big hand for a hearty shake and bicep squeeze, then gestured the stranger should join him.

The man pulled up a chair as Hector closed his notebook and slipped his fountain pen in his sport jacket's pocket. He checked his deadly Rolex for the time—making sure Ian and the others weren't apt to return anytime soon. He said softly, "Tell me this much, up front. Is Denkins really your name?"

"Of course not," the stranger said softly back. "You know the drill. Frankly, after what you and Prescott Bush pulled in 1958 in Nashville, the Central Intelligence Agency is exceptionally wary of you and your allegiances, even now. You're regarded as some sort of a rogue male to the present administration. As you've figured out by now, I'm Company— CIA. I'm not, however, authorized to give you my name, only to tell you there will be terrible repercussions for you if you do not cheerfully and immediately turn over the microfilm in question if it comes into your possession. Your Limey friend Mr. Fleming aside, the Pacific is Uncle Sam's province these days. It is not a field of operation for the Brits or their fucked-up intelligence services."

Perfect. Another threat, from another *interested party.*

Hector smiled ruefully and rapped his knuckles on the countertop. His Japanese neighbors looked over, mildly shocked by the sudden noise, though apparently not surprised at its source. Almost as one, they turned and lowered their heads, forcing attention back to drinks and plates.

Rubbing his jaw, then getting a cigarette started, Hector said, low and mean, "Starting off with threats is no way to treat a so-called rogue male, Agent. You must know that. And, anyway, I've got others threatening me, too. You're far from first in line on that front, old pal." A meaner smile. "You're far from the scariest, either. Unlike some civilians back home, the acronyms FBI and CIA don't give me the same sort of butterflies they might engender in just any old American rube."

The agent nodded. "Point taken. You've got quite a history, as we've both acknowledged. We tapped the phone call at the hotel several days ago. We heard that nasty exchange with the Hungarian. Rest assured, we already have Mr. Hanrahan and Miss Vicente under top-level surveillance. They're unwittingly safe, and we'll keep 'em that way. That I promise you."

Still more wonderful news.

On his dullest day, Jimmy Hanrahan was sharp enough to spot a tail and so would probably be left paranoid and angry regarding the mystery of who was suddenly shadowing him *this* time.

And Alicia? If she somehow tumbled to the fact Hector could still cast a dark shadow of intrigue and menace over her and her children—and that he could somehow do that even across the expanse of the Pacific Ocean? Well, that certainly wouldn't do anything to help his dearly held hope of one day winning her back into his life.

The Company Man smiled and held up his hands. "You're right. None of this hardboiled stuff is the way to go for two like us. Instinctively I knew that, and even made the very argument to my bosses." He crossed his arms on the table and leaned forward confidentially. "I promise you again, we won't fail in protecting your friends. And against orders, I will tell you my name is Scott Bollard. I'm Agency since fifty-six. I've studied your file and read many of your novels. I suppose you might describe me as a fan in every sense."

Hector supposed they'd see about those assertions, too, in time. For now he said, "Last time I checked, we're allies with the British. The CIA and SIS are particularly cozy. We and the Brits have that so-called, 'Special Relationship,' after all, right? Why not just let them get it via Ian and share in the dirty, deadly wealth?"

Agent Bollard shifted in his chair and looked around. "Come on, Hec—you read the newspapers. I'm sure given his past efforts for his government—and his lingering intelligence ties—Mr. Fleming has opined to you on troubling matters over there. He probably tried to alibi or to gloss them. The fact is, we simply don't trust the British with something as devastating as the Flea Bomb. From where we sit, British SIS seems to be a sieve of classified information, most of it flowing straight to the damned Russians. These recent defections—Burgess and Maclean—are obviously alarming. And, confidentially, we believe there are more defections or at least further un-coverings of significant KGB moles in the SIS to come in the very near days ahead. Hell, please don't get your back up about this Mr. Lassiter, because she's certainly a dish, but they didn't even realize what they had hiding in their midst in the person of your rather traitorous recent bedmate, Miss Branch. With all of that taken together, you have to agree the British don't inspire much in the way of confidence any more. That Empire is over."

Mention of Haven got Hector's mind going on something else. "About Miss Branch—do you think she killed that man on the plane?"

"Hell, we're fairly certain she did."

Hector noted Scott was clinching his fists as he confirmed that grim fact. "I'm going to guess your next question and tell you flat out that Terrence Hunt was Agency. I knew him. He was okay. If that bitch killed him, and if I ever get a shot at her?"

"I'd been told by someone that Hunt was actually named Sebastian Keene and that he belonged to something called the Black Dragon Club," Hector said.

Agent Bollard scoffed. "I'm guessing you were told that by either Haven Branch—for obvious reasons to build mistrust in Hunt, and by extension with the Agency—or by Mr. Hiroshi Takahashi."

"The latter," Hector said, deciding to play ball on that point. "Tell me, Scott—and please, going forward, it's 'Hector', okay?—was Hiroshi what he claimed to be? Some arm of Japanese security or the like?"

"Debatable," Scott said. "We think he was double. Either way, I think Branch was complicit in his murder, too—chiefly by assassinating his assassin in order to gain trust and face with you and Mr. Fleming."

"Maybe," Hector said. "Either way, you seem to know nearly everything, Agent."

"We have eyes and ears same as everywhere," he said, shrugging.

Hector thought, *If I had a nickel...*

Scott said, "Will you cooperate? Can I trust you to do the *patriotic* thing, to do the *right* thing, Mr. Lassiter? I've studied your file, as I've said. You're not the usual leftist one finds when one scratches an author of the typical Hollywood ilk. You're actually said to be pretty conservative in your politics and outlook."

"I've got no politics, but you know the threat to my friends," Hector said.

"And we're protecting them, just as I've told you. Top talent is on the case. You have to trust we will do whatever is needed to keep 'em safe. We'll do that just as ruthlessly and effectively as proven necessary."

"I'll think hard on it," Hector said. He held up a hand and said, "Please don't press more than you have—I already lean your way, of course. Better us than them makes sense. It's just very…well, it's complicated. I'll be hurting a dear friend's feelings if I deny his government this damned thing. Please, try to understand."

Scott smiled and nodded. "The threat to your friends back home aside, I also get that you don't want to offend your British friend. Mr. Fleming is archly patriotic—as much as I think you are—only he makes no pretenses to the contrary. It comes across in his novels in an almost poignant way—this stubborn refusal to see the sun has long ago set on the British Empire. Of course I understand the place you speak from, Mr. Lassiter. But you need to understand my position, too. The stakes are unimaginably high. If the Russians somehow were to lay hands on the Flea Bomb, and if they turned it loose in Iowa, or Ohio… Maybe even in New Mexico? Then it's all over, and for all time."

Maybe he really did see Hector's end of things. And anyway, the American spy earned points for his use of "poignant." Hector shook his hand and said, "So I'll just trust that all of your eyes and ears will keep you on the page going forward?"

"Sure, trust in that. But also, just in a pinch…" The Company Man reached into his overcoat pocket and pulled out a small, reel-to-reel micro-recorder. It was the smallest tape recorder Hector had ever seen: not much bigger than a pack of Maverick playing cards.

"State of the art device," Scott said proudly, "and plausible for a writer to carry. You know, for voice memos and the like. But it's also a two-way radio. I'm at the other end, always.

It's encrypted, so it won't accidently come across on some taxi driver's dispatching radio. There's no danger of local cops accidently tapping in."

Scott spent about five minutes showing Hector how to use the thing—both as a tape recorder and as a communication device—then said, "Do you need a gun?"

"The British have already provided me with a Walther PPK," Hector said.

A sad smile. "Those goddamn sentimentalists. So they gave you James Bond's current gun, in other words. Jesus Christ."

The CIA looked around, then reached into his other coat pocket and slid something heavy and wrapped in handkerchief across the table. Hector could feel what it was, of course, if not what type of firearm, exactly. He quickly put it in his pocket.

"Never can have too many rods in a situation like the one you're in," Scott said. "That's a Smith & Wesson Model 36. It's what the Secret Service uses. Better our gun than that German trash. It's already loaded and has no registration numbers. I'll have additional ammunition sent up to your room. It'll arrive in a hollowed-out edition of The King James version of the Bible. No snoopy Buddhist housekeeper will dare touch that tome."

Hector thought that over—at least the British had also provided a holster. And his gifted Rolex watch was growing on him—definitely a far-sight better than his battered old Timex. He felt a bit short-changed by his own spooks.

The two men shook hands and Hector settled up. His mind was of course going in new directions now, so his writing time was clearly well and truly over.

His new gun weighing heavily in his coat pocket, Hector went upstairs where he treated himself to a hot shower, then took a restless nap. That resulted in another imagined tangle of arms and legs with Brinke.

There came a not-asked-for nor even particularly useful offered insight as dream Brinke rested her damp cheek above his racing heart and ran fingernails through his graying chest hair.

She smiled and said, "Don't look so gloomy, darling. After all, by definition, betrayal is only possible where first there is *actual* love."

About four, Ian, Dikko and Tiger returned. The quartet gathered in Dikko's bathroom this time, the taps turned full up again.

Ian was clutching a book of English translations of Basho's poetry. He said, "Bashing up on some of this, so to speak. Tell me, Hector—writer to writer—does this speak to you?" Ian then read:

> *"Tired of cherry,*
> *Tired of this whole world,*
> *I sit facing muddy sake*
> *And black rice."*

"I'm afraid it really doesn't," Hector said to Ian. "Speaking of poets, we've been wandering Japan for a week and then some. When do we cross paths with our old friend Mitsuharu Kaneko?"

"Fear we're still trying to come to an accord there," Ian said, pocketing his book of Basho's works. "I'd far rather do it sooner than later, and I expect you feel the same, of course. But Mr. Kaneko is concerned about the violence that's become attached to our quest—most particularly to you, my dear

Hector. That exploding leg did terrible damage to all trust. These headlines are chipping away at our poet's belief in our dependability to take possession of this deadly information he holds and to move it to safe and appropriate hands. For the moment, our poet's playing very hard to get."

Ian hesitated. "There's something else I must confide now. Our poet friend has taken possession of Miss Devlin's things you came to collect. Evidently that happened some many days ago."

Hector was seething. "How long have you known about that?"

"Just an hour or so." Ian sighed. "I don't know the poet's motives for doing that Hector. I see you're furious and I share your feelings. This is all getting very muddy and messy."

"Terrific," Hector said. "Just wonderful. So what comes next while we wait for this poet to presumably find some fresh trust in us and to give me what is mine—I mean Brinke's writings, of course."

"He's to ring us up again tonight," Ian said, "In the meantime, I think it's appropriate to at last check out our Hungarian friend's health farm. Hearing no objections, we should do that first thing in the morning, I think. Are you game, Hector? Death respects a disdainful eye, yes?"

3

HERE'S MUD IN YOUR EYE

Sitting in the back of a cab with Ian—Dikko and Tiger were in their own hack trailing somewhere behind— Hector said softly, "So, this new Bond you're over here to re-search—I'm hearing rumblings you mean to kill Bond at the end?"

Ian shot him a look. He clenched and unclenched his fists, then said, "Old friends have clearly been talking out of school. Besides, you're the man who killed Heath Dirk—killed him quite unequivocally and outright, as I recall, and with no possibility for reprieve or resurrection *ala* Mr Conan Doyle's Sherlock. Hell, even the poor protagonist of your first novel, *Rhapsody in Black*? My God, what you did to *that* poor chap, leaving him to fall into a lingering darkness? You've never been shy about leaving your heroes bloody and desolate. Or even *dead*. No sentimentalist, Mr. Hector Lassiter."

Ian sniffed and said, "And, anyway, I can hardly kill the infernal goose just as he's starting to at last produce his golden eggs, can I? Ann, ironically and especially now, wouldn't have that either, not a bit of it. Kill James Bond? No, what I see is something more Doylean, more Sherlockian by design. Something closer to *The Final Problem* leading to *The Empty House*, so to speak."

Hector tried to make sense of all that. He said, "You've always had a knack for titles, Ian. I've always envied you that. What's this one to be called?"

Ian smiled and said, "*You Only Live Twice*. It's taken from a humble, left-of-the-mark haiku I attempted a time back. Got the syllable count all wrong, but I do still love the phrasing and the sentiment. Goes like this: 'You only live twice. Once when you're born and once when you look death in the face.'"

Yes, Hector thought, his British peer certainly did have a way with his titles. He said—and meant it, "That's pretty damned wonderful, Ian."

Béla Gustav Herczog's health facility was situated in the flashy, tawdry midst of a kind of red-light district of twisting, narrow alleys and mean-looking storefronts where actual felines lazed in front of the cat houses.

The smell of sulfur hung nastily over at least this part of the city that was studded with bathhouses offering variously hot water, sand, sulfur or mud baths—a cloying, smelly variety of so-called "*onsens*."

Hector thought he might be days getting the rotten-egg smell out of his nose and perhaps even weeks washing it from his clothes.

According to Tiger, in the bathhouses, men and women bathed nude together in the gray-brown ooze of the smoking pools.

Irresistibly, Hector imagined Brinke, who was always something of a libertine or at least a kind of hedonistic adventurer, moving naked among these Asian strangers—her pale, long and curvy body a kind of wonderment to the native bathers.

Would Brinke have taken an Asian lover here or there, male or female?

Quite probably, and quite probably both, Hector decided.

It occurred to him that he wasn't even sure when she had actually made her passage through this place.

Had Brinke sampled Beppu's wicked offerings before she met Hector? Or had it perhaps instead happened between February and December 1924—their near year apart? During that frustrating period when Brinke was on the run, rebuilding her life and establishing a new identity, hiding from French police who did not quite believe the fiction of her apparent death in the frozen Seine on a long-ago February night.

Brinke had also been running from a malevolent female British mystery writer dedicated to her very real destruction—a terrible woman who also had not quite fallen for that very strategic "murder" Brinke had engineered.

His head once more filled with thoughts of his first wife, Hector distractedly toured the grounds of the facility with Ian. For the most part, it seemed to present itself as a kind of honest spa or clinic, although the smell of all that sulfur was now truly getting to Hector—threatening to make him at least sick to his stomach.

Béla Gustav Herczog's dwelling place sat at the far eastern edge of the facility, its turreted, multi-story upper reaches just visible above the treetops.

It was far enough away from the sulfur pits to perhaps be spared some of the stench. Hector couldn't imagine even perpetual proximity eased one's awareness of the horrible stench—it was simply too relentlessly overpowering.

There were no obvious paths or signs pointing the way to Herczog's castle—for that was surly what it was, and very much modeled in the Eastern mode.

At last feeling they had the landscape of the clinic and castle grounds down —a kind of working map in their heads—Ian and Hector wandered over to a consultation house to see about perhaps booking a massage or maybe even enjoying something a bit more "robust" as Ian put it. Particularly since it seemed among the services offered was something called "soapland," a mysterious phrase—enigmatic, at least to Hector—that put a wicked smile on Ian's face. "I've heard of these," he said, clearly delighted. "We simply mustn't pass it up now that we know it's an option, Hector."

But fate wasn't on Ian's side this day—or, to be more specific, it seemed that Ian's heart simply wasn't in the carnal challenge, so to speak.

Once he provided an honest accounting of his recent heart attack—that admission taken with his outward appearance and the distressing, impossible-to-disguise pallor that further bespoke his failing body's frailty—Ian was very regretfully informed by a smallish, clear-skinned young Japanese woman that she was so very sorry not to be able to "service" Ian.

Hector, while feeling sorry and upset for his friend, found himself wondering whether their regretful spa consultant had enough command of the English language to grasp the potential spectrum of meaning in her use of the phrase, "service."

Hector, on the other hand, was cleared for the full service, *if* he wanted to pony up the necessary yen.

Ian smiled ruefully and shook his head. He whispered in Hector's ear, "Clearly, the great bad man is cowering off behind his walls somewhere, and this clinic is hardly the equivalent of my little place atop my Piz where Blofeld makes his lair in the coming Bond you recently read. And, anyway, I took a mud bath in Vegas once to research the experience for *Diamonds Are Forever*. It was a rather horrid experience I'll confess now, although, admittedly, it lacked the scenery and sensory experience *you're* promised, even with this wretched smell of rotten eggs hanging so sourly in the air. Go off and enjoy yourself, Hector, and try very hard not to catch anything Western science can yet cure. I'll meet up with you at the hotel later. Will this stand as our plan?"

Hector wasn't so sure about whether or not he'd be enjoying the full "service" to use their consultant's word, but he did entertain the possibility that sitting in the hot ooze might take some of the pain out of his still rather sore body.

The bruises had faded to near nothing, but the beating he'd sustained so many days ago—and the slightly cracked ribs from the impact after the explosion at the airport—still dogged him with mild pain. Again, he rued the loss of his youthful self's ability to bounce back from such traumas.

Mostly though, he was very relieved Ian's vanity wasn't pushing him to insist upon a mud bath that might spike his heart rate and at last give Ian's much-talked-about "Iron Crab" its final, fatal pass at the British author's diseased heart.

"I'll try to be back no later than seven," Hector said. "We'll get some good sake and a meal, then we'll call our poet friend and insist upon a rendezvous. At very least, tomorrow, regardless of anything else the world may throw at us, I'm claiming Brinke's writings from that son of a bitch. That's my promise and present to myself and this poet had no right to mix up in that."

They shook hands and, only half-comprehending what he was agreeing to, Hector handed over the money to the pretty Asian *consultant*.

He was directed through a rustic wooden door. As he followed the indicated path to the bathhouse, Hector gave it some more thought: It had been a long and sorry time since he'd paid for sex—well, one was always *paying* for sex in some way, if one looked at it in a certain cynical light. But Hector hadn't paid *outright* for the service in a very, very long time, and those times that he had done so, the experience hadn't been even particularly good. Maybe because, to invoke that phrase again, his heart simply hadn't been in the act and neither had the woman's.

But he told himself that this time the money was paid and what he let himself derive from that compact would be his own choice and one made in the moment. If it amounted to simply a hot bath in this smelly ooze and a hosing off afterward—maybe some caressing hands or bare feet walking on his aching back—all of that he would accept and savor as he could.

As an old man greeted him and he exchanged his shoes for slippers at the door, Hector told himself it really didn't have to be more than that simple bath and maybe a massage, not at all.

The women who was to care for him was named Kazaori, which he, was told, translated into something along the lines of "Leaning in the Wind."

She had virtually no English, but the other woman who had taken his money assured him there would be little risk of misunderstanding and, really, it was just best if he put himself in Kazaori's hands and to know that by the end of their time together, Hector was guaranteed to feel quite relaxed and, her words, feeling "very much soothed."

The girl was a kind of revelation—petite, pretty, and certainly no more than twenty-five or twenty-six. She was also paid for, in full, as he reminded himself.

At his age, one never knew how many fine young ladies lay in store along life's narrowing, increasingly unpromising road.

Hector's earlier resolve to sanguinely bypass sex had already fled as the pretty young thing led him to their private bath area and said simply, "He is to undress, please."

She pantomimed the act of stripping and then she undertook that process herself, slipping out of a silk kimono—her only clothing.

Hector briefly turned as if shy, but really just to hide his guns in his coat pockets before continuing to strip himself.

When he was naked too, the lovely Kazaori proceeded to bathe him, head to toe.

After, she had him move to a tub where she joined him, sitting facing him as her hand drifted under the water to grasp him, stroking him for a time, then, as she moved to kiss him there, Hector shifted so she wouldn't have to have her face touch the water.

So far, their language barrier, as promised, was little impediment to what Ian might have described as their *robust* interactions.

Correctly sensing he was close to climaxing, Kazaori stopped and they rose together from the water. She next directed him to move to an air mattress on the floor. There, she covered them both with a slick lubricant—some concoction she called "nuru gel."

Kazaori preceded to rub up against and slide over Hector's body, front and back, using her breasts and other private areas to massage all the various bits of him.

Again, as she sensed she might push him over the edge, she once more bathed Hector and then herself. After toweling off, she gave him a long, lingering massage before putting a condom on him and at last riding him to an aching climax.

Kazaori, too, seemed to reach the same kind of bliss, but as she was a professional, Hector wasn't quite sure if it was an actual "little death" or instead a blessedly convincing bit of play-acting to spare an aging *gaijin's* ego.

She said in English, "Happy end, yes?"

The writer in him rebelled at the concept but he smiled and said, "Very happy, yes."

When he had more or less recovered, she kissed Hector with a feather-brush of budding lips on his mouth, then washed him a last time and led him to another room where she held his hand as he slowly lowered himself into a mud pit.

She pointed at a clock on the wall to indicate when she would return for him—in about fifteen minutes. She said she would again wash him off upon her return, help him to dress and then send him on his way back into the world feeling she "most sincerely" hoped, as something like a "new man."

As he sat sweating in the hot mud, feeling it ooze uncomfortably into various crevices and cracks and but also undeniably at last drawing some of the stubborn aches and faint pains from his abused bones, Hector decided it might be a real act of will to stay in the hot mud for the full fifteen minutes.

He could feel his heart beginning to race a bit and raised himself a bit to get his heart and lungs above the hot and steaming surface of the mud.

But it proved he didn't need to worry about sticking it out for the entire quarter hour.

After just less than five minutes, two hulking Japanese men in ill-fitting suits entered Hector's private mud bath and pointed at the shower with Hector's Walther.

One of the giant men—both, Hector had already decided, were surely current or recently retired-Sumo—pointed at the shower stall and said, "Wash up, fast, then put this on." The big man held up a black kimono that he then tossed onto a shelf.

Hector tried to brass it out. He said, "Sorry, but there's clearly a misunderstanding of some kind. Kazaori promised she's coming back to—"

A curt nod of a bullet-like head on thick neck cut him off. "No," the big Japanese man said. "That's not how it is, of course. You will not see her again." His English was quite assured.

The giant stranger said, "Just please stop wasting time, Mr. Lassiter. Stalling buys you nothing. An important man wants to see you. He is a man who doesn't like to be kept waiting."

4

THE ROOT OF ALL EVIL

The two imposing, obese men led Hector into a large, traditional Japanese room with facing, sliding walls currently pushed open to afford a pretty view of the gardens and the lightly-falling and sweet-smelling rain. He'd been right about that much—the sulfur smell didn't reach the main living quarters, or at least it didn't on this rainy night.

As he stood barefoot in his kimono, flanked by the two big men, Hector sized them up again. He judged that even in his prime he wouldn't have stood a chance against one of the leviathans, let alone both—not in any hand-to-hand confrontation. One of the two topped out at six-five, easily.

The other stood perhaps six-four. Despite the rolls of fat, Hector also sensed there was mature, substantial muscle underlying all that blubber.

Hell, Hector wasn't sure two or three well-placed bullets would stop either of these monsters in time to forestall serious damage to himself. And, anyway, he had no guns at the moment. He was still naked under the black silk kimono; the bundle of his clothes sat neatly folded on a black lacquered table on the far side of the room.

That table: Hector looked around again for something, some item of décor or simply *anything* that might give insight to Béla Herczog.

But the room was as neutral as some of the traditional hotel rooms or inns he'd experienced on this trip with Ian across Japan: Just a smattering of traditional prints of unremarkable Japanese scenes or settings. There was really nothing individual—nothing to provide insight—in the room at all.

The soft sound of steps, then a tall, thin bald man in black pants and a black polo shirt entered the room. The man wore black slippers on his slightly pigeon-toed feet.

The new man's skin was of a sallow-brownish hue reminding Hector in a sad and pointed way of Ian's unhealthy pallor.

The skinny man's naked scalp was veined over with blue and purple spider webs. His mouth was a sour slash—no prominent upper or lower lip. The eyes were deeply sunken into dark, wide-apart orbits and were pale gray, the irises surrounded all around by the whites of the eyes—rather like Mussolini's appeared in photos when *Il Duce* was captured on film in moments of rage or spittle-spraying zeal.

But it was the man's withered right arm that captivated Hector's pale blue eyes. The small and stunted arm barely came even with the man's normal, unremarkable left elbow. Vestigial fingers dangled limply from under the edges of the loosely fitting right sleeve of the black polo shirt in a kind of repellent flipper. A birth defect? Something resulting from his birth mother's exposure to some ancient chemical forerunner to Thalidomide, perhaps?

Either way, Hector was glad to see that this man, at least, wasn't particularly imposing, despite being more than a shade taller than Hector.

A voice the author recognized from that phone call at the hotel days before said, "Mr. Lassiter. I'd really hoped we'd not come to this bitter, final place."

Hector smiled uncertainly and said, "Can we really be said to have come to *anywhere*? We haven't even been properly introduced, Mr. Herczog. Listen, would you mind terribly if I was to—"

The left hand rose, quieting Hector. "No, we'll not waste time with any of that. I'd hoped at one point we might work together after a fashion. I'd hoped that you would at least cooperate and cheerfully hand over to me the materials related to the Flea Bomb. But then I began to gain access to your various dossiers via Haven Branch and so many others—the files kept on you by the British and by your own government secret forces.... Even by the French and the Russian secret services."

Herczog waved his good hand and shrugged. "After at last wading through all of these materials, I decided you will never bend to my will, not happily, nor will you ever do so constructively. *That's* when I decided to try and eliminate you at the airport. It seemed prudent to simply and swiftly remove an inevitable complication. But that effort unfortunately failed. Then my associate, Miss Branch, begged me to let her try her little ruse with your mutual kidnapping. She was convinced she could manipulate you toward unwitting cooperation. That gambit, too, went lamentably awry, and when she should come under my hand again, as she inevitably will?" He drew his left hand across his neck. "I abhor ineptitude."

The man with the withered right arm moved to a small wall cabinet and opened it. He pushed aside Hector's bundle of clothes to make room and poured Satori over ice.

Without offering Hector even the invitation of a possibly tongue-loosening drink—this was another very bad sign, a mortal harbinger, the novelist decided—the bald man said, "When Miss Branch failed with her melodramatic masked ruse in the garage, I made my little phone call and decided to try and motivate you through the simple and straightforward promise to kill your friends and former lovers if you didn't agree to facilitate my will. I then sat back to wait and see what effect those far from idle threats would have."

Hector shrugged. "And I think we would have to agree that the jury is still out on all that, as I have done nothing but try to satisfy my curiosity about who you are, and to get a look at you and your operation here—doing so as a paying customer, I'd add. I'm hardly skulking around or hiding my identity toward some dark end. Not like you."

"Silence," Herczog said, the whites again showing all the way around the pale gray eyes. "What you have done is to ferret out my identity, and then to dare to come straight into my keep. That portends enemy action and, based on your past escapades and a willingness to use lethal force when and how you see fit, I regard your presence here and now as clear indication of your intention to *assassinate* me in my own home."

The man gestured at Hector with his glass. He said sharply, "No, Mr. Lassiter, your intent and lethal threat are all too clear to me. You mean me harm, so I will simply kill you first. Mr. Fleming is tired and sick—I think it will not be terribly difficult for my Black Dragons to wrest from him the microfilm once it passes into his faltering hands. He also has a wife and a child whom I can threaten as easily as I threatened that Irish trash and that Mexican whore of yours back in California. So you see, Mr. Lassiter, you are now imminently expendable in my eyes. All actions have consequences and yours have gotten you killed today."

Hector decided to try and keep the man talking a bit while he raced to figure some way out of this mess—before he was summarily escorted out and tossed into a stinking fumarole by one of the giants looming either side of him.

"You can't *really* think possessing this damned weapon can truly change the political fortunes of Japan," Hector said. "This threat of starving the West is certainly bad enough, but we still have the big bomb—probably many hundreds if not thousands of them, by now. We could make your whole adopted country look like Nagasaki or Hiroshima in just a few terrible minutes. And, anyway, the Japanese government is still somewhat held in check by American interests. I can't imagine you and your Black Dragon cult have the skills or the scientific knowledge to bring this Flea Bomb off on your own. That prospect seems to me totally out of the range of possibility."

Béla Herczog laughed and drank more of his Japanese whiskey. He picked up the bundle of Hector's clothes and tossed them at the novelist.

Winching, Hector gingerly caught his clothes, hoping that if the cigarette pack given him by the quartermaster Burton was still in his suit pocket it would survive such reckless handling—would weather concussion from his catch.

"Get dressed, Mr. Lassiter," Herczog ordered.

As Hector complied, the man said, "As you so often claim to be true of yourself, I'm not really much of a political animal, Mr. Lassiter. Politics are ephemeral. While I love Japan and find its aesthetics and appetites most closely conform to my own, I am, at base, a realist. Like you, I have concluded Japan will never be an imperial force, not like in the old days, not ever again. Similarly, I concede that I have more years behind than ahead of me, and so I will enjoy my time here, endeavoring as I can to experience the Japan I formerly loved while giving a wide berth to the Westernized abomination much of this country has become and will further continue to under your country's presently indirect but lamentable and unavoidable stewardship."

Hector tucked his shirt into his pants, then zipped up and fastened his belt. He noticed for the first time his explosive cigarette pack, along with his recorder-radio, sat on the table next to the bottle of Satori whiskey. They were covered by his clothes, originally.

Hector looked around frowning—his shoes were nowhere to be seen. Conforming to Japanese tradition, he expected they must be awaiting him by some door through which he was expected to make final passage on the way to his execution.

Hector slowly picked up his sports jacket, subtly patting pockets—only his comb, two lighters and room key and fob remained in its pockets. Pretty thin pickings in terms of potential weapons.

Staring out at the rain, showing Hector his back, Herczog said, "For me, those who covet the Flea Bomb for its perceived political power—Miss Branch representing a fine example of this delusional type—are merely useful tools. I don't want the bomb's schematics for political reasons, nor for games of power. Rather, I see in it profit potential on an unprecedented scale. Call me the ultimate capitalist. I will sell this thing not just to the highest bidder, but to *any* qualifying bidder. I will do that, over and over."

A terrible smile tugged at the corners of the near-lipless mouth. "And after all, how much of a threat can the thing pose if same as *everyone* on earth has possession of the weapon? Isn't that the very underpinning of the terrible stalemate that allows those in America and Russia to sleep at night with all of those bombs you referenced proliferating on either side of your Cold War? I speak of course of this terrible balancing act of annihilation so chillingly labeled 'mutually assured destruction'."

The man sniffed and contemplated his cocktail tumbler clutched in his single, functional hand. He said softly, "They declare money as the root of all the evil in this troubled world. Apparently, so is the concept of exclusivity. No, Mr. Lassiter, I think we can agree the world will actually be demonstrably better for my profit pursuit of the Flea Bomb. It's the thing held in jealous exclusivity that poses the most dire threat to the innocent—if any such creatures really still exist in this world anymore. After all, your own glorious democracy no sooner developed the atom bomb than it felt immediately impelled to use the monstrosity, not just once, but twice, and in murderously short order—murder on an unprecedented and instantaneous scale."

Hector had nearly finished dressing. He fastened his Rolex and slipped his hands into his pants pockets, trying to act nonchalant—unafraid. He said, "You know full well that when even these pro-Japanese converts like Haven Branch learn how you've played them, this little hideaway of yours will very likely become your tomb, yes? Everyone is apt to turn on you, to seek your extermination."

A harsh laugh. He said, "That's the pulp fiction writer in you speaking, Lassiter. That's the fantasist with the too big and crazy imagination. All blood and thunder and overgrown-adolescent nonsense. My God, these silly books you write, Mr. Lassiter…? At least your friend Fleming has the ability to deny his untoward fantasies when called upon them by critics. He can say Bond is just a mere fiction and escapist fare. But how to defend or deflect such criticism when you actually use *yourself* as a character in your own novels, as you have done these last years? The man who lives what he writes and writes what he lives, indeed. This sad ego projection of yours named Hector Lassiter who moves like some aging lothario and *bon vivant* through your fictional world, cosseting his appetites and animal passions with liquor, expensive meals and too young women—what a sad and clumsy ego projection he is, indeed. What embarrassingly naked wish-fulfillment."

The one-armed man poured himself yet another drink. Clearly, he was an alcoholic, Hector decided, *bent on getting there and soon*, as a recovering alcoholic friend had once put it in describing that numbed, elusive state that all problem drinkers chase like opium smokers chase the dragon.

Herczog said, "I hope you appreciate that I at least gave you a chance to go out like that man with his low drives and animal passions that you write so much and so nakedly about. I let you have a last bit of time as a man with that delectable young flower before sending you to your death, as I will do now. If nothing else, exploiting your lust made it that much easier to strip you, quite literally, of your defenses. Now, I'm really quite finished with you, Mr. Lassiter. Allow me therefore to at last formally introduce your attendants."

Smiling and bowing at his outsized minions, Herczog said, "Please to meet Mr. Amon Wada and Mr. Chikao Kida. Mr. Wada and Mr. Kida are retired Sumo as you'll already have deduced from their splendidly imposing physiques. Mr. Wada, particularly, was once a quite famous *Rikishi*—a

Sumo wrestler. Now his skills are wholly mine. You see, Mr. Lassiter, though venerated and honored while in public life and competition, the prospects for such wrestlers once they leave the ring are quite bleak indeed. Their lifestyles and diets drastically shorten their life spans. Their old age is usually one riddled by myriad health concerns, by arthritic aches and paralyzing pain before they finally succumb to some fatal attack—usually of the heart—and well in advance of their non-sumo Japanese peers."

Hector could easily believe that last: He estimated Mr. Wada went two-hundred and seventy pounds, easily. Mr. Kida, who still wore a topknot, seemed closer to three-hundred pounds. Both men seemed ready to explode out of their matching black suits and even their black wingtip dress shoes.

Herczog continued, "So these former champions, happily for us all, are now devoted to my service and well-compensated for little missions like the one I have called them here to perform for me tonight."

Béla Herczog smiled at his Sumo wrestlers and said, "Mr. Wada, Mr. Kida, you will escort Mr. Lassiter on a one-way visit to our private nocturnal Crocodile Hell. Please do so right now. Mr. Lassiter has made it clear he is no longer of any use to me, as I've argued. He is, in fact, a threat to me, as I have also made clear this evening. This is a justifiable act on my part, so if Mr. Lassiter resists before you get him there, shoot him in the head and complete his journey to that particular Hell even if it means you're simply transporting his corpse. Is this all understood? I much prefer him to meet his death with eyes wide open—deep down, as a writer, I think even he might appreciate that gesture—but if it's his lifeless body you feed to the crocodiles, that will be his decision, ultimately."

5

SUITCASES WITH TEETH

The last of the light was quickly failing as they reached *Oniyama Jigoku*—a particularly special "Hell" that Tiger had off-handedly remarked was noted for more than the usual stinking sulfurous pools of varying hues that drew all the tourists, foreign and domestic, to Beppu.

This particular "Hell," the Japanese journalist had confided, was also noted for using its extremely warm waters to facilitate the breeding of more than eighty different variations of crocodile—some of those species among the largest and most fearsome in the world.

Dusk now fallen, the Sumo wrestlers keyed themselves into the empty park with a chilling familiarity bordering on the routine: The tourists were long gone and there wasn't even a security guard on duty to patrol the place for the evening.

Warily walking ahead of Mr. Wada and Mr. Kida, Hector had to assume Béla Herczog had paid well for his prideful, after-hours run of this horrid place—it was a kind of paid-for killing ground. The two massive former athletes clearly felt fully assured that this was their own private Hell, so to speak—their nocturnal devil's playground.

According to Tiger, rumor also had it the odd, suicidal Japanese man or woman would occasionally break into the park after hours to hurl themselves into the crocodile pools.

They were swiftly and wholly devoured soon upon breaking the water's surface, Tiger said. No evidence was left by morning to appall or to frighten the next day's visitors— not a scrap of flesh or clothing would be found.

Running escape and attack scenarios through his feverish mind, trying to think of some viable way out of his seemingly hopeless situation, Hector found himself absently reaching into his pocket for his Zippo and Pall Malls to calm his nerves—to focus his mind through familiar routine and sorry muscle memory.

But he inadvertently grabbed hold of the wrong cigarettes— instead pulling out the explosive pack of supposed Japanese smokes given him so many days ago by the strange little armaments quartermaster, Alec Burton, and which Hector had asked for before being escorted out of Herczog's palace. Béla Herczog had agreed that a condemned man certainly deserved a last smoke or two and handed the pack over.

A grunt followed as Hector's hand dipped into his coat, then there was a vise like grip on his arm, just below the elbow. Mr. Wada confiscated the cigarette pack from Hector. "You won't need that, but *I* might—smoking suppresses the appetite, and I'm still trying to shed some weight. I have a child on the way. I'd like to see him grow up. And, anyway, in less than a minute, you surely won't need anything, not ever again, you know."

The Sumo wrestler again had said all that in far better English than Hector had once anticipated or had any reason to expect to hear. Despite that fact, the ride over had been one spent in an eerie silence, jammed up tight against

Mr. Kida in the backseat of a claustrophobic, two-door Toyota Publica.

With the two Sumo wrestlers packed inside along with six-two Hector, the tiny car had seemed more than a little like some overstuffed child's toy.

Hector gestured at the cigarette pack and said rather too desperately, he knew, "Your boss felt *differently*. Please let me smoke."

The Sumo shook his head and said, "He is him and I am me. I am here now and he will never know of any of this."

The ex-Sumo roughly thrust the confiscated cigarette packet into own his right suit coat pocket. At first Hector winced, fearing the man might break the fragile vials inside with his rough handling. But nothing like that happened and Hector dejectedly re-pocketed his Zippo.

That other cigarette lighter—the one that was effectively a lethal, single-use torch—was still there in the same pocket, but it struck Hector as a fruitless weapon measured against these two equally lethal wrestlers.

In a drizzling cold rain, they approached the statue of a huge, nearly naked red devil with yellow horns and a protuberant yellow belly button. The demonic idol was perched atop a squat stone by an iron gate.

From behind that gate, more curtains of steam rose toward the moon.

Hector could hear commotion in the water to the accompaniment of gulping reptilian roars and vibrato belches, some of which sounded more than a little like the gunning of motorcycle engines. Hector assumed it was the overlapping sound of all of the crocodiles, calling out in the night.

From stands of calmer reeds and weeds, the more soothing sound of crickets trilled.

Mr. Wada opened the squeaking, rusting gate with another skeleton key and Mr. Kida motioned with a gun that Hector should lead the way along a narrow, wooden boardwalk opening on to similar rickety walkways.

The other pathways separated—or in a couple of cases, actually crossed over—neighboring, steaming hot pools. Each of the concrete-walled water basins below abounded with now strangely motionless white-gray crocodiles. Hector estimated that a few of the huge reptiles would measure more than fifteen feet long, nose tip to tail.

Hector tried to recall all that he knew about crocodiles. There had been alligators in Florida proper, of course, but dwelling in Key West as he had for so many years in the 1920s and '30s, Hector rarely encountered even those predators.

As he surveyed these lazing in the moonlight, watching the men with lustful intent, Hector found himself irresistibly drawn to the giant crocs' yellow-grey eyes with their vertical slit pupils, almost evoking the eyes of felines. Then he remembered that, yes, crocodiles indeed preferred to hunt by night. And now along had come Hector Lassiter, set to be offered up to the beasts in this twilight time when they were at their most feral.

Mr. Wada gestured at one of the biggest of the reptiles and said, "That one is a saltwater crocodile. They are the biggest and meanest of the breed, and I mean anywhere in the world, man. They eat anything they can reach, even other smaller crocodiles. So I recommend you try to land close to one of them—then put your head close to its mouth. That will end it fast for you. Otherwise, they like to get you by the leg or by an arm, then they jerk you under. They roll over and over and can tear off your arms and legs just by twisting them clean off, one at a time, before they go for the rest of your body."

Mr. Wada grinned, showing two gold, front teeth.

Hector looked again at the giant, armored crocs—resembling nothing so much as dinosaurs as they lazed languidly in their steaming pools, motionless save for the slithering, tracking motion of their dead, cats' eyes that followed the three men—the three figures they surely regarded as food, but currently frustratingly out of reach.

Losing hope, Hector thought, *These are what are going to finally kill me, these goddamned, vile suitcases with teeth.*

Wetting his lips—his mouth was now very dry, though his palms and the rest of his body were quite damp—Hector said, again rather desperately to his own ears, "Whatever that man you work for is paying you, I can promise my government will double it. Let me leave here, and I'll see that you're well compensated and given protection. I can promise you my government will—"

Another short and harsh chuckle that brought him up short. Mr. Wada said, "All you can promise me talking that way is a quick death. Please just be quiet now, Lassiter. After all, you're already *shini-tai*. You just don't seem to admit it."

"I don't speak your language," Hector said bitterly. "And, anyway, why do you speak such good English?"

"In wrestling terms, *shini-tai* means you're already a dead body," Mr. Kida explained.

So, the other spoke English, too. Mr. Kida added, "And *we* speak English so well because *we* were born in Hawaii."

"Then we're *fellow Americans*," Hector said. "You should be on my side, per force."

Mr. Wada scowled at that patriotic plea and motioned again for Hector to lead the way along a particularly rickety, arching wooden bridge that spanned the largest of the steaming pools teeming with crocodiles. The wooden planks groaned under the weight of the Sumo.

Hector guessed this particular crossways must be used by tour guides or the like to feed or perhaps to rouse the crocodiles to some activity for the sake of entertaining daytime visitors. Either way, it was clear to Hector this was meant to be his terrible destination. His time was at last up.

Nearly devoid of last scraps of hope, the novelist slowed, then half-turned to measure distances. He visualized himself successfully executing the move he had in mind, then Hector again drew back a clenched fist as if to telegraph a punch.

Mr. Wada merely laughed and raised a beefy arm to block any ineffectual blow that Hector might hurl his way.

Instead, Hector lashed out with his left foot, striking the big sumo wrestler in the side. He was aiming for the pocket where the explosive pack of cigarettes now nested.

Impact—the soft but telltale sound of tinkling glass. Deadly chemicals were already mixing.

Mr. Wada grunted, then clutched unsuccessfully at Hector's ankle.

But Hector was already moving as swiftly as he could away from the Sumo—running headlong toward what appeared to be a virtual dead-end, but really, in the moment, Hector was simply intent upon putting as much distance as he could between himself and the still-startled ex-wrestlers.

As Burton the quartermaster had warned, the actual interval between the impact of Hector's kick and the resulting explosion was appallingly scant.

A hot rushing gust of air robbed Hector's lungs of oxygen, then slammed him down hard on the wooden planks and set his ears to ringing.

As he watched, Mr. Wada seemed for a moment to evaporate or even to disappear into the rising steam, but that steam was now a livid pink.

Mr. Kida—standing immediately behind his vaporizing comrade—let out a short, harsh scream, then seemed to actually shrink in stature.

Hector realized the blast had struck Kida below the knees, essentially atomizing the man's lower legs. More disturbing to Hector was his realization the rickety bridge upon which he stood uncertainly was also beginning to collapse under them.

The bridge's strengthening arch had not just been compromised by the bogus cigarette pack's explosion, but severed.

With its center now gone, the bridge's isolated, surviving spans were overwhelming their failing anchors and moorings at either end of the crocodile pool.

Hector immediately began running back toward the now-missing section of the failing bridge, determined to hurdle the three- or four-foot gap in order to reach the other side and continue his dash to safety before the entire structure collapsed into the now frenzied crocodile pool chummed with so much Sumo blood.

But Hector fell perilously short of his goal. To his horror, his hands slapped the far side of the severed bridge just as its ragged edge splashed into the crocodile pool. He was in the water up to his knees.

There was another terrible commotion as the twisted knot of crocs sprang to thrashing life, darting with lashing tails toward the tendrils of blood spreading out across the smoking surface of the water from the remains of the Sumo wrestlers' ruined bodies and the new turmoil created by the bridge's final collapse.

Somehow, Hector managed to get one foot squarely planted upon the back of Mr. Kida, who was still thrashing around, trying to grab hold of the bridge himself even as he bled out from his terrible leg wounds.

Hector used that fleeting purchase to push himself back up the edge of the sinking bridge. He managed to grasp one of the now-sideways rail supports, hauling his feet out of the water just as a large crocodile took a surging snap at Hector's dangling legs. Hector booted the thing in its sensitive eye sockets with his heel.

In a kind of terrified frenzy, Hector grabbed another "rung" and hauled himself further up the ruined bridge that had now become a kind of makeshift ladder, slanting, as it did, at a near forty-five degree angle into the bloody, steaming pool of feasting reptiles.

From somewhere above, Hector heard bending nails and rending screws—a rusty groaning as the compromised remains of the dry-rotted bridge threatened to pull loose from their last moorings to crash into the deadly pool.

Hector at last hauled himself up to safety, rolling onto an adjacent, and *intact* catwalk just as the last of the bridge gave way.

Standing atop that surviving pathway, panting and doubled-over—hands on knees and still trying desperately to get his breath—Hector listened as Mr. Kida gave a last, terrible shriek, then was dragged under the surface by countless, impossible-to-escape and tightly clutching jaws.

There were more terrible thrashing and belching noises from the crocodiles as they gorged on their unscheduled evening meal.

Weak-kneed and shaking, Hector surveyed himself. There was no blood to be seen, but his pants were soaked below the knee. Of course his shoes were sodden, too. But that hardly mattered with the mounting rain.

The important thing was that he was still alive and so still dangerous to the one-armed man he meant to revenge himself upon this bloody and rainy night.

Shivering in the quickening downpour, Hector realized the keys to the little car that had brought him to this terrible place were in the pockets of one of the men now roiling in the stomach juices of God-only-knew how many of those giant carnivorous reptiles gorging down there.

But that didn't really matter, either: His old friend Jimmy Hanrahan had long-ago schooled Hector in the art of hot-wiring cars.

So long as he remembered to drive on the proper side of the road, Hector was fairly confident he could find his way back to the health clinic where Béla Herczog would be expecting the little car to return to him with his killer Sumo inside.

Yes, this was Hector's instinctive plan of action: He would drive straight back into the belly of the best.

Once there, he would put the son of a bitch Herczog down for all-day and then some more.

6

TO HELL AND GONE

After just a few false turns in the driving rain, Hector eventually found his way back to the Hell's Gate Spa.

As he approached the imposing wrought iron fence, invisible electric eyes tripped on an array of floodlights, bathing the approaching vehicle in white light. Hector pulled his coat collar up to obscure his face and waited for someone inside to push the button to open the gate for the familiar car.

Several nerve-rattling moments of silence and motionlessness ensued. Hector began to fear he'd be flanked with men with guns, maybe more retired Sumo.

With a groan and a clang, the gate suddenly separated at its center and swung inward with a continuing muted squeak from its corroded hinges.

Gusting rain blanketed the windshield. Hector resisted turning on the wipers—that would only give a clearer view of the interior and probably of his face. It would likely make it equally clear that where three had left in the cramped little car, only one was returning.

Palming the wheel with his left hand, he followed the winding path leading to the five-story white and black turreted garrison. Hector reached into the glove compartment and retrieved the American gun given him by the CIA agent— the gun he'd seen Mr. Kida stash there on the ride over. His Walther was somewhere in the croc pool, now.

So much for playing James Bond manqué tonight, he chided himself.

A lone figured draped in a dark wind-whipped kimono was standing in front of the castle under an umbrella, waiting for his minions to return. One kimono sleeve whipped wilder in the wind—that nearly empty right sleeve. Clearly, it was Herczog, and just as clearly he was confident enough in his Sumos' effectiveness and loyalty to feel comfortable greeting them in solitude.

That was a lucky break for Hector. He'd heard enough about these places to know the last thing he needed was for Béla Herczog to escape back into his *yamajiro's* central keep— surrounded as it likely would be with tell-tale nightingale floors and the Japanese variation of bone-breaking oubliettes— see-saw floors to drop the unwary into a pit, or perhaps instead depositing them upon a waiting nest of clustered and sharpened bamboo staves.... Or, maybe it would just deposit the unwary into some chute ending in a white-hot fumarole.

As he palmed the wheel, taking another brief and meandering curve away from the castle, Hector activated the little car's high beams, hoping to make it that much harder for Herczog to make out shapes or silhouettes in the absurd little Toyota.

The figure framed in the headlights bowed, squinting against the cold rain and called out, "It is done? Lassiter is no more?"

Hector hauled himself out of the little car, the gun gripped in his left hand. It only took at instant for Herczog to realize the biggish man at the wheel was not one of his hulking ex-Sumo celebrities-turned-enforcers.

Béla Herczog let out an inhuman shriek and pulled something from under his kimono. Hector, despite holding his gun in his left hand, fired first.

Another yell—Herczog's gun struck the ground and then went off, taking out one of the Toyota's headlights.

Hector gave chase in the bracing rain. He fired a warning shot as the other man started to drift toward the stairs and the entrance of his castle. Hector once again figured if Herczog made it inside, his own odds of ending up maimed or dead increased geometrically.

Snarling, Herczog veered left into shadows, slipper-clad feet crunching on manicured gravel. He was leading Hector into his maze-like garden that weaved between all those stinking and scalding fumaroles, probably hoping Hector, unfamiliar with the path in the dark would stumble into one of the pits to be instantly incinerated.

Herczog screamed out, "That shot you fired will bring more of my men, Lassiter. Leave now—run, and you may yet live."

Hector dismissed that threat. The rain was so heavy the sound of any shot would be lost under its infernal pounding—assuming anyone else was actually roaming the grounds of Herczog's castle, which Hector sincerely doubted.

Before he might lose sight of him in the dark, Hector took aim at the man's left shoulder—he'd have gone for a leg or a hip if that black kimono didn't obscure such close targeting—and squeezed off another round.

There was a terrible squeal and the man pitched forward onto a gravel path between two steaming fumaroles.

The rain had also increased the density of the steam plumes coming off the lava pits and Hector briefly lost sight of the man in the low-hanging fog when he hit the gravel: he instead followed the sound of the man's five clawing fingers and his madly scraping feet.

As he drew closer to the bald man's figure emerging from the mists, Béla Herczog rolled onto his back, groaning, and tried to lash out at Hector with his feet. The one-armed man snarled, "You have no authority here! You shot me in my home! The Japanese police will—"

No patience for any of that, Hector took aim between the man's eyes, then shifted a foot to the right and pulled the trigger, kicking up pebbles next to the man's head.

"*Please*," Hector said, "this is no citizen's arrest. This is simply a public service, as far as I'm concerned. Loose ends from the last war."

He reached down and knotted his fingers in the man's sodden kimono, hauling him to unsteady feet.

Sensing what was coming, Herczog said again, "You can't possibly dare to do this! I have important friends, not just here, but also back home in Hungary!"

Hector was having none of that. "I thought *this* country was your home—your home of *choice*. Anyway, this isn't a trial, and I'm not interested in playing judge, either. Only executioner."

Hector gripped the man by his wounded left shoulder, eliciting another sharp scream. Herczog took his last shot: "If you do anything to me, Haven will never forgive you, Lassiter! And I still have my men, watching your friends back home— have you forgotten that?"

Hector just shook his head. "You say that about Haven like it still matters to me. And even if it did, you already made it clear you mean her dead, too. As to your threats against my friends? I'm choosing to embrace that ancient strategic philosophy of cutting off the snake's head, then simply standing back as its body whips and dies. And anyway, the CIA is now watching those of yours who are watching mine. But, all that aside, there's that one other, immutable truth, Béla."

His chin trembling, Herczog stammered, "Wh-what *other* truth?"

"We have a pithy saying back home," Hector said. "No body, no crime."

Hector gave that a solid second to sink in, then he straight-armed the man in the Oriental robe.

Tipping back on heels, his wounded left arm wind-milling, Béla Herczog toppled into the larger of the two steaming sulfur pits at either side of the gravel path.

Hector quickly retreated several steps to avoid the burning and sulfurous backsplash as the man plunged, screaming, into a hissing bluish fumarole.

There was a terrible burping noise, then a fresh burst of steam billowed from the hole that ran to the center of the earth.

Standing over the steaming cloud, Hector lowered his gun and took a last look around to make certain no guard or sentry had perhaps heard any of the gunshots or the high-pitched screams as the terrible man made his way down into his private Hell.

Although satisfied he at last had the place truly to himself, Hector still resisted the temptation to penetrate the almost certainly booby-trapped and fortified lair of the Black Dragon Club leader.

Instead, blinking back the rain, Hector returned to the ridiculous little Toyota. He was intent upon going in search of his hotel, a hot shower and another solid, Western-style drink.

Driving through the bucketing rain, Hector thought of the sound and the smell of the man catching fire as he sank down into the sulfurous hell mouth.

A quote by Mark Twain he'd been tasked to memorize in grade school suddenly came to Hector: "Go to Heaven for the climate, Hell for company."

7

OUT OF JAPAN

Mitsuharu Kaneko, now gray-haired and his face heavily lined and weathered, was not the large-living, woman-obsessed intellectual of the mid-1940s that Hector fondly recalled.

The sixty-seven-year-old poet had just ordered another round of sake. He was expounding on his poet's life—reminiscing about his explanation to a recent interviewer regarding the unending life-of-the-wits existence he baldly perceived himself exemplifying.

"We marvel how we've been able to spend our life with an unexpected line of work," he said, "but realizing that we've reached such an age as to be able to do anything about it even if we thought about it, we decide to compel ourselves to find something worthwhile, albeit reluctantly, in the years ahead of the life we didn't want. That's what we usually do. There's something about us human beings that is piteous and lovely."

Trying to get his head around that observation, Hector studied the old poet in polite glances.

So far as he knew the man's biography, Kaneko struck Hector as a Japanese Orson Welles of a sorts: an other-worldly prodigy who'd dropped out of countless schools and abandoned many educational disciplines and paths—eventually actually painting pornography for a time to fund his travels—all that before finding his poet's voice. The Japanese poet seemed to Hector the most consummate of autodidacts.

"This I truly believe," Kaneko said. "To oppose is the only fine thing in life. To oppose is to live. To oppose is to get a grip on the very self. When I'm in the east, I want to go to the west. My greatest hate is all people feeling the same."

So far, Kaneko had charmingly and stubbornly deflected all of Hector's attempts to discuss Brinke's writings and his questions regarding their possible whereabouts. For his part, Hector had been able to maintain some semblance of civility, but his patience was waning, his self-control eroding under the steady assault of the Japanese liquor and all of the unsought philosophical insights.

As if to underscore that fact, Ian hefted his cup and said, "The man drinks the first flask of sake. The first flask drinks the second. Then, the sake drinks the man."

With grandiose seriousness, Ian rose and, leaning on his cane, excused himself to seek the restroom. Dikko followed along, majestically focused on not falling as he drunkenly trailed Ian.

When it was just the poet, Tiger and Hector, Kaneko's manner abruptly changed. He leaned forward and said very seriously, "I sincerely apologize for what I felt I had to do regarding your wife's writings, my friend. I had to take drastic action when you disappeared for those several hours after having been kidnapped just a few days before. All the evil in the world seemed suddenly centered here in Beppu and I felt I simply had to do something momentous to protect this terrible secret. Japan should not have this weapon. We proved ourselves capable of the greatest treachery with our surprise attack on your country in 1941, Mr. Lassiter. It was a terrible perversion of Bushido Code. Our conduct during the war, and our treatment of your prisoners hardly distinguished us." He raised his bushy eyebrows. "Too many who caused all that, or who apologize for it, still have positions of influence and power, I am sorry to confess."

"I appreciate you saying that," Hector said. "But this man Herczog is dead, and by my hand. I watched him burn. Brinke's writings are very important to me; they are important in ways I can't express." Hector shook his head and said, "I was supposed to meet an inn keeper and claim them. This seemed so easy and straightforward. How did you come to have control of my wife's writings?" Hector couldn't keep a hint of menace from his tone.

"It is not so straightforward, not at all," Kaneko said. "Miss Devlin's writings were never really in that inn-keepers hands, you see. Not really. The writing was undertaken when Miss Devlin was a guest of mine, during the early 1920s. I believe it was 1924. We knew each other from a time even earlier than that. She was always something of an Orientalist, I'd guess you might say. Our Brinke was seeking sanctuary after fleeing Paris, hiding from some murderous fellow writer, she claimed. So she lived with me for a time. She knew she could trust me and that I'd protect her, as I had similarly done many years before."

He let that hang there.

Hector resisted the urge to inquire if he was implying they'd been intimate. Like Hector, the poet had that certain reputation as a great lover of women. Kaneko said, "The innkeeper was a kind of middle-man, in the parlance of your country. I desperately wanted you to claim this terrible thing and give it to your government, Mr. Lassiter. All those years ago, Brinke painted a very intoxicating picture in my head of the kind of man you are. Reading your books in translation in the intervening years secured that image in my mind. It set me on a course, a path I'm still committed too. Particularly as I've watched the British sink steadily in importance, stature and competence. I quite deliberately decided to use Miss Devlin's writings as a means of insuring your particular cooperation.

"You see, when I at last met you in the flesh, in 1945, you impressed me, very much so," he said. "I thought then of confiding to you about our mutual friend—our exceptional Miss Devlin. I'm sure we would have got to that and her writings would likely have become yours in due course all those years ago. But events with the microfilm's loss overtook us. And you and I are of similar nomadic impulses. Time passed. When the microfilm was at last recovered I saw a fresh chance. It is now hidden among Brinke Devlin's posthumous writings that I have held for so many years. I choose this moment to tell you that to ensure you'll take the necessary next and last step required to claim the writing, *and* the microfilm. I choose this precise moment to tell you all this in order to spare Ian's ego. He's an apologist and champion of his country—it positively screams through as such in his writing. But Britain is a spent force, and one now riddled with enemy agents and provocateurs. And everyone but everyone wants this terrible secret."

Hector said testily, "So why not simply ring up the CIA and offer this thing to them, straight up?"

"Because your country's government is vast and not without corruption of its own. You're a man of good character. A man with connections and a distinguished espionage history in the OSS. I trust you can vet the recipients on your end in a manner that I, as a practical reality, cannot. You'll see that this terrible thing passes into the safest American hands. I believe that. It's really that simple, my friend."

"Where are Brinke's writings right now," Hector asked, trying harder to keep his tone cordial. "Where exactly is my next destination?"

"Istanbul," Kaneko said. "I happen to have a trusted friend who will soon be there. Another writer, as it happens… At least that's so when he's not acting. He's been cast in the next Bond movie. I know that you were also planning to visit the filming in Turkey with Mr. Fleming. It seemed like a kind of—what is your word?" A smile as he remembered and said, "Yes, *kismet*. Destiny. And it was the only destination of yours in the near-term known to me, thanks to an aside by our friend Ian."

"But that's *months* from now," Hector said. "I'm entitled to my wife's writings. I can hardly be expected to come all the way here only to be nearly killed several times over and told half-a-year from now I can enjoy the privilege of making this same potentially deadly trek again. And what *then*? What if the Russians are suddenly all over the scene, or the Chinese?"

"I was overcome by events and by justified fear," Kaneko said staunchly. "By the same token, I'm not a cruel man, not at all. And it strikes me you have had no concrete proof of the existence of Miss Devlin's so-called lost writings—some of her other belongings, clothes and such, I fear, have fallen prey to moths and insects and had to be disposed of. Now only her writings survive, but for such as us, what else is there, really?"

Reaching into his pocket, the poet said, "I retained this single article as proof of their existence and as a meaningful gesture of trust and agreement. It is also an unabashed enticement, of course. And you may also choose to regard this as an apology of sorts, if you will, for this further inconvenience and terrible, regrettable test of your patience."

He slid a small, black notebook across the table to Hector.

The novelist's heart raced: He'd seen similar books of its size and manufacture in Key West—it was a favorite notebook brand of Brinke's. He reached across the table with a trembling hand and slid the book toward himself.

He opened to a page and—*yes*, by God! It *was* Brinke's handwriting—no doubt about any of that.

Kaneko said, "Put it away, now, I beg you. Our friend is returning."

Hector searched Tiger's face, and said, "Whose side exactly are you on?"

He got a shrug in return, then Tiger said quickly, quietly, "Ian and Dikko are my friends. But Japan is my motherland, and this man is one of our finest poets and a man of great conscience and wisdom. Now, hide the journal, Lassiter."

Hector did that, feeling like it was the world's largest sum of found money, and one eager to burn a hole in his pocket. He wanted nothing more than to excuse himself immediately to the restroom to begin reading the book. But he knew instinctively that once he cracked its spine, he'd simply *have* to read through to its end.

Kaneko said quietly, urgently. "You *will* go to Istanbul then? You will meet with my friend, Mr. Shaw, who will give you the other journals, as well as the manuscript for Miss Devlin's lost novel?"

Hector's blue eyes narrowed. He said simply, "Of course. What choice do I have about any of that?"

The night dragged infuriatingly on. Ian began pressing the poet harder on the issue of the microfilm's present whereabouts, and, for Hector's sake, the present whereabouts of Brinke Devlins' writings.

The poet deflected, saying only that he'd placed his trust in a kind of cutout who would make both of these answers known to the poet in the course of time, when things had again convincingly cooled down. Kaneko would, when circumstances at last seemed right, then and only then pass along word to Ian and Hector about where the goods could be collected.

Clearly angered, Ian turned to Hector and said, "I'm really dreadfully ashamed at how calamitously I've quite failed you in all of this old man. I'd trusted this brother writer to be a man of honor, however—"

Impugning Kaneko's honor was a bridge too far, so to speak—and a terrible breech of Japanese etiquette. In Western terms, it was roughly equivalent to grounds for a duel.

Ian seemed to catch himself and immediately began to back-pedal. "That was off-sides," he said quickly. "I—"

Tiger quickly raised a hand and said, "The sake has simply drunk the man and claimed his tongue. I'm sure Mitsuharu knows that, too."

The poet bowed and said, "It's late, none of us are young anymore, and so it's time we took our parting before true offense might be given or taken."

Alone in a cab together, a clearly exhausted Ian said thickly, "I'm so sorry this blew to pieces, Hector. I'm terribly sorry none of this panned out. Part of me thinks we should follow Mitshharu home and use more vigorous means to impel him to cooperation. If you want to do that, it's the least I can do in penitence. I'm game, dear fellow."

Hector restlessly rubbed a thumb over the journal in his pocket.

He said softly, "I don't think that poet is any more effectively in control of matters than we've ever been, buddy. You had a phrase in *Casino Royale* I've always been taken with—something about being 'carried away by the gale of the world.' We shrug and soldier on."

"This was a terrible bust," Ian said bitterly. "Ashes on all fronts."

Not from where Hector stood. He was burning to say his goodnight to Ian in the hotel lobby and then spend the night between the covers, so to speak, with Brinke's writings— whatever their subject.

An hour later, after a quick, hot shower and a call downstairs for a bottle of red wine, Hector at last settled down in bed with Brinke's journal.

He took a deep, calming breath and then turned the first page.

It was dated February, 1924. It appeared to be Brinke's *in situ* journal of their love affair's early-going arc. Its first page had been recorded the morning after the night Hector and Brinke met and promptly became lovers.

It flowed forward from there, ending with her eventual passage into Japan to reunite with her old "friend and kind of spiritual mentor" Kaneko.

It wasn't fiction, by any stretch, of course. It was nothing that would ever be publishable in that sense, although it would represent a kind of gold mine if Brinke ever found a worthy biographer.

For Hector, it was an intimate, wrenching insight into his life love's view not just of the world, but of Hector Lassiter, the man and emerging novelist—long before the two became twisted up into the same strange thing in the eyes of the reading public.

For this one slim volume of Brinke Devlin prose, Hector was a most singular audience.

Throughout the book were studded first impressions of Hector in various settings—social, vengeful…passionate. These were the insights Brinke was having into Hector's character in the heady rush of their budding love affair. She had scribbled down countless bits of phrases of his, myriad casual but pungent asides… "Hectorisms" she called them.

She spent pages recording her impressions, sensations and memories of their early lovemaking. Her words brought Paris and their snowy, sleety first nights together with a terrible vividness that left him shaking.

The dreams he had that night about Brinke after closing the covers on the thin journal nearly swamped Hector.

He awakened at four in the morning, panting for breath and bathed in sweat. To put it in Ian Fleming terms, Hector was utterly shaken and stirred.

He ordered up some more black coffee and tried to write himself out of the inchoately panicked state in which he'd awakened.

Brinke's new words seemed to have returned her to him in a kind of half-life that deeply unsettled her widowed husband.

He vowed to find some pep pills to keep himself awake on the plane back to the States.

It would be unseemly waking up screaming on the flight after another too-vivid dream of Brinke.

Brinke's journal was constantly in his hand or his coat pocket. He could almost swear that it radiated a pulsing heat against his twitching thigh.

Goddamn Istanbul now seemed same as a lifetime away to Hector.

8

MURDER ON THE ORIENT EXPRESS (1963)

In the *Wasteland*, Ezra Pound's stiff-ass Brit acolyte T.S. Eliot asserted April to be the cruelest of the months.

It was the very month the James Bond production crew had picked to begin the filming in Istanbul of the second of the 007 films, *From Russia with Love*.

Between crowds of gawkers, incompetent local crews and a dying principal supporting actor, Eliot's April estimations seemed apt enough.

Things weren't going much better by the time authors Ian Fleming and Hector Lassiter arrived at the troubled film's set in June.

As he packed, Hector decided he should probably go armed from the get-go this time.

He'd managed to hold onto to his nifty, deadly Rolex and crazy flamethrower lighter, so those went into his much-traveled leather suitcase.

The CIA gun he'd managed to retain—something he could afford to lose—he hid away in a box of his own books that he shipped on to his intended hotel in Istanbul. The books were gifts to some of the filmmakers and actors with whom Hector was already acquainted.

Rather than travel directly to Turkey with Ian, Hector instead decided to treat himself to a kind of nostalgic idyll on his way to the Bond film set.

Ever since her journal fell into his hands, Hector had continued to be a haunted man.

Brinke was a nearly constant, palpable presence, still costing him sleep and sufficient appetite to result in the need for new notch holes in his belt. The thought of the impact that several more volumes of new Brinke Devlin writing might have upon him left Hector with a deep sense of foreboding. Indeed, a couple of times, he nearly begged off the trip to retrieve the goods, fearing their probable toll on his health and sanity.

Yet, he couldn't do *that*—couldn't simply leave Brinke's lost prose dangling in the wind and to be lost when the venerable Japanese poet at last went to his reward.

So Hector flew first to Paris and spent a week there walking the city, visiting surviving haunts and hanging about spectral landmarks that probably held little or no meaning for anyone on earth now save Hector Lassiter.

Other, better known cultural and historical sites hadn't fared so very well, either.

Hector stood outside the former site of his favorite Parisian bookstore, Shakespeare and Co., and nearly wept.

His dear Sylvia Beach, librarian, bookseller, publisher, postmistress and boyhood crush, had passed in October at seventy-five.

Oh, Alice B. Toklas was still around at least, but Hector wasn't remotely prepared to open *that* uneasy door.

As he thought more about it, Hector realized hardly anyone from that time other than a certain too-wise Paris detective still stalked the earth. On his last night in Paris, still chasing ghosts and shared memories, Hector rang up Aristide Simon.

The two met for a pleasant dinner at a newish, smart place called *Le Relais de Venise*. They reminisced over fine red wine about Hemingway and Gertrude Stein and all the good old, long-gone days and the grand crimes the Frenchman had cracked since he and Hector last significantly crossed paths in the early 1930s.

Aristide was now frail and hunched and bald. He required the support of Hector's arm in addition to his cane in order to navigate the rain-slick streets of Paris after dinner.

As they were returning to the retired inspector's home, Aristide suddenly paused and gripped Hector's arm tighter.

The ancient detective said, "One thing that has haunted me to this day. Maybe you will do me the favor of at last shedding some telling light on this mystery. You insisted to me long ago that your friend—your lover—the Devlin woman, did not die in the Seine as I insisted that she certainly had. I scoffed then, much to my ensuing shame. I've long ago come around to your way of thinking about all of that. Please tell me this, Hector— did that woman in fact endure beyond February 1924? I'll confide that I hope so. She was remarkable, in her way."

Hector smiled and nodded. "She did survive. And she was also quite innocent of all you suspected her of having done. We met up again in February 1925 in south Florida." His smile then dimmed. "Sadly, she didn't live to see October 1925. She was killed by another. It happened in Cuba. Pardon my French, but fucking life imitated art."

A shaking veined hand was pressed to Hector's heart. Aristide patted Hector's breast and said, "And that is a terrible something you certainly know much about, this sometimes bloody intersection of life and the imagination."

Hector shrugged and said, "Anyway, nobody's ever really dead so long as we remember them. Isn't that how we comfort ourselves?"

Aristide just smiled thinly and shook his head. "Come, come, Hector—you truly ask that of a fellow cynic? Neither of us is that romantically deluded."

The grand old Orient Express—the actual train everyone thought about when confronted with that exotic, storied name—had shut down in 1962.

Now there was a train under the approximate brand name that made a twice-weekly run from Paris to Istanbul—the so-called "Direct Orient Express."

Hector sat in the dining car of that somewhat more humble train, quite alone and nursing a rum St. James, mostly for more stubborn, sentimental reasons.

He tapped the ash from his cigarette and drummed fingers on his just completed proof copy of Ian's *You Only Live Twice.* The novel's ending—and a certain contrived obituary for Ian's long-suffering hero—tantalized Hector.

Staring at his own ghostly reflection imposed over the darkening passing countryside, Hector braced himself for another nightly visitation by Brinke.

He thought about how things could flip on a dime. He marveled once again at the fact that where he'd once delighted in the renewed acquaintance, as he drew closer to this rendezvous with more of her writings, he had a mounting sense of dread—also one of profound exhaustion regarding Brinke Devlin.

He awakened each morning after his sleep-starved nights spent with dream Brinke feeling more depleted than he'd been when he'd crawled between the sheets.

He was continuing to lose weight and also the concentration critical to his writing because of sleep deprivation. The latter alarmed him the most, of course.

In a very real sense, this nocturnal Brinke with whom he verbally jousted, flirted with and, inevitably, *loved*, had become a kind of all-too-literal succubus—an honest to God life-force stealer.

Yet, it was his beloved Brinke, and so…?

Hector saw his dim and ghostly reflection in the glass reflexively shrug.

The dining car was nearly empty—just Hector, a couple of solitary drab gray men who looked like business travelers… there was a pregnant woman whose red hair spilled from under a rather unremarkable scarf as she sat facing away from Hector. When he looked up again, he saw someone had joined the mother-to-be—presumably her child, as Hector could only see the very top of the head of the little person at her side.

Yes, just these random, nondescript fellow passengers and a rather boisterous family of Turks who were settling up, and—a blessed turn—at last preparing to leave the dining car-lounge.

Once the rowdy family was gone, Hector figured on permitting himself a single glass of good red wine and breaking out his notebook to continue work on what he was increasingly coming to view as his last novel to appear under the Hector Lassiter byline—a *big book* he was toying with calling *Toros & Torsos*.

On this first night of his multi-night train journey, Hector calculated a solid two-thousand miles or thereabouts to get that book under something like control.

And, anyway, given his dread of sleep, he might as well spend that time here as in his private sleeper. Yes, that was the plan now that he thought more on it. He would just sit and watch the scenery roll by, all the while scribbling away and guzzling strong black coffee to stoke the creative fires until the sun came up.

A shapely shadow fell across his notebook. The hairs on the back of his neck rose. How many times had he lived this same scene? How many times had it ended darkly, tinged with eroticism and death?

His mind already went in that direction because of the decidedly hourglass proportions of the shadow passing over him.

Hector closed his just-opened notebook and slid his fountain pen back into his sports coat pocket.

The woman was tall and wickedly curvy—dark brown hair, dark brown eyes and a full, sensuous mouth. Her cheekbones were high and defined, and the faintest Cupid's bow up-tilt at the edges of her quite enticing upper lip lent her mouth the appearance a sort of perpetual sexy yet mocking half-smile.

At first glance, Hector put her age somewhere between forty and forty-five. Thinking of Haven Branch and some others since, doing the math, Hector calculated he was at least a solid five years past being picked up in bars by women who didn't have some ulterior and inevitably dark motive.

On the other hand, that daunting notion of time spent alone in a sleeper berth with succubus Brinke left him feeling desolate and, yes, even reckless.

Yes, if this woman was indeed going to come on to him, it surely was some kind of put-up job, he told himself. But even if that was so, this evening's edition of reckless and slightly drunk Hector decided he was very much open to that gambit as the rails sang softly under them.

Game as he was for the game, Hector wasn't interested or patient enough to engage in the usual, too familiar dance and repartee, not for this trip to the well. This one time, he embraced the old filmmakers' axiom: "Get in late and get out early." No exposition, in other words; no dawdling.

He gestured she should slink into the seat opposite him. She did that, rather obediently, placing her arms on the tabletop and drawing them together at the elbows, deepening the enticing valley of tawny flesh between her generous breasts, so very much on display in a low-cut, black cocktail dress with gold trim that traced its dramatic, quite revealing neckline.

In New York or Paris the dress would have been plenty daring. Barreling toward Islamic Istanbul, it was positively scandalous.

Cutting off all the usual potential feints and opening lines, Hector rolled the dice and presumed he was already known to this middle-aged vixen.

He said, "I'm Hector Lassiter, author and screenwriter. I'm on my way to meet up with an old friend to observe some location work on the filming of one of his books and to lend a little quiet, off-the-books dialogue help for the script. I'm wagering you're here, not because you love my books, or have any real particular interest in me, but because somebody directed you my way. Is that so? There'll be no hard feelings for telling me I'm right about any of that, I swear." He gave her what he hoped would be regarded as a charming smile and searched her brown eyes.

Hector paused, holding up a hand to ensure her silence, and said, "A moment." He signaled to the waiter to refresh his drink and to bring one for his company.

Not even waiting for her to voice an order, Hector gave her another long, appraising look, then ordered her a glass of 1959 Barbaresco. He raised an eyebrow and was granted a sexy and bemused smile.

She spoke English with an Italian accent: "An excellent start, Mr. Lassiter. And, yes, I have been sent to, *er*...to meet you."

"Right, and now that much is out of the way," Hector said. "Or we have met in a way. I need to know your name, darlin'." He smiled, then added. "Parenthetically, that dress is really quite something. Your choice, or...?"

"All mine," she said. "As for my name, that is Vannina Anna Maria Bello. I'm an actress, though not a particularly popular one. Not yet, anyway. Do you speak Italian?"

"Not so much," Hector lied. "And I'll confess now I don't recognize your name or know your work." A sad smile. "I'm sorry for that."

"I, of course, know of *your* film background. It was frankly one of the appeals of being asked to approach you like this." She blushed. "I don't do this kind of thing as a sort of career, you know. If you were any other man, with any other background, we wouldn't even be talking now."

Hector nodded his understanding. "I'm sure we can do something to find you film work in the States if you get over there if that's your personal aim here in meeting me. I'm pretty confident I can make that happen. And you don't have to do anything more than you've already done to achieve that. I want you to be clear on that point—no strings."

She smiled politely at their waiter and accepted her glass. She sipped and said, "It's sublime. You certainly know wines."

Hector decided this one time to highlight his age. "I've had a long time to practice, to research."

She sipped more of her wine then said, "I really don't know who I'm working for—if you can even call it that—nor what they want, exactly. This was a kind of coincidence, I suppose. A happenstance. I *happened* to be on the train, and I *happened* to be approached to approach you. There was nothing more asked of me than that. There were no…" she struggled, looking for the right word. She bit her lush lip, then settled on, "There was nothing *untoward* asked of me. I'd have said no if that was an expectation. I'm no prostitute, Mr. Lassiter."

Hector smiled and said, "I'm *so* glad. And, frankly, I'm a little afraid for you now, darling. A lot of bad people are interested in me and my little trip to Istanbul. They are the most insidious kind of people. The sort that would have no hesitation about using a fetching beauty like yourself as a sort of disposable tool. You should know that up front."

He lit a cigarette and looked around the dining car. He didn't see anyone who seemed to be watching them. He said, "Well, for better or worse, you've made contact now, my darling Vannina. So now the next step will soon be asked of you, somehow, some way, I'd wager."

"Why would so many people care about your trip to Istanbul, Mr. Lassiter?"

"Hector. And that's a very long and sordid story that wouldn't reward you with insight or anything that might help your mysterious employer who isn't an employer in your eyes. If there is any such thing in this kind of mess, just know I'm on the side of whatever passes for angels. Anyone who isn't on my side is on that of the Devil. That's simply my point of view, of course, but it's not open for debate. Tell me now, how was this approach to approach me engineered, exactly? Who hired you just to say hello?"

"A woman at the station, just before we boarded. I was told I would be paid five-hundred dollars, American, simply to strike up a conversation with you. Anything after that was strictly to remain my business. I took the money, very confused, but frankly very excited to meet a man with your film connections. You know—not to have to go the casting couch way. I took the offered compensation and I didn't look back. It's kind of found money, you might say."

"That's all very strange," Hector said. "We need to talk more, of course. This woman, was there anything remarkable about her? Anything worth remarking upon?"

"No. She was tall. A little overweight, maybe. She wore a long black coat and a black hat with a veil. I never saw her face. She didn't offer a name and I didn't ask."

God, Hector thought. She was clearly daft to take the strange deal. And, she was also likely utterly disposable in whoever's eyes, just as he'd said.

And a slightly portly woman handler? That made no particular sense—certainly it couldn't have anything official at its back.

Hector supposed that just because Béla Herczog was baked bones in the sour gut of the world by now it didn't mean the surviving Black Dragons might not press on without their Hungarian demon's head.

But could even that bunch really know his reason for coming to Istanbul? He'd been left alone, after all, between Japan and now.

Of course, it could simply be the fact he was reuniting with Ian that might reignite fresh interest. That proximity might give certain obsessed types freshly hopeful and foul ideas, he supposed.

What was Ian's turn of phrase for that very variety of phenomenon? Oh, yes: "Nothing propinques like propinquity."

Hector said, "I'm not tired, and in fact I'm more than a bit hungry, again. So I'm going to presume to order us a light dinner. Over the course of that meal, I really need you to think hard about your next steps, Vannina. You need to think about that as if your life depends upon it, because I suspect it very well might. The fact you have no clue whom you're working for just now indicates to me it has to be someone malignant—intent on covering tracks."

She shivered a little as that last sunk in.

Hector got out another cigarette. She reached across and presumed to take one for herself. Hector lit hers and his own. He said, "Whatever is to come, it's something that bodes nastily for both of us, pretty Vannina. Of that much, I'm all but certain. Oh, and I'll confess now that I do know more than a bit of Italian."

He smiled and raised his glass. "I'll make this simple pitch now that you're best to throw in with me and to put all your trust in me, tonight. When dinner is over, if you're convinced otherwise, we'll shake hands and then retire to respective corners." He smiled, took her hand and leaned across the table to kiss it. "And, after that, well, let the Devil take the hindmost, yes?"

"And my alternative?"

"Wait and see what otherwise develops," he said gravely. A shrug, then, "*A mali estremi, estremi rimedi.*"

Vannina gradually seemed to warm to a still unresolved alternative.

More wine, some small talk of Italy…. A lot of back-and-fourth about Hollywood and screenwriting. At least that chit-chat left him with the strong sense she was exactly what she claimed—an aspiring actress.

She also really knew his novels—but in translation.

The train was slowing as it rolled into some in-between–bigger-places station. Being so far from his destination, Hector simply wasn't paying much attention to the train's pace and progress up to this point. This stop was just another bygone place he'd never see or know; one where some would get off, while others got on the train.

But somewhere already on this train, Hector had decided, was this fetching and unfortunate creature's would-be "controller," to resort to the sordid language of the spy trade.

But now, if Vannina was known to have made contact with him, perhaps others would be boarding the Express along the way.

Freshly assessing their company in the dining car—he dismissed the pregnant woman with her back facing him as well as two of the three presumed businessmen, instead settling on the possibility of one gray-haired, solitary man who seemed very much alone—Hector said softly, "There must have been some kind of protocol for the next step once you met me. What was that? A particular compartment you were to call on, or…?"

She nodded emphatically, dark hair brushing her bare shoulders. "Not at all," she said. "I suppose they meant to watch and then contact me. Maybe they're watching even now."

To her credit, she didn't look around to confirm that fact. Indeed, Vannina seemed properly wary and so she instinctively played it just as cool as Hector would have counseled her to under the circumstances.

Ian had once written in his one of the Bond books—was it the Russian one?—there's always something exciting going on aboard the Orient Express.

Vannina gave him a long, hard look, then said, "There's fear in yours eyes—fear for me, I think. I should never have gotten on this train, and I certainly never should have agreed to sit down with you, should I? You're weren't kidding about any of that, were you?"

"No," Hector said. "You certainly shouldn't have done either of those things." A sad smile. "But how could you really know?" He reached over and closed a hand over hers. "That's just spilt milk now. *Acqua passata non macina più.* And hell, hindsight's *always* twenty-twenty, isn't that right? You know the old American cliché? What would it be in Italian? *Col senno di poi è venti venti*, yes?"

Her pretty face took on a grave expression. "I really am in danger now, aren't I? The more you joke and try to talk around it, the more I begin to fear it's even worse than I can imagine."

Hector weighted responses and settled on, "You have a compartment of your own?"

"Couldn't afford it."

"Then I'm going to be bold. Let's collect your things, and get you moved into my cabin. I have a private compartment with a spare bunk. Again, this carries no strings. The bed will be yours and at least you'll be safe behind locked doors." He smiled again and added, "And I swear I don't snore." The smile took on a certain edge. "Or so I've always been told."

"And then…? It's a long way to Istanbul, which is where I'm going." A funny smile. "More luck, good or bad, I suppose—as you say it's your destination, too. But my hope was to go there to try and get some work on the new Bond film. Again, it seems my meeting you is a kind of *kismet* in the parlance of the place we're headed."

"Then I simply insist that we're going to remain inseparable, at least until Istanbul," Hector said, taking her hand. "You're just going to have to put up with my constant companionship. We'll keep it room service going forward. My strategy is this: If we can get you to Istanbul, and if we eventually part ways there, well, then your agreement or pact with these people, whoever they are, is likely voided because I think whatever interest they have in me is firmly tied to that city. It makes tactical sense to me to do what I've proposed to you."

There were other tactics involved, of course, at least from Hector's end. Someone wanted the two of them to meet, only that much was clear. Hector decided it best just to facilitate all that and force whatever crisis might lay in wait.

Vannina thought about it and said, "Yes, it makes sense, to me, too." To her credit, she said it with an uncertain smile.

On their way back to Hector's compartment, they stopped to collect Vannina's things. As he hefted her suitcase—really more of a footlocker—and remarked on its weight, she wrinkled her nose and shot him a look. "Surely it's not *that* heavy," she said.

Hector would beg to differ but lugged the thing down the narrow common aisle. With a last look around to make certain nobody saw, he opened the door to his compartment and stowed her big suitcase in a corner. The bulky thing took up precious real estate in the compartment.

Before they'd left the dining car, under the guise of settling their bill, Hector had arranged for caviar and a bottle of chilled champagne to await them in his compartment.

Smiling at the surprise and holding one finger up, Vannina said, "Can we abandon at least one pretense now?"

Hector smiled back and set to work on the cork. "Oh, I'm forever and always in favor of *all* abandoned pretenses," he said, wondering what she was getting at. "It's practically my religion." He smiled and said, "Of what, precisely, are we letting go in this case?"

The cork gave with a loud pop that sounded a little like a gunshot and gave her a start.

Collecting herself, she nodded at the bottom bunk. She wrapped her arms around his neck and kissed him hard, taking charge. Briefly pulling away, panting, she said, "I've *always* hated sleeping alone."

They actually made love in the upper berth—it rode far smoother than the lower, where they had fleetingly started out tangled in one another's arms.

In the afterglow, over champagne and caviar on toast, Hector pushed for more answers:

Again, how exactly *were you approached to approach me?*

Please try hard and provide to me every *detail or remembered scrap about that mysterious woman who made the pitch for you to introduce yourself.*

Vannina's reflections and efforts didn't provide any new data to chew on. So they shared some more champagne, then made love again.

After, feeling a bit crowded—her generous breasts were a happy problem in the narrow bunk—Vannina migrated to the lower berth.

Hector was vaguely aware of her doing that. He was at last properly exhausted from making love to a flesh and blood woman after too many weeks—hell, call it for what it really was, too many *months*—of Brinke taking him in his increasingly troubled dreams. This one time, he thought he might really sleep in peace.

Hector rolled over toward the wall and the soothing welcome of the greater darkness to be found there. He'd have preferred a proper bed—king or queen size that would have allowed him to at least reasonably spoon up against a warm, nude Vannina, pushing further away Brinke's randy ghost, if she still somehow proved persistent on this increasingly rare real-world carnal night.

As sleep was at last claiming him, Hector thought he heard the soft squeak of hinges.

He didn't think much about that as he remembered locking and twice checking the compartment door, but now, fully roused, he felt impelled to roll over onto his left side.

Jostling around, trying to be quiet, Hector turned in his narrow cot, tucking his right arm under his pillow—an ancient habit. Usually, he kept his gun under there, but of course his weapon presumably awaited him in Istanbul. For now, all he had was a trick lighter and a watch and they were not on his very naked person.

Hector gradually started to drop off again, then the squeak of hinges again pricked up his ears. The cabin door was securely bolted as he'd already assured himself—of exactly that much Hector was certain.

The window was certainly no option for entry.

Another soft but steady squeak. *What the hell* was *it?*

Hector opened his eyes, letting them adjust to the dark. In the light through the window—the moon casting its light over the silent countryside—Hector realized that Vannina's big, heavy suitcase was now partly open.

Maybe Vannina had gotten up, taken some things from the case and gone to the compartment's little lavatory?

But then Hector realized the suitcase was actually *still creaking open.*

In a cold, dawning realization fired by the terrible implication of the suitcase's undeniable movement, Hector wished he had a gun. His armpits were damp with tension.

Stingy moonlight on metal emerging from the suitcase—light glancing off of some kind of gun, Hector supposed, characteristically leaping to the worst-case scenario.

The suitcase wasn't that large—it could only house a monkey, or a child, surely.

Then it clicked:

Or a *dwarf.*

Guns were the great equalizer, regardless of one's size, of course.

Even a little man would be lethal if he brought a firearm into play in such cramped space as Hector's train compartment, this tight little space heavily scented with sex, caviar and champagne.

His mind racing, Hector understood it all too clearly—the idea was *never* to use Vannina in any significant sense beyond simple sex. Her role had simply been to gain access to Hector's compartment in pretty much the manner that had unfolded.

They—whoever they were this time—were again using Hector's reputation as a womanizer against him.

Impulsively, Hector hurled himself off the bunk and slammed squarely atop the nearly wide-open suitcase. It was a kind of calculated risk in that he had no way of knowing in which direction the gun might end up pointing upon the moment of impact. It struck Hector as a fifty-fifty proposition: he'd be shot, or he would not.

Six-foot-two, one-hundred-ninety-pound Hector landed squarely atop the suitcase, slamming the lid down with a terrific thump that fleetingly stirred Vannina. Possibly she would have awakened at that moment—probably she would have—but the train plunged into a tunnel at the very moment Hector thudded atop the case.

In every human throat, there is a precious, precarious bone called the hyoid. The little man's throat was positioned *just so* as the luggage lid's edge found the emerging little man's throat.

Hector lay still atop the case and listened to the dying little person inside—he dearly hoped it wouldn't prove to be a child, some other innocent like Vannina lured into bloody intrigue.

Sweating, Hector held his breath, awaiting the telltale death rattle of whoever or whatever had hidden inside the big trunk.

When the last rattle came and then quickly went, Hector rose. Vannina sighed and stirred again as the train left the tunnel and the moonlight again lightly illuminated the compartment. Hector fleetingly took a perverse pride in having knocked her out sufficiently to sleep through their tiny intruder's rough dispatching.

Then he remembered the little corpse still in her suitcase and the smiled died on his lips.

Hector opened the luggage and indeed found a very tiny, very dead little man inside. The tiny corpse looked very much like a discarded ventriloquist's dummy but it had a five o-clock shadow; at least, he consoled himself, he hadn't killed a child.

Patting down the little man's pockets, Hector found a wallet. At first glance, there was nothing terribly useful inside other than a fat roll of currency. Found money.

The train briefly entered another tunnel, then shot out the other side and the dim light again returned. Hector looked the little man over again—he wore a child's-size black suit and patent leather shoes, but his gun was a man's-size forty-five. Hector recovered three spare clips from the little man's left-hand pocket. At least now he would be adequately armed heading into Istanbul, he assured himself.

If the little man had friends on the train—and he surely must—Hector's advantage against them had just sharply improved.

In another pocket he found several small listening devices that had peel-away adhesive tape strips on their backs.

This, Hector decided, had been the little man's *real* aim: to get inside Hector's compartment, then festoon the cabin and Hector's belongings—the things he'd be most apt to carry around on his person—with myriad bugs.

The little man's dead glassy eyes accused Hector. The moonlight through scudding clouds almost gave them a kind of malignant, flickering life of their own.

Disgusted, the author looked around and then tried the window. It wouldn't open far enough to accommodate the disposal of an adult body, but he decided their would-be assassin would just slide through the gap.

Hefting the little dead man, Hector slid the little spy through the window's crack, then gave him a hard shove out into the cold night.

Hector made a sour face and tried to keep his imagination in check—trying very hard not to visualize what the little man would probably look like after going under the wheels.

The cold air whipping through the window at last awakened Vannina. Pulling the sheets over her bare chest, she said, "Is something wrong, darling?"

"Just letting in a little fresh air. Feeling like a late night drink. You'll come?"

After a shared bottle of wine, they at last returned to his compartment.

Along the way to the dining car and back, Hector had attached the half-dozen or so little bugs to corridor walls and the underside of a serving cart being pushed along the aisle by a blue-suited attendant. He'd adhered them to the coats of passing fellow riders and, after briefly excusing himself, even to the base of a common-access commode.

Just before she once more fell asleep in the bunk under him, a very sleepy Vannina asked huskily, "Do you really think you can find me some work on the new Bond picture, Hector?"

"Back home I can find you work, and for certain," he said. "As to the new 007 film? Suppose we'll have to see what pull Ian or I might have with Mr. Broccoli and Mr. Saltzman. You're beautiful. Bond is about beautiful women. This seems very much within reach to me."

As Hector was about to drowse off himself, he heard urgent, frantic voices outside the door.

Someone—a train official of some kind, he figured—said urgently, "How could we possibly have *lost* a passenger in motion? I don't *care* how small he is, he's not a child and so this isn't some silly game of hide-and-seek. Find him, damn it!"

Hector fell asleep with a wry smile on his face.

For once, blessedly, he didn't have a single dream of Brinke.

9

SOMETHING WICKED
THIS WAY COMES

Sean Connery, dressed in his immaculate gray Anthony Sinclair-tailored James Bond suit with pale blue shirt and black knit tie, nodded for another *bira*—a *beer*—and said to Hector in his juicy, Glaswegian Scots accent, "I've read your stuff, Mr. Lassiter. Much of what I've read I've quite loved. Let's say I can pry a little money out of these fat producers' pockets. If so, would you maybe option something to me? I have a novel or two of yours in mind. God knows I don't want to end up type-cast as this silly character for life. Your characters are much closer to the ground than Mr. Fleming's."

Hector tapped bottles of Bomonti with the cinematic version of Ian's James Bond and said, "By all means. Whenever and whatever you want, Sean. You should know up front, I have a ruthless maxim regarding any and all film options: my book, your movie. If your option money spends, I smile, shake hands, and get the hell out of your way. If the damned thing somehow miraculously comes out okay in the end, I'll deliriously say so to the press and raise a glass in tribute. If it's a dog, I maintain a respectful silence."

Sean smiled and said, "Very good! I do so appreciate a fellow professional. We're a dying breed."

Hector had been a week in Istanbul—this now shabby, threadbare ghost of Constantinople, as he thought of it.

It seemed all dust, blast furnace winds, hucksters and dodgy religion to Hector.

He'd hobnobbed with the Bond film producers, done a little uncompensated and un-credited script doctoring just for the hell of it and for free drinks.

He'd also nearly lost Vannina Bello in the very early going after a man with a knife came at them as they were exiting a seafood place along the Bosporus during a sight-seeing blitz.

It hadn't seemed at the time like anything remarkable—nothing tied to old unfinished business of one sort or another, nor to old enemies.

The attack hadn't even struck Hector as being credibly tied to the Flea Bomb in any way.

No, it had been—or so Hector had decided in the moment—a simple case of random street crime. It was just dumb bad luck that it was they who had nearly become victims. Happenstance, Hector told himself, that was all.

But Vannina's candid words in the wake of that attack cut close to bone: "I see now the journalists are maybe right about you and the collision between your life and the page, so to speak," she said bitterly, her chin trembling in fear. "If this is how things *always* are for you, then I can see now why you're still a bachelor...*and* a widower. This was all terrifying, yet you seem to take it almost in stride, even now. That leads me to believe it's *not* an uncommon thing for you. Now I fear that maybe you even savor this sort of thing."

It was an entirely sensible point of view, he had to confess that was so.

But, in the end, he soothed her into staying on with him, sharing his room and bed while waiting for an opportune moment to effect an introduction between Vannina and the Bond producers. He needed to do that much for her in recompense, he told himself.

But if things were somewhat rocky for Hector, they were far more tumultuous for the cast and crew of *From Russia with Love*.

The beloved Mexican actor Pedro Armendáriz—a man who once portrayed Pancho Villa—had been cast as James Bond's charismatic ally Kerim Bey, a large-living man who expected to "die from living too much."

He'd been chosen for the Bond film by director Terence Young at the passionate urging of the legendary American film director John Ford. It developed in time that Ford well-knew that Pedro was afflicted with cancer; Ford *didn't* know just how ill and he didn't share that tidbit with Young while angling to get his ailing friend a well-paying job to help see to medical bills.

The fact Pedro was *terminally* ill emerged only after the crew was deep into filming. The filmmakers rushed to complete the dying actor's scenes—actually propping Pedro up at later points—so he could finish the film and his family would be left precious money. For some wide shots or those involving walking, others stood in for the actor as a terrible, painful limp became more pronounced.

Doctors on the scene offered their grim opinion the actor had only days—maybe only hours left. It was a grim race against the clock to complete Pedro's character's doomed journey. At various points, even the director actually began to fill in for the dying Mexican actor.

Ian, who had arrived in Istanbul ahead of Hector, had purportedly bonded with Pedro, pretty much from the gates.

According to Connery—he confided it to Hector over some imported single malt one night shortly after the author reached Istanbul—Ian and the Latino actor had spent a long time talking candidly about Hemingway and the merits of his recent suicide. Their overheard talk deeply rattled those who'd witnessed the nakedly fatalistic exchange.

Armendáriz was quite approving of Papa's actions. Sean, somewhat frustratingly from Hector's perspective, couldn't account for Ian's take about any of that.

Shortly before Hector's arrival, Pedro had completed all the filming he could handle, then flew to Los Angeles where he was booked into the UCLA Medical Center for treatment of a rapacious cancer localized somewhere in the region of his hips.

On June 18, Armendáriz fatally shot himself in the chest with a gun he'd somehow smuggled into the hospital.

Upon learning the bitter news, Ian said, "Bravo."

For his part, hearing of Pedro's suicide by gunshot, Hector of course thought again of Ernest Hemingway. One way or another, all of Hector's roads seemed somehow always to lead back to Hem.

And on that grim note, there was also and quite depressingly the matter of Ian. He was dressed more casually this trip, favoring flannel or corduroy slacks and sweaters, but still smoking too much for a man with his damaged, dying heart. He still drank far too much, as well.

Ian looked *so* much worse to Hector's eyes than he had in Japan.

Hector kept hearing Dikko's voice drunkenly slurring the phrase "*Death in the face*, old boy. You see it, too, don't you? Don't you dare lie and say you don't, you bastard!"

Faced with so much morbidity—and finding Istanbul not so much to his liking—Hector instead focused like a laser on the actor and recently awarded novelist Robert Shaw. The English born but Celt-raised Shaw struck Hector as a kind of dissolute kindred.

It was clear to Hector writing was Shaw's great love. Acting was a kind of uneasy and perhaps even lamented means-to-an-end for the stocky thespian. The very embarrassment of acting—the need to strip oneself of every scrap of inhibition in order to achieve anything approaching an honest and therefore worthy performance—gave cover for Shaw's favored excuse to justify his undeniable and profligate alcohol abuse, Hector early decided.

Hector suspected it was also a bit of some tragic genetic predisposition to alcoholism plaguing Shaw. He thought that based on certain things the actor-novelist had confided about his alcoholic father's death.

Either way, Hector had made a point to ferret out and read Shaw's first two novels, particularly the recently award-winning *The Sun Doctor* after the Japanese poet Kaneko had confided that Shaw would be Hector's next link to Brinke's lost writings. As a result of that reading of the actor-novelist's work, Hector found himself—along with a few worthy critics—regarding Shaw as quite a serious fiction writer.

Since their first meeting, Hector had been toeing up to confronting Shaw directly about Brinke's writings.

But he'd had to wait to do that at a time when he was safely away from Ian.

So far, Hector was still weighing whether to betray his government's wishes and share the Flea Bomb spoils with Ian—which was, of course, essentially the same as sharing the thing with the British government.

Tonight, the actor and Hector were at last dining alone.

Not for the first time, Hector noted how Bob Shaw tended to draw looks from their fellow diners. Bob had been cast as the evil assassin and moon-driven killer Donovan "Red" Grant.

The producers had made the dark haired actor bleach his hair a ghostly blond-white—probably figuring the better to contrast with dark-haired (and toupeed) Sean.

In opposition to his role as a taciturn stone-cold killer, the real Bob Shaw struck Hector as a warm, smart and genial guy—at least that was so with the proviso that Bob didn't dive *too* deeply into his cups. Properly lubricated, Shaw could sometimes border on being an unpleasant companion.

Given Shaw's skills as a writer, Hector eventually pressed him for an explanation for his more noted acting career.

Bob, good-looking and very present in a brutish way, just smiled and said, "Let's face it, old man, there are hardly more than a hundred published novelists in England who can get up the price for a decent meal," he said. "Tell me that's not so. I'm sure you could say pretty much the same for American authors. You're in the lucky two percent, I'd wager—you know, the rare ones who can actually live on their writing."

Hector shrugged and said, "Hell, I can't deny it. Few enough manage to make a real go of it. So, I guess, I'll wish you to break a leg on this film."

Bob laughed and raised his glass for a tap against Hector's. He said, "This place is rather not to my tastes—Istanbul, I mean. Too busy. Too crowded. I'd prefer to be wandering the Highlands. Touring Ireland on a bike or something."

"I tend to agree," Hector said. He looked around and said softly, "When can we talk about Brinke's writings? When can we make that exchange?" Hector again despised the desperate edge he detected in his own voice.

Bob Shaw studied him with pale, steady blue eyes. He said after a time, "We'll do that when I know I can *safely* hand it off to you. I know enough to grasp what I'm entrusted with, old man. I will not have this thing on my conscience. I also know a good bit about all the terrible things that happened to you in Japan. I can't risk any repeat of that kind of thing and the loss of the goods. You follow?"

"I follow," Hector said quietly. "When you're good and ready, of course."

What else could he say?

Given Ian's determination to have the damned recipe for animal and plant death placed into British possession, Hector felt it best to test those very waters with the man currently holding the goods. After all, Fleming and Shaw were countrymen.

Hector said, "Have you been tempted to make a copy, or, rather, just to hand the thing over, straight away as the saying goes, to your own government?"

Bob gave him a hard look. Hector couldn't figure out what was going on behind the man's eyes. Eventually the actor said, sounding truly perplexed, "*My* government? Hell, I don't trust the English as far as I could throw the bastards. But let's give it a few days and make sure there are no unfriendlies around, okay?"

"Okay," Hector said. "Makes perfect sense." Hell, he'd waited *this* long.

The two men shared some local food and one too many drinks. Nearing the end of their meal, Hector asked, "How'd you come to know the Japanese poet, by the way?"

"Mutual writer friends," Bob said. "I'm a writer first, really, at least to my own mind if you haven't already gathered that. The acting, if anything, feels like a somewhat embarrassing way to make a living. It doesn't come easily or naturally to me, most times. I was talking about this very thing to Sean—he's a pretty bookish guy, by the way, but more of an autodidact. Sean and I come at it very differently." A frown. "I mean acting, you know." Hector knew.

After more talk of writing and acting, they set off back to the Hilton Hotel Istanbul—this modernist, grid-like high-rise hotel that seemed jarringly out of synch with the surrounding old city.

Hector towered over towheaded Bob, and it gave him certain advantages in spotting potential tails—but Hector saw no sign of anything like that as they made their way back to the Bond film company's present base of operations.

The following afternoon, over lunch, Hector at last effected an introduction between Vannina and Cubby Broccoli. Husky and ebullient Cubby promised to see that he would make something happen for the aspiring starlet. "After all," he said, smiling broadly, "it's a Bond film, and it's Bond's world we're just lucky enough to live in for a while. Pretty girls only need apply. And, anyway, you're a fellow *paisano*."

Later still, Hector and a now-giddy Vannina decided to walk off their lunch in the only slightly quietening Grand Bazaar, gaining access through the Nuruosmaniye entrance to the enclosed network of shops.

Vannina almost resisted making the trip with him, remembering their near street robbery of a couple days before, but eventually gave in. She was grateful to Hector for what she already regarded "my big break." Vannina pulled him close and said, "Thank you so much for this, Hector. Meeting Mr. Broccoli was more than a thrill. Perhaps even a life-changer."

"Window-shopping" as they wandered the Bazaar, they were besieged with myriad offers by peddlers willing to deal. One particularly insistent little man in one of the more luxurious quarters of the place made heroic efforts to interest him in one of his lavish oriental rugs.

It was full-court press on the part of the vendor, and Vannina didn't help matters by too nakedly fawning over the man's exotic wares.

Hector more practically emphasized the fact they were tourists, and, anyway, he lived in a desert and the rugs, beautiful as they were, would clash.

The man wouldn't take Hector's no for an answer and instead focused all efforts on Vannina. After several moments of his hardsell, she finally squeezed in, "I don't have a place of my own." She smiled and shrugged and said, "No floor."

The man looked defeated for perhaps three seconds, then beamed, showing two gold front teeth and produced a small mahogany box with a flourish. He opened the box to reveal a tangle of gold necklaces, broaches and rings.

They were clearly hand-made and Hector knew enough about precious metals to know they weren't knocks-off of some kind. He picked through the offerings and held up a golden pin—a bucking horse. "I was a cavalry officer a lifetime ago. So this seems like luck to me. "You okay with this?"

Vannina held it in her hand and said, "A little too cowboys and Indians for me." She seemed fascinated by a particular golden bracelet her hand drifted to more than once.

Hector picked it up and haggled a bit, eventually agreeing to the purchase.

She kissed him hard on the mouth and thanked him for the gift.

Hector took her arm and led her deeper into the Bazaar. He stopped to buy them both a Turkish tea, hoping to chip away at least a bit of his current mild state of intoxication. He really must cut back on the *raki*, he chided himself.

After they'd finished their tea, they linked arms and began to grope their way back toward the entrance, aiming for a return to the hotel.

Smiling up at him, she said, "Are you certain you don't want to detour for a little boat ride on the Bosphorus first?"

"I'm sure," Hector said. "We have *other* options, don't we?" He pressed his fingertips more firmly and familiarly against the small of her back.

"Oh, yes, *those*." A cunning smile.

They stepped back out into the light. There was immediately the returning sound of bustle outside the market. Their eyes struggled to adjust to the light.

A motorcycle gunned its engine, then there was a single loud crack that chased birds from the surrounding trees.

Vannina stumbled, then turned and placed both hands on Hector's shoulders, nearly tripping him as he bumped against her, chest to chest.

She searched his face, her chin trembling.

Vannina tried to form a word—his first name perhaps, Hector thought, even as his hands wrapped around her trim waist to give her support.

Something slick and warm reached his hands. She looked down between her breasts, which prompted Hector to do the same. There was a spreading crimson stain.

She collapsed in his arms as he screamed out for somebody to call for an ambulance.

Vannina was dead long before any help arrived.

The police had been a *different* challenge and on several levels, of course—it took some time just to find an English speaking detective.

After three hours in police custody, Hector was at last released to Ian and Bob Shaw, whom he'd called when at last permitted the use of a phone.

It seemed the would-be actress had been killed by a single shot from a rifle, probably fired directly across the street from the entrance to the Grand Bazaar.

Ian said, "Who would do that? And why?"

Hector shrugged. "I have no idea as to who. And regarding the why?" He shared another shrug.

Bob shot Hector a look, but held his tongue.

When he at last returned to the Istanbul Hilton, it was a very lonely room and one filled with piercing reminders of Vannina: there sat her luggage; over there her other things, scattered carelessly across the bathroom countertop—lipstick and perfume…a never-to-be-needed-again toothbrush.

The phone rang. Hector scooped it up and said, "Yes?"

It was a male voice, with a slightly familiar accent. It said low and teasing, "It could as easily have been *your* heart that stopped its beating tonight, Mr. Lassiter. You might have been the one my sniper killed. If the microfilm should come into your possession, and if you fail to give it to me, it will most certainly be your heart, next time. Yours, and perhaps Mr. Fleming's… Maybe the hearts of a few of your new moviemaker friends. Maybe the heart of Mr. James Bond himself. Imagine the sensation and hullabaloo that would spring from *that* audacious act."

Biting his lip until he tasted blood, Hector said softly, "Finding the microfilm isn't in the cards this trip. That's ancient history. But let's pretend some miracle somehow occurs to that end. How do I find you to let you know?"

"No need for that. I'm *watching*. I still have eyes and ears, even here. If—no, let's say *when*—the time comes, I will assuredly find you."

The man at the other end of the phone hung up.

Hector racked the receiver and, cursing to himself, still numb from Vannina's murder, walked to the picture window, staring out at the night lights of Istanbul.

He thought of Vannina even as he braced for another nocturnal visit from Brinke.

That, he somehow knew, was inevitable on this dark and bloody night.

Maybe they'd both come to him in dreams this night. Maybe they'd do that this night, and all his nights going forward.

10

BRINKE OF DESTRUCTION

The street was the usual flurry of vendors, hawkers and shady characters.

The longer Hector stayed in the crumbling, cramped confines of the former Constantinople, the more he realized its deteriorating, shadowy streetscape stoked a festering sense of paranoia.

It was a city seemingly made for spies and intrigue.

Hector mixed in a little more water and sipped his anise-flavored *raki* while fitfully reading Ambler's *A Coffin for Dimitrios*. He wasn't sure why it had taken so long for him to get to this particular Ambler—particularly given its author protagonist and his similarities to Hector (*God, even that surname…?*).

But other factors conspired to disrupt his concentration upon what Hector thought to be a very fine novel and a clear inspiration for *The Third Man*.

The novelist looked up from the book about another novelist and at last spotted Bob Shaw making his way across the narrow, busy street.

Bob had a black attaché case gripped in his left hand. He might have been taken for some kind of European business traveler but for the fact he was dressed rather more like a London dock hand on this off-set day.

Hector stared at that case, his pulse quickening.

There couldn't be very much in there, of course.

There would be the holograph of the novel whose existence the poet Mitsuharu Kaneko had confirmed to Hector.

Maybe there were would be two or three more journals or diaries—hardly more than that seemed possible. Although Brinke was certainly prolific—nearly as prolific as Hector— she hadn't been *that* long in Japan for her last visit, after all.

Forcing his attention from the briefcase, Hector searched the streets for signs of anyone possibly trailing the pale-haired actor-novelist.

So far, nobody struck Hector as remarkably suspicious.

Indeed, for three days, Hector and Bob had established this exact pattern of meeting for lunch over drinks—bolstering a façade of having at last found a particularly pleasing restaurant they'd chosen to make their haunt.

Ian, dubious about the place, nevertheless dutifully tagged along each day with Hector.

Ian enjoyed talking with Bob about writing and his lonely time spent growing up with his alcoholic doctor father and nurse mother on Scotland's blustery Isle of Orkney.

This time, Ian for some reason decided to at last remark upon Shaw's briefcase. By design, Shaw had also carried the briefcase with him the past few days so it, too, wouldn't seem anything particularly remarkable, this most important of times.

Only Bob and Hector knew that on those previous trips the case was empty by precaution.

This day, however, the attaché case was supposed to contain "the bloody goods" as Bob described them.

Fixing a new smoke to his ebony cigarette holder, Ian said, "That damned attaché case again. My God, have you heard our thespian's reasoning for toting the thing around constantly like that?"

Hector said softly that he didn't.

"Well, I confronted him about it finally last night over some rather disappointing *Çiğ köfte*. It seems Mr. Shaw now *always* means to carry it about. When I called him on it last evening, he muttered something about staying in character— that horrid phrase. He said it's Red Grant's constant companion as he tracks Bond through Istanbul and so it must remain Shaw's constant accessory in order to inform his 'performance with the proper verisimilitude.' I swear those were his exact words."

Ian sniffed and looked dumfounded. "It's rather too like your pretentious young American actors and their so-called ghastly 'method' approach to acting. I'm horrified to think that vogue might be taking hold among British actors, too. Haven't you Americans done enough damage to Western culture already?"

"Appalling," Hector said, distracted, hoping it would be taken as convincing commiseration. "Unthinkable, really." Still no sign of any unfriendly sorts, at least not street-side.

So far, Hector had kept Ian in the dark regarding his hoped-for imminent retrieval of Brinke's writings—the precious parcel that would also freight the malignant strip of microfilm so precious to all those evil sorts full of infernal and passionate intent.

Hector drew a deep breath of relief as Bob at last entered the *kebapcı*. Now the zone of risk was limited to the inside of the establishment. Hector had already scoped his fellow diners and detected nothing to give any kind of pause.

As Bob closed the door behind himself, nobody rose or rushed to intercept the blond actor—there was no scramble by anyone to clutch at the case he carried.

Smiling and nodding as he spotted Hector, Bob weaved through tables to their booth and placed the case on the floor between his feet, gripping it between the toes of his shoes, then sat down and eyed Hector's drink with a kind of covetous drinker's glare that Hector had seen in the eyes of so many writer friends in bars and taverns the world over.

Smiling, Hector said, "I took the liberty of ordering up a fresh round of *raki* for three. Should be arriving momentarily, buddy."

Grinning, the actor clapped Hector's shoulder and said, "You're one of the really good ones, Hec. But hell, you already know that, don't you?"

As the actor said that, something bumped the tip of Hector's shoe. He realized that Bob had toed the attaché case under the table to Hector. Shifting his feet, Hector closed both toes of his shoes against either side of the attaché case and completed its journey under his chair. He clasped his ankles tightly against it.

It required a real act of will on Hector's part to refrain from settling the tab on the spot—from making his excuses and bolting off to the Istanbul Hilton to hole-up with Brinke's writings.

Then Hector remembered the kind of energizing and sustaining force that single slim journal given him in Japan had seemingly instilled in succubus Brinke.

What would *several* new volumes result in when it came to her potency to cost him sleep and peace of mind?

Suddenly, some time spent slumming with his fellow writers and some *raki* or *kırmızı şarap*—red wine—to wash down some *iskender kebap*, seemed strangely appealing.

What did that imply?

And did he *really* care what it meant as he frankly feared for himself because of phantom Brinke's deepening hold upon him.

The fresh round of *raki* and a pitcher of water—*su*, as Hector now knew it was called here—arrived.

Going a bit stingy on the water, Bob raised his glass and said, "*Şerefe!*" and shot-gunned his first drink. He nodded at Ian and said, "Or, in deference to your recently revealed to be half-Scottish spy, *Slàinte.*"

Ian just smiled thinly. It was left for Hector—who'd frequently spent a month or two most years since the last war vacationing the Highlands and fishing its lochs to respond, "*Do dheagh shlàinte.*" Ian said, "As a matter of fact, I intimated Bond's Scottish roots all the way back in *Live and Let Die*. You may remember I wrote—"

There was a commotion at the door of the restaurant.

Five men dressed in matching black pants, long-sleeved turtlenecks and black ski masks crowded in, brandishing Kalashnikovs.

Hector groaned as a sixth man, dressed in the same manner but taller and thinner than the rest, strode in behind them. He carried a simple forty-five in his black-gloved right hand.

Three of the men with the automatic rifles ordered all of the diners but Hector and his companions to rise and move to a rear party room where they would be held "without harm if cooperation is offered." The wait staff and bartender were also ordered into the back.

Most rose to comply. A lone pregnant woman at a corner table didn't do that. She had raggedy red hair and wore thick-lensed glasses. Something about her spoke to Hector, but he couldn't put his finger on it, beyond vague memories of Vannina speaking of having been paid by a portly—perhaps actually a pregnant?—woman to approach Hector on the train to Istanbul.

The pregnant woman moved to join the men.

It clicked suddenly as some straggling or infirm diners, all of them tutting, some of them weeping in fear, moved to the back room to be held hostage.

Ian cursed sharply. Robert Shaw looked to Hector and said, "We've cocked it up good. God, but I'm truly sorry for this."

Ian looked puzzled. Hector's mind was racing, reaching for angles, strategies. He eyed the tall man with the forty-five gripped in his hand and said, "So, who the hell are you, Stretch?"

The stranger said, "I'm the man you thought you killed several months ago," the stranger said quietly. "You murdered my strong right arm and strategic doppelganger, so to speak. A hard man to replace, but not the real article, Mr. Lassiter."

Ian said softly, "Béla Herczog...."

"Just so," the tall, masked man said bowing ever so slightly.

Hector turned his attention to the pregnant woman. "This medusa with you—I have a theory. "Why don't you shed the wig, sugar? It *is* Haven under all that war paint and rouge, right?"

Haven slid off her wig, revealing her black hair and said, "Just so, darling. I am very sorry, Hector, but you know what this means to me. Turn over the case, and we'll find the film and let you keep your wife's precious writings. I promise if you cooperate and do that you'll leave here with all you really came for."

The real Herczog shot her a look. "*No*. No, that is not how we proceed. I have no way of knowing if there's been subterfuge. We take it *all*. If this man resists, shoot the actor first. If he still resists, kill the English thriller writer. God knows he's not long for the world anyway."

Hector looked at his friends, dry-mouthed, his big and usually steady hands trembling.

Shaw was bearing up well enough. Ian seemed not to have registered the death threat. Instead, his eyes accused Hector. He said venomously, "Are you telling me you were here to receive the Flea Bug manuscript and you were going to do it under my very nose, Hector? I thought we were friends! I thought we were *allies*."

A soft, sad chuckle. Her gun pointed between Hector and Ian, Haven Branch said, "Poor, poor raggedy old Ian. I have real affection for you, I really do. But based on intercepts, I'll tell you what Hector never would. To his credit, he would do that precisely because he's your true friend, but also every bit as much a loyal, proud American as you are English, Mr. Fleming.

"Hector's under orders to keep the Flea Bomb out of British hands with the same zeal he'd keep it from Russia or Red China," Haven continued. "The so-called 'special relationship' is on the rocks if not outright dead. Burgess, Maclean and now Kim Philby—yes, the former head of British Intelligence once based in this very city in the 1940s— is a defector, too. They are only the tip of a terrible iceberg, dear Ian. MI5 and MI6 are a Soviet sieve, and the Americans well know it. From the Americans' point of view, handing the Flea Bomb to you is the same as handing it straight to Russia. I'm saying that so that Hector doesn't have to." Another sad smile. "I'd hate to come between old friends."

Ian was left desolate at a stroke.

Hector glared at Haven. His gaze strayed from her smoldering black eyes to her torso. He said, "That bump part of the disguise, too?"

Haven shook her head with a mocking smile. "No, it's all too real. How's your math, Hector?"

He grew cold all over, inchoately and immediately accepting the unmistakable implication of her statement. Their child was inside her. He tried to get his head around that and found he really couldn't.

Well, anyway, he could hardly kill her now, could he? But the others? They were a different story, if he could only find the opportunity.

Béla Herczog held up a gloved hand. He said to Hector, "Your friend's lives hang in the balance, Lassiter. Hand over briefcase now, please. If you cooperate, and if you do so cheerfully, perhaps I will see about having the Devlin woman's writings sent 'round to you eventually—through *channels*, of course—once I'm convinced they hold no secrets of value to me."

Hector nodded. He held up his hands and said, "I'm going to reach into my right pocket now, very slowly. Just getting my lighter, and some cigarettes."

Haven said, "It will calm his nerves. Let him do that." As if to bolster her position in vouching for him, she moved her aim from between Ian and Hector, pointing the barrel of her gun squarely at Hector's forehead. "We can trust him to do that much."

Not waiting for Herczog to assent, Hector reached into his pocket and pulled out his pack of Pall Malls and both of the lighters in his pocket. He obscured the one given him so long ago by Burton in his left hand while lighting his cigarette with his Hemingway gifted Zippo that he then placed on the table in full view of the armed men.

Hector said to Herczog, "You said that one-armed man I pitched in the fumarole last year was your stand-in. You said he was your kind of second-in-command. I assume, therefore, he spoke for you back in Japan? That he accurately articulated your own arguments and thoughts as much as one man can for another?"

Herczog shrugged. "You're wasting time. Don't make me shoot this actor and cost your producer friends money having to re-film all his scenes."

Bob arched an eyebrow at Hector and dared to pour himself some more *raki*. He did that with a very steady hand. He downed it and said, "Seems my fate is in your hands, Hec."

Hector smiled encouragingly and said, "Haven, you should know this man you've thrown in with isn't after this weapon on behalf of Japan. His stand-in whom I indeed killed made it quite clear to me this son of a bitch means to sell the plans for the bombs to any and all who can meet his asking price. He's no idealist. He's a terrorist and an opportunist. That's all. The Black Dragons are essentially a real life version of Ian's SPECTRE—an outfit dedicated to lining its own pockets at any cost. I believe you're an idealist, darlin', But this man is very much the opposite. I'm speaking truth to you, Haven."

But to what end are you doing that, Hector asked himself. It was surely the very question now passing through Fleming and Shaw's minds.

Even if Haven accepted Hector's assertion, she was every bit as outnumbered and outgunned as Hector and company.

Béla Herczog waved a hand dismissively and said. "Well, it looks like Mr. Broccoli will be needing a new villain." He shifted his aim to Robert Shaw's head.

Hector held up both hands, his cigarette dangling from between his lips.

He'd decided on a course of action. It was unthinkable, yet some selfish small part of Hector's being—the terrible survivor in him—actually welcomed the outcome he was striving for now.

Hector slowly reached under the table and picked up the attaché case with his left hand. He pushed aside his glass and plate to make room on the table, then sat the case down flat on the tabletop and, not waiting for approval or permission, deftly opened its clasps.

As he did that, lifting the lid, he said, "I should at least glimpse my wife's writings you may or may not deign to send back to me eventually."

Herczog said, "So help me, I'll kill all three of you if you don't give me that briefcase right now!" He began to move closer to the table, reaching out.

Hector opened his left hand, took aim, and depressed the actuator on the cigarette lighter given him by the British intelligence quartermaster so many months before.

He flinched as the long flash of flame burst from the end of the lighter with a terrible hiss, licking the precious papers in the suitcase and setting them ablaze.

Screaming, Herczog tried to slam shut the lid and extinguish the flames.

Haven shot the man in the side of the head—a spray of red and a flurry of exploding black wool.

The contents of the attaché case were fully ablaze.

Hector didn't dwell on that—hell, he actually felt some relief for the papers' destruction.

Perhaps, he thought in the moment, Brinke's specter would loosen its suffocating grip on his imagination at last.

Even as he thought all this, Hector drew his gun from under his sport coat and took aim at one of the two masked, armed men who'd remained behind with their boss. Haven downed one; Hector the other.

Ian scooped up Bela Herczog's discarded gun and turned in his chair, shooting the first of the armed men to enter from the back room.

That left two who escaped through a back door.

The writers looked around at the shambles and bloodstained mess of the dining room. The scorched attaché case's contents were now black, curling ash—nothing to be salvaged... not a scrap.

Haven gave Hector a desolate look, then, shaking her head and keeping aim at his right eye, she backed out the front door and quickly lost herself in the crowd.

Ian looked from the charred contents of the briefcase to Hector. His eyes said it all: *Ashes, dear boy. Ashes.*

Bob said, "Gents, I really think it's best we leave here before those folks in back find their backbones and get a better look at us."

Sound logic.

The trio hurried from the bloody ruins of the restaurant to also lose themselves in the crowd gathering out front, some of those cupping hands to glass to better glimpse the carnage inside.

Circumstances required that the actors share a dinner with the crew that night.

Ian was scheduled to fly out the next day. Hector was planning to stay on another day or two, but he was already rethinking that strategy.

The night proved to be a bit of a hash. Producer Cubby Broccoli put the arm on Hector at the bar. He said the next Bond film was already in the pipeline and would be *Goldfinger*.

He was thinking seriously about offering the role of the titular villain to Orson Welles.

"You know Orson, right? Could you approach him for me, Hec?" Cubby wrapped an arm around Hector's broad shoulders. "You know—prime the pump, so to speak?"

Hector nodded, looking dubious. "I'm not sure Orson and I are talking this year."

Disappointed, Cubby said he understood and then made it clear to the bartender all of Hector's drinks were on the film production's tab.

Hector stood at the bar with a vodka martini garnished with three plump, skewered olives, watching Ian. The English author looked bone-weary. Emptied out. He'd tried to beg off dinner in favor of a meal at his hotel.

When the producers insisted he instead come out for the more formal affair, Ian expressed his sincere hope for a quiet place. Instead, it was all bands and belly dancers this raucous night.

Co-producer Harry Saltzman ordered food for everyone— some spicy and heart-burn threatening native fare.

Ian held his head and whispered to Cubby and the lovely Dana Broccoli, "I don't *want* any of this food. It's noisy. I want a Spanish omelet."

As Hector watched, worrying after Ian, Cubby Broccoli spent what seemed like a half-an-hour trying to describe a Spanish omelet to their uncomprehending waiter. Cursing softly, Cubby rose and went to make the dish himself. Hector loved the man for that in the bittersweet moment.

Hours later, at last back at the Istanbul Hilton, Hector made the decision to leave on the Orient Express back to Paris the next morning. (Ian was flying back to England; the mess and mayhem of this bit of tourism had drained him quite utterly, he said.)

The film crew still had several weeks to go in Istanbul.

The authors sat in the hotel lounge—blessedly quiet—and talked about next projects. Ian was tentatively planning a new Bond he intended to call *The Man with the Golden Gun.* "One way or another, this one," he said firmly, if a bit direly, "will certainly be the last of them."

The British novelist then added, "I still feel quite cross toward you, Hector. Some of what Haven said about Britain is hard to deny just now, but nevertheless...."

Hector held up a big hand. "Wherever you ultimately land in regards to your feelings about me, buddy, please know this much is gospel: I was *never* going to give that microfilm to *anybody*, Ian. I'd decided sometime ago that if I managed to walk out the door with the case intact, I'd come straight back here and up to my room. I'd find that damn film, then I'd have used Hem's gift lighter to torch that wicked bitch to hell and gone. *That* was my plan. Nobody should have the goddamn thing. Isn't that the very definition of *détente?*"

"Just so," Ian said at last. "And I believe that is exactly what you intended. It's what happened more or less, after all. Though I'm so sorry for you having to have to destroy Brinke's posthuma. That's a tragedy."

Ian reached over and closed a cold, trembling hand over Hector's. "But all is now forgiven. Think you might get to England later this year? Or, better, maybe come to Goldeneye when I'm next there? I know Noel would love to see you again."

"My best to Mr. Coward," Hector said. "I don't know, Ian. Let's see how the world turns."

They tapped glasses and Hector said, "Farewell to old war business, yes?"

"Last goodbyes, yes, indeed," Ian said. "Of course, there's rarely ever any good about goodbyes."

He gave Hector a solemn look. "I know it's bad for my heart, but we both know I can't endure a half-life and I'm very much on borrowed time, now. If I listen hard, I hear the Iron Crab's claws clacking."

Ian managed a smile that almost caught the incandescence of younger Ian's grins of yore. He said, "Please, do get at least a little tight with me tonight, Hec? Won't you do that?"

Hector weighed that prospect and all its risks. He said from the heart, "I'd like nothing better, Ian."

Several hours later, his windows thrown open to let in the scent and chill of the Istanbul night, for the first time in many months, Hector dozed and had no dreams of Brinke.

He awakened for the first time feeling rested and whole… if just a *slight* bit saddled with a faint but nagging sense of guilt for his good night's sleep and peace, and the implication of their cause.

And, of course, he had more than a bit of a hangover, too.

11

EVERY MAN'S DEATH (1964)

On Wednesday, August 12, Hector was in New York City, putting on his game face to endure an afternoon with some hot-shot kid editor who was trying to mess with Hector's new novel. The kid editor had crazy ideas; personal political notions he wanted to have find form in Hector's book.

The wunderkind hoped that perhaps he and the "venerable pulp scribe"—those were the kid's actual words, ill-advisedly delivered baldly to Hector's face—could bond and talk through his fresh vision for Hector's novel at Yankee Stadium as his favorite team hosted the White Sox.

Somehow, the kid had gotten this wildly mistaken notion Hector gave a damn about baseball, or hell, about *any* sport.

Never a happy spectator, Hector liked to think of himself steadily writing and creating while sports fans gawked and fattened their asses as they squandered the precious days of their finite time on earth playing gnoshing voyeurs. Hector had too much work to do, too many books he meant to leave as his legacy and evidence of a life if not *well* then at least *fully* lived.

Apart from his utter disinterest in the so-called "national sport," Hector's heart wasn't in the prospect of the sure-to-be-disastrous rendezvous for all kinds of other reasons.

The whole damned world seemed to be going through another of its spastic upheavals and, therefore, who of any real value or worth to the sorry world had the time or attention to squander caring about goddamn baseball?

Hell, even now, there was a race riot unfolding in Elizabeth, New Jersey.

South Africa had just gotten the boot from the Olympic Games for its racial policies.

In England, Charlie Wilson—infamous for his role in the so-called "Great Train Robbery"—had somehow escaped from prison in Birmingham, causing a terrific ruckus in the British press.

Then that *other* sorriest of the sorry news found Hector. It did that all the way from England—this last, and worst bit of breaking news; an announcement to bury any and all worries about Charlie goddamn Wilson.

It was, admittedly, hardly unexpected news: Hector had bracing for it for many months, hell, maybe for a couple of years.

The first published report that reached Hector was datelined from Canterbury.

It seemed that following a too rich meal and a tragically taxing day at some golf club, Ian Fleming had suffered another heart attack.

This was the one that at last saw the Iron Crab firmly grab hold of Ian's diseased heart and give its terrible, final squeeze.

Ian somehow "lingered overnight" before "succumbing" the following day.

The last recorded words of James Bond's creator were piercingly prosaic—allegedly some uttered comfort for his caregivers. Dying Ian was said to have affably apologized to his ambulance drivers, "I am sorry to trouble you, chaps. I don't know how you get along so fast with the traffic on the road these days."

James Bond's creator was no more.

In a last, bitter twist of fate, Ian Lancaster Fleming died on his young son's birthday.

Hector sat mourning in an Irish bar just off Times Square, swamped by drunken post-game ruckus and the afterglow of a profanity-laced kiss-off of his would-be kid editor.

Despite the crowd, Hector was still terribly alone in his head—a near constant reality for any writer when he really stopped to think about it.

He then remembered a quote from the ill-received Bond novel published the year that Ian and Hector went to Japan. Ian's rare, female narrator confided, "Loneliness becomes a lover, solitude a darling sin."

Only a professional writer could have composed those lines.

Hector sat with a thrice-read *New York Times* report of Ian's death and thought, *People dying who had never died before, damn it all to hell.*

Hector settled his tab, binned the newspaper, then went off to find another bar.

The next one would hopefully be frequented by attractive, available women in whose company one could perhaps forget other things for a time.

Months passed; more dubious decisions and a mounting number of career setbacks.

In autumn 1967, after many years of intensely flirting with the notion, Hector Mason Lassiter at last set out to "kill" himself.

Oh, he'd played with the idea many times and at many stages of his life since the age of forty, or so.

In 1958, Hector had actually briefly assumed another man's identity, trying the concept out—a dry-run that tellingly didn't kill Hector's obsession with an eventual radical reinvention of self.

But it had seemed too soon, then.

Hector thought that he still had some important books to publish under his own real name—novels to secure Hector Lassiter's literary long game.

So he stalled…kept his head down and wrote about that *other* Hector.

Of course Brinke's 1924 staged self-murder loomed somewhere in the back of his mind every time Hector entertained undertaking what amounted to his faked murder-suicide.

Feeling she'd all but played out her string as the mystery writer Connor Templeton—and faced with unwarranted but mounting French police interest—Brinke had impulsively, yet *effectively* faked her death in Paris.

A few months later, she'd settled in Key West with Hector. On Bone Key, over the astonishing period of just a very few months, Brinke composed three very different sorts of novels under a different name, essentially enjoying a second life as a writer.

Hector came to see Brinke had been an instinctive survivor—a model for artistic and actual self-preservation until capricious fate ended the lucky streak she was enjoying through the fall of 1925.

Hector wanted to think he could be the same—a survivor and a noted male author but one who would not stagger down quite the same destructive path that had swallowed up Hem and Ian.

Mired in a well-intentioned but foundering marriage to a pretty young Scottish widow for whom he too belatedly saw he was completely unsuited, Hector began to lay the groundwork for his own death and resurrection with his soon-to-be-ex-wife Hannah's actual cooperation.

He called in favors from local New Mexico cops, coroners and drinking buddy reporters.

Hector devised for himself a *La Frontera*-style staged murder-suicide and a concomitant and very quiet Tijuana divorce.

This last came with heavily buttressed but cheerfully offered alimony settlement thrown in.

Palms were greased and last favors called in.

The stage was set and the trigger at last was pulled on a venerable old Peacemaker.

October 1967:

Thurgood Marshall was sworn-in as the first black Supreme Court Justice.

A Disney cartoon of a Kipling work was released.

Three Apollo astronauts were killed in a launch pad test gone terribly awry.

Elvis got himself married, and the film adaptation of *You Only Live Twice*—a mess of a movie bearing no resemblance to Ian Fleming's tortured, haunted novel—was still burning up the box office.

Its star, Sean Connery, declared the movie to be his last Bond.

In October of that same wicked year, Che Guevera died before a firing squad—rumor had it Hector Lassiter's old German nemesis, Klaus Barbie, might have played a role in Che's capture and extinction.

As for Hector Lassiter himself, the novelist was declared dead to the world in late October, the victim of an apparent death-bed interview gone horribly crossways for interviewer and interviewee.

Obituaries were written; vexing opinions on the Lassiter career were proffered.

All of the author's known works were briefly, gloriously brought back into print in snappy, uniform editions.

Then, just a few short months after, a new and enigmatic— an even *reclusive* author, some would say—made his acclaimed debut.

Novelist Beau Devlin and his striking, much younger Latina wife, Alicia, took the money from his first novel's sale—as well as its attendant lucrative film right's option— and purchased a pretty house set high above a cliff side on Hawaii's largest island.

For a fleeting time, it seemed that life for Hector had renewed itself.

With nearly all of his best friends dead and his thinly fictionalized world passing into history, there seemed a chance for a true, new beginning for the author and the man, a world full of possibility, and, God willing, one devoid of shadow.

For three years, more or less, that all proved to be true enough.

12

CODA: PATRIOTISM & THE SPY WHO LOVED ME

In November 1970, three years and a few days into his new, sweet life, the seventy-year-old novelist "Beau Devlin" suffered a short, sharp flurry of rabbit punches.

The first came the day before Thanksgiving when word reached Hawaii novelist Yukio Mishima had died in the most ghastly and public fashion imaginable—a failed military coup and an apparent ritual suicide to eclipse even the horror of Hemingway's far more private, so-called "*seppeku* by shotgun" nine years previously.

The ghastliness of Mishima's death far outstripped Hector's "murder-suicide" in New Mexico three years before.

On November 25, Mishima and a small band of rightist coconspirators—members of a Mishima-formed private militia called *Tatenokai*, or "The Shield Society"—inveigled their way into the offices of the commandant of the Eastern-Self Defense Forces.

The commandant was promptly taken hostage, lashed to a chair, then forced to listen as Mishima strode out onto the balcony of the Defense Force's HQ to address a crowd of angry soldiers gathered below.

Dressed in a severe military tunic, a white bandanna emblazoned with rising sun bound 'round his head, Mishima stood out above the crowd below and railed on for several minutes, waving and pointing with gloved hands. His speech had been calculated to impel the soldiers to join in his coup.

If that was really the author's aim, things went terribly wide of the mark.

Mishima's jaw-dropping actions drew the harshest scorn.

The catcalls of the soldiers and the chop of overhead helicopters all but drowned out the ranting novelist's last publicly voiced words.

In terms of Yukio Mishima's own literary long game, Hector figured the drowning out of his crazy speech had maybe been a favor.

But then, after returning to the barricaded office of the captive commandant, Mishima dropped down onto the floor, and performed the unfathomable ancient act of ritual *seppuku*, slicing open his belly.

As he crouched there agonizing and hunched over his pulsing, disgorging entrails, his co-conspirator and alleged lover, a young man named Masakatsu Morita, failed in his several bloody attempts to sever Mishima's head with a cleanly executed sword stroke—the traditional and expected benevolent act of delivering the *coup de grace* that the Japanese called *kaishakunin*.

Disgusted, another of the Shield conspirators—a tougher, more enigmatic young man named Hiroyasu Koga—deftly decapitated Mishima with a single stroke of the author's samurai sword before turning the bloodied katana on the hapless Morita, who had subsequently *also* failed in the execution of his belly-cutting.

(One native correspondent, as Hector read in a subsequent, translated news account, noted Morita had written Mishima in 1968, seeking admittance to the Shield Society and professing his patriotic commitment to *die* for Mishima, if that was deemed necessary. The two similarly possessed men, in accordance with the samurai tradition, had actually written "death poems" before embarking on their farcical, lethal coup.)

Hector sighed: Writers as spies, martyrs and as would-be revolutionaries? And now as latter-day samurai?

It was all juvenile insanity…*wasn't it?*

Contemplating the blood-and-thunder melodrama and waste of Mishima's political stunt—not to mention his grisly suicide—Hector thought irresistibly of Byron and the British poet's equally dubious efforts to bring about Greek independence.

All that had been another bizarre and quixotic scheme orchestrated by a somewhat fey and delusional man of letters—a writer seemingly bent upon bending the weave and woof of history to the author's idiosyncratic will.

A writer proposes, Hector thought, *and God coldly disposes.*

Byron, only thirty-six, died of sepsis. Mishima had been forty-five when he went to his highly personal Valhalla.

A widely publicized and close-up photograph of Mishima's severed head had burned itself into Hector's brain. That sorry vision was quickly followed by a remembered image of Pancho Villa's rotting damaged skull, then of a too-well-described revelation of Hem's near headless body sprawling in the entryway of Ketchum Idaho home.

Hector massaged his temples, trying to drive the bloody collage of severed heads and bloody torsos from his mind.

After watching as much of the Mishima coverage on television as he could stomach—as well as having read countless, breathless newspaper accounts of the man's last hours—Hector shook his head and deeply sighed again, staring for a long time out the window at the restless Pacific and wondering at all the waste and stupidity.

He was truly dumbfounded that such an accomplished writer could undertake so bizarre a course of personal and *public* self-annihilation.

But then, brooding more on it, Hector gradually remembered Hem's crazy efforts to run his own guerilla unit in occupied Paris, which in turn evoked discomfiting memories of Hector's equally dubious undertakings along similar lines, even as he, just like Hem, had traveled under the cloak of "war correspondent."

Point a finger, and you point three back at yourself—wasn't that the old folk saying?

But Hector, albeit under a different name, was still very much alive, and now well past such crazy gestures, he insisted to himself.

Still, a quote by Mishima that figured in one of the accounts of the Japanese author's death hung stubbornly in Hector's head: "If we value so highly the dignity of life, how can we not also value the dignity of death? No death may be called futile."

In the end, Hector simply couldn't agree with that point of view. After a few more hours lost to brooding, he pushed thoughts of Yukio Mishima and patriotic, fatalistic acts from his mind.

After all, a holiday loomed.

On Thanksgiving Day, Hector Lassiter celebrated and feasted with his growing, come-late-in-life family. They enjoyed a golden, sunny holiday together.

But the sun and fun proved fleeting enough.

The next morning, Hector received a phone call, just a few minutes after he had completed his daily session at the writing table.

A familiar female voice—the British accent mellowed, but still very much present—said firmly, though affably, "I know who you really are, *Beau*. I don't mean to use that against you, not at all. I'm not intent on sharing your secret with the world, so, Hector, please don't hang up on me. I beg you to hear me out."

Before he could say anything, Haven Branch pushed on: "The world has changed *so* much, or at least that's true of that place I thought meant so much to me, once. But that's all changed as our Japanese writer friend's death has made all too clear to me. Certainly you've changed, and I have, too. Things that once meant everything—or at least seemed to—mean comparatively little to me now. I see how fleeting a happy life can be. So I'm here on the big island, and I'm not alone. I'd like for us to meet a last time."

Haven hesitated and he could hear the uncertain smile in her voice as she got to the heart of the matter. "You see, Hector, there's someone I'd very much like for you to meet. You *will* do that, won't you? Just for an hour or so? I swear to you, I mean you and your family no harm. I'd just like you and this other person to spend some time together."

Hector's mouth was dry; his palms damp. "This person I'm going to meet…?"

"I think you well know who it is. But he won't know *how* it is. That's the one favor I ask of you. That's the only condition I place upon you." She took a breath and said, "Will you do that for me? Will you do that for *him*?"

Hector said it from the heart. "Of course I will."

Hell, he was doing it every bit as much for himself.

Maybe Haven had chosen the rendezvous site to twist the knife, or, given her long love of Japan, perhaps she wanted to give that "someone" context for the act that set Japan and America at war with one another nearly thirty years before.

Either way, as scheduled, they met at the Pearl Harbor visitor's center.

Haven, still slender, still quite attractive, was standing by an anchor that had been recovered from the wreckage of the ruined U.S.S. Arizona.

Hector looked around for a young boy or girl, but saw nobody that immediately fit the probable template he had in mind for Haven's child. No, strike that: for *their* child. Him, Haven had said several times on the call, he remembered: *We must have a boy*, he thought.

Haven's wore her black hair a bit shorter and she had a dashing white streak that came off her right temple and fell in a kind of careless comma toward the still cleanly drawn line of her jaw.

The dark eyes appraised him and said, "You look well, Hec. Years younger than a man of seventy. If I didn't know the timelines, I'd put you in your mid-fifties."

He smiled and hugged her close. "You're still a liar, but also still a beautiful fibber."

With his left hand—a glittering gold band on that ring finger—he presumed to lift her same hand to his face. The third-finger of her left hand was naked.

"I'm really just better alone like that," she said. "Far happier unattached."

He said, "But do you need money? Some kind of support for...?"

She shook her head. "We're perfectly *fine*. "I'm a journalist, now." She hastened to add, "But not the kind that spies or lives life with an eye to how it might read later."

"That's good," Hector said softly. "But the child—what does he or she think became of their father?"

"The story given is the father died in a senseless act of violence for which he was not himself responsible," she said. "A crime victim, of sorts. It's even true, in some ways."

That landed like a kind of gut punch, but Hector just nodded and said, "Right."

The balmy wind—it was in the low eighties this day after Thanksgiving—fingered her hair. Brushing it back from her dewy forehead, she said, "Of all the places on this earth where you might have settled down, why did you choose here to make your second life, Hec? Or do you prefer that I call you Beau?"

Hector followed her lead to a bench looking out on the harbor. He sat down beside her. He said, "Deep down, I'm still Hector Lassiter, and those closest to me still call me by that name. It's who I really am, of course. Who I'll always be, and to the bone."

He looked around and said, "As to this place? I've always favored islands. This is like Key West only with elbowroom. Tell me, are you still Haven Branch?"

"Still. Quietly. Like you, most probably think me dead. Everyone—MI5, the Black Dragons—they've moved on, it appears, and I'm now left alone."

He couldn't help himself anymore—the curiosity was eating him alive. Hector said, "The child—a boy or a girl?"

"*We* have a son," she said proudly. "He's a splendidly handsome blend of us. He has your eyes and your face, but with darker hair—the blackest hair, like mine. But the resemblance to you is strongest, hence this fiction that you're *distant* blood." She frowned. "Well, I guess fiction isn't the right word for it. Not at all."

He said thickly, "So as part of this lie agreed to, I should be a Branch?"

She shook her head, a somber look of reflection taking her. "No. I'm out of the espionage game—all the way out, but other things can happen in this sorry world, as you well know. Some illness, or some stupid traffic accident could strike. If he *should* ever find himself alone or in need, I'd like him to have some way to find you—his one known relative. *If* he ever feels compelled to reach out. It must be on his terms. I'm firm on that, Hector."

Still not thinking particularly logically, tantalized by the prospect of this son he'd soon meet, Hector muttered, "So then I should be Hector Lassiter this one last time?"

"Lord, no," Haven said, looking truly appalled. "Surely you know how it is now regarding *that person*, even though it's just been a few years since he *died?*"

She said it almost as if Hector Lassiter really was somebody else. "You know what I mean by all that," she said, waving a hand.

He wasn't sure that he did know what she meant *by all that*. So Hector asked her to elaborate.

Haven took his hand and cradled it on her lap. She said, "Deep down, I'm sure that you *do* know what I mean. I'm talking about all that business that was dragging you down— the fallout from using yourself as a character in your later books, for one thing. The man who lives what he writes and writes what he lives. There's a whole generation coming up— Heath's generation, and, yes, that's his first name—young people who already believe or are erroneously taught that

Hector Lassiter is and always was a fictional character. It's kind of perfect in its way if you can step back from it and see it in a certain light. My God, Hector, you're actually passing into the mist of your own myths. You essentially wrote yourself out of your own life and straight into pop-culture legend."

Hector had nothing to say to that, not in agreement or in rebuttal. His mind was still very much elsewhere. He repeated, "Our boy's name is Heath?"

"I told you at our start how much I loved that name, and its inspiration. And it's a small connection to the 'real' you, of course. It was really the only name I considered for our boy."

His mind racing, still grappling with all of it, Hector echoed a joke of hers from long ago. He said, "Heath Branch. Haven Branch. At least it makes the monogramming of towels that much easier."

She squeezed his hand. "You should know he already shows flickers of having some ambitions as a writer. I think he has a real talent for it. Heath tells me these wild stories he makes up to try and put himself to sleep. They really only excite him to terrible wakefulness. But I desperately want him to be an author who just *writes*—not one who plays spy or sees a life of action as a means to feed his muse."

Hector wasn't convinced it could ever work that way for *any* writer—life was always fodder, in the end, and one chased sensation and experience to fuel the fiction. Surely they *all* did that. Wives, children and friends too-often became collateral damage to that terrible impulse in an author.

But he didn't offer that opinion now.

She smiled and said, "John Butler Yeats—you know, the Irish poet's father? Well, he once said that in his son William's a-birthing, he'd given 'a tongue to the sea cliffs.' In having a child with you, I feel like maybe I've done the same for the East." A shrug and a smile. "I suppose time will tell.

"So, to your earlier question—regarding how I'll introduce you—you'll be the man you are now, the writer who writes one way and lives in quite another fashion," Haven said. "You'll be Beau Devlin to him, in other words."

A funny smile. "How do you think Brinke would have felt about your taking *her* name?"

"She'd be fully in favor," he said. "I think Hem might even have suggested it once." Hector changed the subject to one much more to his interest. "So you're both living somewhere in Japan, I take it?"

"Somewhere, yes. But we travel, and widely. I'm more of a feature journalist—I write a lot of travel pieces—and Heath can frequently come along. For one so young, his passport is already a delirious shambles of customs stampings. That said, I'm not sure how much longer we'll stay in Japan. It's sadly becoming more Western every day. Mishima was right in so many ways. Japan is losing its soul."

"Maybe, but Mishima was a kind of philosophical Luddite in other, key ways," Hector said firmly. "I'd say he was an anachronism with all that samurai stuff and becoming so enthralled with the ancient and increasingly irrelevant Bushido Code. Would be a little like me running around the United States like some itinerant soldier of fortune, beholden to no one, packing a six-gun and living by some creaky old version of a cowboy's code as I imposed my singular will on the world."

The unconscious irony of that assertion swiftly and soundly swamped Hector.

Hell, that *had* been his life, in some sorry-ass ways, at least until 1967 or thereabouts. And, hell, he still had his

Colt Peacemaker after all, well-oiled and always loaded, but currently safely tucked away back at his Oahu *spread* because Hector Lassiter had lingering enemies and couldn't they, just as Haven Branch had now done, one day find him?

Haven had the grace to pass over Hector's dubious dismissal of Mishima.

She said, "You know, I never got to extend my condolences to you about poor Ian. If only he'd been able to live differently, how many more books—Bonds or otherwise—might we have had?"

Indeed. How many? The same could be asked of Hem, of course. And of Mishima. None of those three writers were prepared—perhaps they were simply not equipped—to be old men, Hector thought.

He said, "Ian took pride in the concept of one day dying from living too much. I think he actually wrote that into some or another Bond."

She squeezed his hand again. "For what it's worth—I mean having it come from the likes of me—I believe you were right to *kill* yourself, darling. I think it actually saved your life."

"So do I," Hector said nakedly. "I'd be on the wrong side of the sod now if I kept being that man, that other writer."

Her expression suddenly changed. "And here he comes. He's a wonder, isn't he?"

Hector turned eagerly, squinting into the sunlight. He agreed the boy was a marvel, even silhouetted as he was by the sun—for the moment, an indistinct but compelling figure to Hector.

Haven pulled a paperback from her purse. It was one of his novels written under his Beau Devlin byline. "I'm going to return to reading this," she said. "It's really wonderful by the way, yet so different from what came before. But you know that. You two take your time, get to know each other as you can."

Standing before him, the boy reminded Hector of the few pictures he still had around somewhere of himself as a child.

Heath was wearing shorts and a dark blue T-shirt. His black hair was worn in bangs and he a familiar cowlick twisted in unruly defiance above his pale blue right eye. He was tanned and fit. He moved with a kind of natural athletic grace. In either hand, the boy held a fishing pole.

Hector introduced himself as Beau. The boy focused on Hector's pale blue eyes—the twins of the eyes the boy saw every time he looked in a mirror—and said, "We're related, mommy said, but I don't know how. I don't think mommy has brothers."

The boy smiled uncertainly at Haven—a new front tooth was just coming in to fill a gap. He asked her, "You don't, do you?"

The accent threw Hector: it was a strange hybrid of Haven's English accent with an overlay of Japanese distortions of a couple of key consonants. More travel might ground that out, though. Hector hoped that would be the case.

"It doesn't really matter so much exactly *how* we're related," Hector said, finding himself trying hard not to let his sprawling Texas pronunciations to bleed through too strongly, then deciding, *No, this might serve as a counterbalance.*

Hector said in a baritone drawl, "It's a confusin' family tree and I don't want to bore you. But blue eyes like ours do run in the family, especially among the men." He pointed at one of the fishing poles. "You do this a lot, kiddo?"

"*Never.* Mommy said you'll teach me. She says you know all about how to fish, Mr. Devlin."

Hector smiled. "Beau. You call me *Beau*. And, yes, I've caught a few fish in my time. Maybe even a lake's worth. Let's go see what we can land here." He rested a big hand on the boy's shoulder and they walked toward the ocean for a lesson in casting.

❧

For more than two hours, Hector fished with his son.

They didn't catch anything worth keeping, but they talked about baseball, which the kid loved and Hector had to fake a zeal for this one time.

They talked about dogs—Heath wanted one, quite badly, but Haven's travels were an obstacle to that.

They also talked a little about writing. Heath posed a child's questions about the craft.

Hector kept the advice simple and easy to remember on that front: "Two rules for success," he said. "Write the story only you can write, son. And you strive to write one true sentence, then you write another and another and just keep on like that."

Hector tried to remember himself at age seven or eight. He couldn't, not really, but he was convinced that even then, he was already aiming to be a writer. He couldn't honestly remember a time when that *wasn't* his goal.

But if he was candid with himself, he wasn't sure he could remember any of Beau's many homilies thrown at Hector about life and such when he was Heath's age.

Still, maybe those few lines of key writing advice would somehow stick if Heath really kept his foot on that particular creative path.

As the sun began to fail—as the Big Island's November rains freshly threatened—Haven at last returned to them.

They said their goodbyes, reluctantly so—at least that was the case from Hector's end. There was a lingering embrace for the mother and a firm handshake for their boy.

Hector watched them walk off together, headed back to their lives apart from him.

Somehow he knew he'd never see either of them again.

At the same time, Hector sensed somehow their luck would always hold. There would be no terrible disease or stupid car accident that would ever send that boy running back to the old man with the palest blue eyes. Hector instinctively knew that would prove so.

When the latest rain came, it did so suddenly, in wind-driven, billowing sheets.

Hector was far enough away from his car that running wouldn't spare him a profound soaking. So, hands in his pockets and head down, Hector walked on through the driving rain, thinking hard about separate lives and second chances.

There are no second acts in American lives, his old Parisian drinking buddy F. Scott Fitzgerald had famously said. Those had proven prophetic enough words, at least for Scott.

But Hector really had learned from Ernest's dire example, and from Ian's, too. Through both of his fellow authors' troubled eyes, in a very real sense, Hector had looked death in the face and chosen a second shot at life.

Eventually—but determinedly—Hector had simply turned his back on that "old whore" death. He turned his back not just on death, but importantly, on *himself*, in the most crucial sense.

Hector had embraced an ultimate and radical reinvention of self whose concept had been bequeathed him by Brinke in one of the last and most important lessons she'd had to teach him.

Mishima had long ago written, "The past does not only draw us back to the past. There are certain memories of the past that have strong steel springs and, when we who live in the present touch them, they are suddenly stretched taut and then they propel us into the future."

Long before James Bond's creator had scribbled down his famous lines in an errant attempt at a haiku, Brinke Devlin had known and proven if one was coldly willing to sacrifice oneself after a fashion, then conceivably one could in a sense live *twice*.

Smiling to himself, Hector slid behind the wheel. He dragged an arm across his damp forehead, then turned over the engine and flipped on the windshield wipers.

The rain, he thought, was like a kind of baptism, and the thought of this blue-eyed, Japan-dwelling little boy who carried his blood and who shared Hector's storytelling drives was like another incarnation of himself—one to be celebrated and even venerated, after a fashion.

Palming the wheel, Hector veered onto the main road and drove home through the pounding rain thinking of Heath, thinking of the life that might lie ahead for this errant son.

He recalled another line from Basho, something that Haven had whispered in his ear, perhaps the very night they'd conceived Heath:

"To live poetry, is better than to write it."

Quite alone, yet somehow quite happy, Hector drove on through the sweet-smelling autumn rain, back to his home and family.

HECTOR LASSITER
WILL RETURN
IN
THREE CHORDS & THE TRUTH
(The final Hector Lassiter novel)

AFTERWORD

About the same time this novel is scheduled to debut in autumn 2015, a new James Bond film will appear— one dubbed *Spectre*. It's a film promising to return to the series' 1960s roots and once again giving us Daniel Craig's brooding, appropriately melancholic 007.

Blessedly, Craig's is an interpretation more in keeping with the spirit of the original Ian Fleming novels, now so very many decades old.

Sitting here on a sultry June evening, I'll confess to hoping that come November and *Spectre's* premier, I'll be profoundly shaken and stirred, once more, by 007.

For some of us guys, it's *still* frankly James Bond's world. The rest of us, particularly we men of a certain age, simply consider ourselves lucky enough to vicariously live in it from time to time.

I was born in July 1962. Around October of that year, my parents apparently felt we at last needed time apart. I was left with my grandparents when my folks decided to take in a drive-in movie.

They had no clue what this flick *Dr. No* was about, but they came, they saw, and they fell in love with James Bond (and my mother with Sean Connery) upon first viewing.

This is, of course, all received memory.

Flash forward: I made my formal, first-person acquaintance with James Bond, in a grand old Columbus Ohio theater, in 1967.

We three went there to see Sean Connery's (first) swan song as 007, *You Only Live Twice*. I remember the broader, set-piece elements of that movie: its Japanese setting, the volcano lair and the car lifted by a giant magnet and dropped into the sea. And I remember being chilled by the spooky murder of a woman by trickling poison down a string and onto her lips while she slept.

From that point forward, in that pre-video, pre-cable and pre-TNT Bond marathon era, we'd anticipate twice-yearly showings of a James Bond movie on ABC on very special Sunday nights.

I watched every one of those films with my father.

Anyone who has actually read the original James Bond novels and then seen the resulting films knows Bond on the page and Bond on film are most often two very different beasts.

Having grown up in the 1960s, in retrospect, I see my own image of masculinity was shaped by three men: Ernest Hemingway, who died in 1961 but continued to publish books at a steady pace into the middle 1980s; James Bond (largely in the person of the swaggeringly Scottish Connery) and my grandfather, Bill Sipe, who was a structural steel worker who wore sports jackets in all weather, smoked Pall Malls and carried a Zippo with a little plastic loader filled with flints for quick re-juices. I dedicated my first-published novel to my granddad.

My grandfather also kept a basement full of pulp literature, including Signet paperback editions of many of the James Bond titles. I'd pick up those Signets from time to time and then put them back down unread. The cover art was muddy and not compelling when measured against the memory of John Barry 007 soundtracks with all their bombast and horns, or against the sexy and vivid film poster images of Connery-Bond and his striking women as painted by Eric Pulford, Robert McGinnis and Frank McCarthy.

My grandfather died in the fall of 1980. He left me his '65 Ford Galaxie and boxes of books and men's stag magazines. Over the course of a mournful winter, I at last read every James Bond book by Ian Fleming, in publication sequence.

Those intense first few weeks living so potently in the head of Fleming remain a favorite reading memory, all these years later. I've revisited every Bond book countless times since, chasing that elusive dragon.

The experience was like a (vodka &) tonic during the long, dreary period of Roger Moore's reign as a flippant and rather fey *English* Bond.

Fleming's Bond was a neurotically subdued and melancholy WWII vet who drifted from affair to affair and expensive bottle to bottle of this and that between assignments.

Ian's Bond was aging in something like real-time and running up against a 35-year-age termination limit for all 00-status agents.

It was pretty clear this was a man who knew there would be no second act in his storied life once stripped of his agency-coveted License to Kill.

When Fleming's Bond murdered someone, he didn't make a quick quip afterward. *Goldfinger,* the novel, opens with Bond in an airport in Miami, getting drunk and contemplating his injured hand, thinking about how it got that way from brutally murdering some luckless, would-be Mexican assassin a short time before.

Thrillers to the core, Fleming's literary Bonds were still far more grounded to reality than their film counterparts.

The film version of *The Spy Who Loved Me* is a nakedly overt and globe-trotting remake of *You Only Live Twice* with Roger Moore dragging the series firmly over the sorry line into self-parody and mockery that Pierce Brosnan would also lamentably cross, time and again, in the 1990s.

Appealing and charming as Brosnan and Moore are as personalities, they were mostly lamentable Bonds.

Fleming's *Spy* is narrated by a Canadian woman who agrees to play caretaker to an out-of-season roadside motel which the owners secretly plan to torch for insurance purposes, fingering our comely narrator as accidental arsonist. All very noir; all decidedly not cinema James Bond.

There are no nuclear submarines, no web-fingered villains living in impossible underwater lairs or giants with steel teeth.

Instead, we get Bond, two thuggish torch-artists for hire, a vampy Canadian, and some raw sex and bloody violence.

It's page-turning pulp noir, really.

We're also granted a revelatory look into the persona of James Bond from the perspective of one of his myriad, nubile bedmates.

When our heroine narrator, about to be murdered—after likely sexual assault—opens a door to find James Bond standing there, blinking back the chilly rain, her first reaction upon seeing this latest stranger at her door is that Bond must be another murderer for hire who's simply arrived late to the scene of her coming slaughter.

Call it *death in the face.*

Fleming's Bond, taken in concentrated form, can pretty much ruin one for much of Albert Broccoli and Company's Bond, at least for a while.

After reading the original novels, the vintage Bond films that resonate most are the first two Connery flicks and the still under-appreciated, but brilliant, *On Her Majesty's Secret*, all three of which hew fairly closely to their source material and to something approaching Fleming's singular conception of James Bond.

In the middle 1980s, when a then sixty-something Moore (cannily self-described at that point as "an occasional stand-in for the stunt men") finally put down his Walther PPK, we got Timothy Dalton, who went into his two films having read all the novels and pushing hard to invest his Bond with the subtext, at least, of the Fleming originals.

Dalton's Bond is truly an assassin, one not particularly in love with his job; at last the Byronic hero his creator envisioned, and not the gadget-reliant quipster who unleashed waves of imitators in the personas of Dean Martin, James Coburn, Robert Vaughn and even Robert Conrad's James West.

When I conceived of Hector Lassiter and his arc over a series of a dozen or so novels, the Fleming Bonds were my central model and primary inspiration.

We're late in the game now, most of the critics have had their say, and so now I'll confess that key influence for the first time.

Precisely one person has ever caught the connection to my knowledge:

A few years back, I appeared at a reading with fellow-novelist Brian Freeman in Ann Arbor's downtown public library.

Our moderator, Robin Agnew of Aunt Agatha's Mysteries—Michigan's finest book store—compared my Lassiter novels to Fleming's Bond novels. Then Robin deftly explained her reasoning for that assertion.

Her thesis was impeccable. I thought sitting there, *At last...found out!*

So here we are, almost at series end. Nearly all has been revealed.

This is the *penultimate* Hector Lassiter novel.

Not by accident, it is also my tribute and heart-felt love letter to Ian Fleming and his darkly seductive, idiosyncratic world.

This installment is also the deliberate table-setter for my series' swan-song, which, not so accidentally, occurs in the same decade that gave birth to Mr. James Bond of Her Majesty's Secret Service.

—CM
June, 2015

ABOUT THE AUTHOR

Craig McDonald is an award-winning author and journalist. The Hector Lassiter series has been published to international acclaim in numerous languages. McDonald's debut novel was nominated for Edgar, Anthony and Gumshoe awards in the U.S. and the 2011 Sélection du prix polar Saint-Maur en Poche in France.

The Lassiter series has been enthusiastically endorsed by a who's who of crime fiction authors including: Michael Connelly, Laura Lippmann, Daniel Woodrell, James Crumley, James Sallis, Diana Gabaldon, and Ken Bruen, among many others.

Craig McDonald is also the author of two highly praised non-fiction volumes on the subject of mystery and crime fiction writing, *Art in the Blood* and *Rogue Males*, nominated for the Macavity Award.

To learn more about Craig, visit *www.craigmcdonaldbooks.com* and *www.betimesbooks.com*

Follow Craig McDonald on Twitter @HECTORLASSITER and on FaceBook: https://www.facebook.com/craigmcdonaldnovelist